SLICE OF LIFE

Howard craned his neck and saw that the creature's clever, wormlike fingers were making adjustments to narrow bands of fibrous material wrapped tightly around his thighs and ankles. He tried to sit up and discovered that his arms were also immobilized. Panic grew in him as he twisted and stretched unsuccessfully.

Giving the bonds at Howard's ankles a final pat, the creature moved out of the range of his vision. When it came into view once more, streams of red-orange fluid were welling from a deep slice in the palm of one cupped hand, the many fingers writhing like a sea anemone's tentacles about the central wound. The machete was in its other hand. Uttering what sounded like a croak of apology, the creature knelt at Howard's side and lowered the gleaming blade . . .

By Geary Gravel
Published by Ballantine Books:

THE ALCHEMISTS

THE PATHFINDERS

THE WAR OF THE FADING WORLDS:
  Book One: A Key For the Nonesuch

A KEY
FOR THE
NONESUCH

Book One of
The War of
the Fading Worlds

Geary Gravel

A Del Rey Book
BALLANTINE BOOKS • NEW YORK

This book is for its editor, Shelly Shapiro, without whose unflagging enthusiasm, illuminating insights, and tactful nagging, Howard Bell would never have found himself facedown in the Fading Worlds.

Thanks are also due, as always,
to Hannah and Cortney,
Ideal Readers.

Contents

CHAPTER I

An Unusual Washroom

HOWARD BELL WAS IN TROUBLE.

He sprawled his six-foot frame in a plastic-wrapped office chair on the thirty-third floor of the soon-to-be-opened Matrix Building in downtown Boston and wondered where he was supposed to be.

Howard glanced at his battered Timex with a sigh. As happened all too often, he had only been half listening when Mr. Foster told him where they would be meeting, and now he was paying for his inattention. With sixty-six floors from which to select he had decided to sit here by the silent intercom and wait for guidance from on high—or on low, as the case might be—rather than wander through the deserted tower complex like the new bee in an unfamiliar hive.

The only flaw in his decision was linked to the intercom itself. Its refusal to operate as expected was the reason Howard had been summoned to the Matrix monolith that night. Unless his boss was having more luck at whatever end of the system he was investigating there would be no instructions forthcoming from the stubborn device at Howard's elbow.

Howard was the night emergency man at Foster's Fix-It Ltd., and with Matrix set to open officially the following Monday, he had been working there for the past four nights, sometimes with Foster and other members of the crew, more often alone. His days he spent yawning over

1

a chattering typewriter in his postage-stamp apartment across the river in Cambridge, correcting, altering, deleting from, and occasionally even adding to the mammoth sprawl of his first novel, now five years into its third draft. By contrast, the Matrix Building had taken just under two years to bring to its present state of near-completion. Even with the constant tide of minor glitches Howard and the rest of Foster's Fix-It had been battling for the past four nights, it was still in better shape than his novel.

He coaxed the last half cup of sludge from his thermos, leaned back, and contemplated his life for the dozenth time that evening. Howard had given himself six months to wrap up The Book, gambling that a stay in the big city would provide him with the real-life experience necessary to enrich certain lengthy passages that seemed to be lacking in depth and color. After that—and the deadline was less than a week away—it was back to the western part of the state and his late aunt's house in the sleepy little college town where he had spent most of his thirty-odd years. As it was, his bank account had dwindled to the point where his last few days in the city might herald the start of a rather lengthy fast. His aunt had left him a small sum of money in addition to the house, and that had given him the courage to quit his part-time teaching job at the college and start work on the novel he had always dreamed of writing. Now, five years later, that money and the savings that had supplemented it were almost gone.

He never would have made it this long, he reflected, if not for his knack of fixing things that other people had given up on. With little scientific knowledge and no formal training, Howard was nevertheless adept at analyzing and repairing an astonishing variety of modern necessities that ranged from coffee grinders to computer terminals. Alden Foster, Howard's boss, called it "a feel for twisted innards," but Howard preferred to think of his ability as a highly developed sense of pattern recognition. Five minutes spent playing with the defective object was usually enough to put him on the right track, and another ten or fifteen spent tinkering often saw the problem solved. If there were sometimes pieces left over when reassembly had been accomplished, so much the better, in Howard's opinion, for it showed that he had been able to improve upon the device while he fixed it, eliminating waste and often streamlining the basic design.

The Matrix job had been a godsend, providing Howard with some much-needed extra cash. According to Mr. Foster, they were being paid out of the capacious pocket of the Matrix president himself, purportedly an incredibly wealthy individual who often employed Foster's Fix-It in his own mansion somewhere outside the city. Normally such minor problems as they had been called in to correct would be taken care of as time permitted after the opening of the building. In Mr. Foster's opinion, the Matrix president was a stickler for detail, a stubborn perfectionist with the capital to back up his demands. After days of arguing with the building's contractors, their patron had apparently had enough and summoned Mr. Foster and his talented henchmen. Howard had been told that they were not to advertise their presence, and that he should report to the building only after the regular day crews had departed. It appeared that the president's actions in employing his private service, while not exactly illegal, were questionable enough that he wished the work accomplished as quickly and discreetly as possible.

Howard was only too happy to comply. Their employer was in a position to pay lavishly for things that were done right, a generosity that Mr. Foster passed on to his employees. Unfortunately, the Matrix intercom system had so far proven intractable, rebuffing his best attempts to set it right.

Howard swallowed a yawn and checked his watch again: 2:10 A.M. He was fairly sure Mr. Foster had said to meet him at two o'clock on the thirty-third floor, but there was a slim chance that it had been two-thirty on the third floor or even three on the twenty-second. Actually, the misunderstanding was at least partly Foster's fault. When Howard's mind was occupied with threading its way through a complicated plot twist at the same time his fingers were unraveling a bollixed circuit, he had little attention to spare for his boss's unnecessarily detailed instructions. The older man had a penchant for military time, as well, something Howard had never been comfortable with. That meant he might not have said two at all, Howard realized, sitting up straight with a frown, but something more like . . . twenty-six? That did not sound right at all.

To make matters worse Howard had to use the rest room.

An elderly custodian had confided to him on their way up in the elevator several hours earlier that, due to a last-minute change in fixtures ordered by the company president, the only functioning facilities in this section of the huge building were a ladies' lounge on the forty-seventh floor and the executive washroom on the sixtieth. The custodian had made it quite clear that the latter was out-of-bounds for ordinary folk like the two of them, despite the fact that the hordes of young Matrix vice-presidents would not begin swarming into the building for another three weeks. Perhaps there was a territorial imperative shared by members of the upper echelon, Howard reflected bitterly, that dictated they must be first to leave their mark on the new corporate hunting grounds.

The lounge on forty-seven it would have to be, then.

Howard scrawled a hasty note of explanation to Mr. Foster, using notepaper embossed with the Matrix crest that he thumbed from a new smoke-brown plastic dispenser. Then he sauntered to the local elevator cluster, one of a dozen arranged in a great circle around the center of the Tower.

The mirror-bright doors admitted him with a soft chime. He punched in his destination and watched lights wink redly as the car began its smooth ascent. Soon the number 47 appeared framed in light above him and the doors were sliding open. Howard reached out on a sudden impulse and hit CLOSE DOOR and 60, his jaw firming as he made the decision to flout the natural order of things by desecrating the executive washroom with his unworthy presence. He might even leave one of the taps running when he was through, he thought recklessly as the elevator doors sighed open several seconds later and he tiptoed down the hall.

He was startled to hear a faint, breathy rumbling as he passed by one of the plush offices that lined the corridor. Peering in at a half-open door he saw the snoring figure of the custodian who had befriended him earlier, the swimsuit issue of *Sports Illustrated* clasped to his ample belly and heavy work boots propped on a worn handkerchief spread carefully on the polished desktop. Continuing past on soundless carpeting, Howard chuckled at his own bravado. Let others kowtow before the rules of the mighty. Howard Bell was no cringing sheep! He reached the heavy wooden door with its scripted brass plate and set his hand grandly on the elegant crystal knob.

It would not turn.

Howard grimaced. Of course it was locked. Why set aside a palatial rest room for the enjoyment of the anointed few if every common laborer in Boston could blithely stroll in as nature called him? He muttered a pungent curse for the legions of fresh-faced functionaries who would soon be presented with the means to pass through that door at will. The keys that would be little more than tokens of elevated status to them represented access to much-needed relief for Howard Bell.

As he stalked sullenly back toward the elevators, he considered returning to the thirty-third floor for his tool kit. He was sure he could put his gift of pattern recognition to work in picking the lock, thus saving himself an ignominious visit to the ladies' room thirteen stories below. There were, after all, certain things one never felt completely comfortable doing—even at two in the morning.

He glanced in again at the sleeping janitor as he passed back down the hall. His eyes widened when they took in the circle of keys lying unprotected not far from the old man's crossed boots. Howard stood outside the doorway and weighed the implications of this new factor.

A mood of reckless abandon seized him. The ring of keys gleamed at him like a symbol of challenge, daring him to take the next step.

Making up his mind in a matter of seconds, he stealthily entered the office, then hesitated on the verge of lifting the keys from the desktop. If he tried to carry them out of the room, the jingling might awaken their rightful owner. Better to slip the required key from the ring with a minimum of noise and leave its fellows behind on the desk.

But which was the required key?

His eyes quickly identified and discounted a house key, a set of car keys—with a blink of surprise to see that it was possible to afford a BMW on a custodian's salary in this town—and a slightly bent post-office-box key. That left only three unaccounted for on a smaller ring of their own that was attached to the main one. One resembled the downstairs front entrance key that Mr. Foster carried on his own key ring, and another was most likely a general passkey for the various offices. The final key on the secondary ring was ornate and golden-gleaming, with elaborate scrollwork and the peculiar addition of three narrow metal bands halfway down its length.

Howard nodded. Just the sort of pretentious object he would have expected. No doubt some local artiste had been paid a small fortune to design a means of entry grand enough for the Matrix executive washrooms.

Silently he pried the metal ring apart and eased the gaudy trinket out, the tip of his tongue protruding slightly between his teeth as he worked.

Key in hand, he backstepped from the room and crept down the hall with an expression of furtive glee on his face. When he reached the door he slid the key triumphantly into the small opening just below the faceted knob. Halfway into the slot the key balked stubbornly and refused to move.

Howard felt like wailing in frustration. He tugged the key loose and inserted it again, but to no avail. Was this meant to constitute an eleventh-hour intelligence test for the junior execs, he wondered, or was each washroom key issued with an instruction manual? He examined the key carefully without removing it from the lock. It was the triad of peculiar little rings partway down the shaft that prevented it from fitting all the way in. Maybe they were designed to slide back when the thing was turned. Gripping the narrow bands with the fingers of his left hand, Howard leaned into the door and turned the key clockwise with strength born of desperation. For a long moment nothing seemed to happen.

From somewhere there came a sharp double click that reminded Howard of a toy from his childhood, a simple metal device cast in the image of a cricket or frog; then there was a feeling of intense cold, and Howard felt a flash of panic as he pitched forward.

The hands that he raised instinctively against the anticipated impact of cold white tile sank to the wrists in a fine powder of warm sand as great puffs of orange dust rose about his face. He lay on his belly for a few moments, then pushed himself up onto his knees and began to sneeze explosively while his head swam in vertigo. When the spasms finally subsided, he brushed a thin layer of dust from his face and turned his head in a slow arc from left to right.

No wonder they keep the door locked, he found himself thinking. There's orange sand all over the place. At the same time he noticed that the aforementioned door seemed to be nowhere in sight. An icy knot grew in his stomach as he raised his eyes to a far horizon.

Before him lay folds and creases of red-orange, a rippling desert that extended in all directions beneath a pale green sky streaked with lemon wisps of cloud. Here and there stood large mounds of reddish earth or rock that were ringed at the base with nodding golden fronds and crowned by masses of ocher vegetation.

Howard was still on his knees, frowning in bewilderment, when a large individual in a gray-green kilt, a matching bathrobe, and a black dinosaur headmask lunged over the small rise several yards in front of him and began pounding toward him across the sand like a runaway Halloween display, something like a curved machete brandished in one fist and squeals of what must have been intended as dinosaur war cries issuing from the gaping beak.

The giant trick-or-treater was barely three feet away when Howard rolled awkwardly to one side; his leg almost ripped free of its socket a second later as the back of his knee accidentally hooked around the shin of his massive attacker.

With a shriek of surprise the great bulk flew through the air, contacting the ground several feet away with force enough to raise a considerable cloud of the orange dust.

"Whoa," Howard said softly, and sneezed twice.

He climbed slowly to his feet and stood watching as the dinosaur-man moved spasmodically in the shallow crater he had created, the long black tail, which protruded from a slit in the rear of his robe, lashing like a sidewinder in the sand near Howard's sneakers.

"Sorry about that," Howard said dazedly. "I didn't mean to trip you, but you sort of startled me with the screaming and everything, and it looked like you were trying to run me over. Boy, that's a pretty wild costume—kind of a triceratops with a Mickey Mouse tail, huh?"

No answer came from the twitching figure. Howard abandoned his attempt at conversation as he noticed the small pool of purplish fluid beginning to spread into the thirsty sand beneath the huge torso. Howard stepped cautiously to the other side of the body. The wickedly curved blade had apparently preceded its owner onto the ground and was embedded to a depth of several inches in its chest.

Its chest?

"Maybe we'd better give this another minute or two," Howard murmured to himself as he knelt to examine the enormous head, which had been twisted violently to one side by the fall. "Of course, I have no idea how quickly time is supposed to pass during this sort of hallucination," he added shakily, jerking back his knee where his jeans had come into contact with the spreading purple liquid.

He marveled at the massive brow ridges that extended into spikes above each tiny eye and at the smaller, almost thornlike projection above the large nostril slits. The mouth arched down into a serrated beak between jutting cheekplates covered by pebbly skin that shone in the greenish daylight as a mixture of iridescent blues and grays above the underlying black. Howard watched the deceptively mild, nearsighted-looking eyes begin to glaze as the spark of life left them. He leaned back and felt his own forehead gingerly.

"I bet I've got a terrific goose egg," he muttered. "Must have hit that floor like a sack of potatoes to put me out so fast. Funny I can't remember the impact. Maybe I've gone right into a coma."

He sat back onto the sand, breath hissing in through his teeth as sudden lances of pain shot through his left hip and upper leg. The air felt hot and very dry.

"God! If I'm in a coma why does it hurt so much?" His words came out in a shaky whisper as he scanned the bizarre landscape. He took a deep breath and lifted a handful of orange sand, which he allowed to sift slowly through his fingers. Suppose he was not in a coma . . . Suppose he had hit his head harder than he thought and it now lay like a smashed watermelon on the clean tile floor. Could this be a near-death experience? He looked around again. Pretty strange set design if it was—and wasn't there supposed to be a bright light? He searched for other options, finding none. Of one thing he was certain: this was definitely not his idea of an executive washroom.

As Howard sat motionless, his eyes roamed the unmoving shape before him, confirming that it was constructed along quite different lines from a human body, being far too broad and short-limbed to pass for a man even if one were inclined to overlook the horned head, clawed hands, and long, whiplike tail.

"I don't get it," he said softly to the hot, dry breeze.

A faint sound tugged at his attention, and he raised his head.

There was something moving rapidly in the distance, and judging by the orange cloud of dust that trailed behind, it was heading in his direction. Howard leapt to his feet, heart pounding like a jackhammer in his chest, and swore at the pain in his leg.

"You'll understand if I put off thinking about all of this for a while," he remarked to the corpse in the sand, his eye on the nearest of the red mounds. He started to hobble toward it, then stopped to squint back and forth between the approaching cloud and the prostrate dinosaur-man.

"Might be a good idea to make you a little less conspicuous," he murmured, "just in case it turns out to be friends of the family."

He leaned down and hooked his fingers into the supple mesh belt studded with small pouches that girded the creature's thick waist, took a breath, and heaved. Dragging the body was easier than he had expected, the tiny particles of sand providing an almost frictionless surface for the hard desert floor that seemed to lie inches below.

Looking back over his shoulder, he saw that the blade—
still lodged deep in the creature's chest—was leaving a
narrow trench in the fine sand.

Golden vegetation stood out from the base of the miniature mesa in a fringe of swaying tendrils. Howard
panted as he dragged the body around to the side farthest
from his approaching visitor and did his best to hide it
beneath the dense growth of overlapping leaves. The underside of the fronds seemed to be slightly adhesive, and
it took little effort to cover the dinosaur-man's body with
them. Still, Howard was sweating from the combination
of heat and exertion when he stepped back to observe his
work. Satisfied, he retreated further, estimating his
chances of reaching the top of the mound unobserved.
Even standing on tiptoe he would be a good ten inches
shy of the tight coils of yellowish moss hanging at the
edge. He shook his head doubtfully and limped in to
where the dinosaur-man lay barely visible under the con-
cealing fronds.

Taking a deep breath, Howard stepped up onto the
corpse, his stomach lurching as he heard the moist click
of blade against bone inside the chest. He stretched his
arms to their limit and was just able to grab a double
handful of the wiry vegetation. He tugged experimentally
and was relieved to find it as tough and springy as the
great mass of steel wool it resembled. As he began to
haul himself up he was startled to feel a slight resistance
from below. Half expecting that the creature had somehow revived long enough to protest its use as a step stool,
he looked down to find that one of the smaller golden
tendrils had managed to become loosely wrapped around
his right ankle. He jerked his leg, and the frond slack-
ened instantly and slid off.

Howard levered himself with a grunt onto the spongy
mat that topped the mound and rolled inward, noting
that the vegetation grew progressively softer the closer
one came to the slightly concave center of the mound.
There was enough room there for him to lie with arms
and legs extended, almost as if it had been designed
specifically to serve as a bed, and he lay there on his
back for a few moments beneath the jade green dome
of the sky. Something that looked like an airborne

manta ray glided lazily overhead on translucent membranes, a long kite's tail of colored streamers fluttering behind it as he watched.

He crawled to the edge of the mound and looked toward the approaching dust cloud. Whatever it was, it had veered off at a sharp angle while still some distance away and was now moving on a course that would soon take it beyond the range of his vision. It seemed to be some sort of long, low vehicle. Shading his eyes with his palm, he was able to make out a row of figures on top, though the distance made it impossible to discern whether they were people like himself or individuals fashioned more on the order of his unwilling guardian below. He had a tentative impression of a variety of shapes and sizes as the carrier receded into the red-orange distance.

When he was reasonably certain they would not be coming back for a while, Howard lowered himself carefully from his refuge and went to further erase the evidence of what had transpired by filling in first the large depression where the dinosaur-man's body had lain and then the trail the two of them had left leading clearly to the base of the mound.

He was using the edge of his shoe to smooth the sand when he caught the flash of something shiny. He bent to find that he had just come close to burying the ornate washroom key. He looked at it thoughtfully and dropped it into an inner pocket of his light jacket.

When he raised his head he saw that the sky was beginning to grow rapidly darker, the tiny sun sinking quickly into a wild sunset of overlapping bands of deep green, maroon, and turquoise. Howard finished obscuring the tracks. Then, reminded by the key of his original mission, he took a moment to relieve himself at the base of a small outcropping of red rock nearby, sparing a glance for his Timex as he zippered his jeans.

"Well, somewhere it's three-fifteen in the morning," he remarked with a sigh to the desert. "Foster's going to think I fell in . . ."

Climbing back to the top of the mound with an assist from the dinosaur-man, he moved to the center of the mossy nest and lay with his arms folded behind his head. He watched as tiny stars began to appear, tracing alien patterns in the emerald-black night.

CHAPTER II

Morning Meals

HOWARD COULD NOT HAVE SAID WHAT FINALLY quieted his thudding heart or calmed his racing thoughts long enough for him to slip into a fitful sleep, but he was instantly aware of the sensation that woke him hours later.

Rubbing his eyes beneath a slowly paling olive green dawn, he wrinkled his nose at the nauseating smell that had dragged him out of his dreams of endless journeying down the corridors of the Matrix Building, his aching feet slogging through drifts of powdery orange sand while the labored breathing of some enormous creature could be heard behind each half-open door.

He gazed with momentary wonder at the sky, already aglow with thin clouds like streaks of yellow chalk. The early morning air was still cool, but when he turned his eyes to the edge of the nest he was sure he saw the ripple of rising heat waves distorting the undulating sweep of the desert beyond. Seeking a source for the terrible odor, he drew his jacket up around his mouth and nose and moved quietly to the rim of the mound.

Howard looked down on a scene that made him recoil in horror and disgust. Below, a soft hissing sound issued from the body of the dinosaur-man, which was almost completely swathed in the golden fronds. Where the flattened tendrils lay against the creature's pebbly hide they had begun to eat into it with some form of powerful acid, thus producing both the rising clouds of warm vapor and

13

the hideous stench that had roused him. Howard could see that the fronds had insinuated themselves into the creature's garments, and the writhing of the taut fabric told him that the ghoulish process was being repeated over every inch of the stinking, dissolving corpse. Even as he watched, the broad bones of head and hands were revealed, gleaming dull gray beneath the golden fronds that moved purposefully across their surface. Soon there was nothing left of the besieged corpse but a cleanly picked skeleton and the shrunken green robe and kilt— for the clothing itself seemed to have remained unharmed, only marked in a few places where the tendrils had lain the longest. The fronds moved languorously over the remains for another minute or two, then relaxed gradually onto the sand at the base of the mound, their golden hue flushed with rose-pink in the areas nearest to the fleshless body.

Howard withdrew from the edge, shuddering as he recalled the tentative touch of the golden tendril on his leg the previous afternoon.

The nauseating odor had dissipated soon after the last morsel of flesh was consumed from the dinosaur-man's corpse, and Howard began to feel an unexpected knot of hunger growing in his own empty belly as he sat in the center of his mossy bed. First he must find some water, he reasoned, a need that began to feel more urgent as he surveyed the arid landscape of rolling hills and shallow depressions. He waited until he was sure the ravenous tendrils had fed to satiation, then eased over the side of the mound and dropped to the ground in the vicinity of the dinosaur-man's remains, making his landing a good three feet from the nearest frond just to be on the safe side.

The wide belt now hanging loosely about the shriveled garments caught his eye as he inspected the plant-things' gruesomely efficient handiwork.

Reaching in to quickly seize a loose sleeve, he yanked the gray-green robe toward him. The fronds offered no resistance, and the clothing tumbled easily into reach, pieces of gray-white bone falling from the sleeve holes as he shook the garments and held them up to the morning sunlight. Sewn into the lining of the robe he discovered a large pouch, in which were concealed other articles of clothing including a vest and shorts made of the same lightweight material as the robe and kilt. The fabric was extremely flexible, and the garments looked as though he could slip them on himself and have a relatively comfortable fit. He decided to roll the clothing into a wide band, which he then wrapped around his waist in case of future need. Then he drew the broad but surprisingly light belt over the band and, after some negotiation with the unfamiliar clasp, fastened it in front.

Nine small pockets were spaced evenly around the belt, each one closed with a tiny clasp bearing a different raised emblem. Howard examined each in turn, finding five to be empty and three of the remaining four to contain items he could not identify: colored powders in two, and a handful of small flattened sticks like fibrous tongue depressors in the other. The final pouch held a wad of viscous, resinlike substance that carried the unmistakable aroma of food when he raised it to his nose. His mouth filling with saliva, Howard touched his tongue experimentally to the brownish gray lump. He licked his lips with a grimace at the taste; then, having no reason to expect better fare within walking distance, he gave a fatalistic shrug to the surrounding desert and took a bite.

Much chewing was required before he could swallow the resin, bursting in the process many small bubblelike chambers that contained an unfamiliar liquid. The substance was apparently a concentrate of some sort, and the smoky flavor was quite strong—though luckily not so unpleasant as to make it inedible. Howard nodded in appreciation, his sampling of the unusual rations having taken the edge off both his hunger and his thirst. As he was replacing the wad carefully in its pouch he noticed that the surface where he had bitten had begun to bubble with activity, as if a new skin were forming to seal off the rupture.

He wiped his hands on his thighs and turned in a small circle, his eyes squinting under the mounting sun. One direction seemed as good as another. Before he departed the area of the mound, he stooped to retrieve the silver blade from where it curved brightly among the dinosaurman's naked ribs. Tucking it carefully between the mesh belt and the sash of green fabric, he stood for a moment looking down at the only companion he had so far had in this strange place, then turned on his heel and entered the desert.

CHAPTER III

A Strange Bedfellow

HOWARD'S FIRST FULL DAY IN THE DESERT PASSED rapidly. Checking his watch shortly after departing the bed-mound, he was shaken to discover that the previous night had lasted no more than six hours from twilight to sunup. It was one thing to accept that he was no longer in Boston; Howard now had to deal with mounting evidence that he was not even on Earth anymore. When the little sun hung directly over his head a scant three hours after dawn he had to believe that a complete diurnal cycle in this desert was accomplished in only half the length of the day he was used to. From then on it was difficult not to feel he was trapped in a speeded-up movie and that Time itself was racing past him as he wandered through the arid waste.

The landscape was largely unvarying, a warped checkerboard of alternating hills and valleys that differed from one another only in details. Howard soon grew weary of marching up and down the gentle slopes like an ant in a sandbox. In addition, his leg was continuing to bother him, though it was not nearly as sore as he had expected to find it.

He saw few living things as he traversed the orange hills and hollows. Solitary kite-rays flapped overhead from time to time, sunlight gleaming greenly through their wing membranes, and their long tails fluttering like ribbons behind them. In addition to the moss-topped mounds he found an odd plant in some of the low pockets that seemed to consist of a dozen or more sticks of dead wood radiating out several feet from a central point. A thin webbing of whitish fibers connected the poles, creating the effect of an abandoned tepee stuck top-first into the sand.

Large outcroppings of minerals appeared on many of the higher surfaces. A transparent quartz containing flecks of black and purple was especially common, along with a glittering deep red stone and a milky white projection that thrust up from the desert like a broken tusk. Small flat crablike things lived just under the sand close to many of the outcroppings, and Howard soon learned to keep his feet up when he rested on the surface of the rocks. The crustaceans, averaging six inches in diameter, were apt to test his sneakers and ankles with surprisingly powerful pincers whenever his feet remained in one spot on the sand for more than a certain length of time.

The golden-ringed bed-mounds were set at intervals that Howard's pattern sense was starting to register as more regular than he had first surmised. He began to get the feeling of larger groupings—no doubt easily discernible from above—in which great circles of the mounds were laid side by side throughout the land of orange dunes. Through experimentation with a stick broken from a deadwood tepee he learned how to gauge when it was safe to approach the golden tendrils and when they had to be avoided. The plants appeared insensitive to stimulus when one found them relaxing limply against the sand. Leaves that stood out from the base of the mound were hungry—as were those that shone with a clear golden color, in contrast to the rosy tints he had glimpsed after the devouring of the dinosaur-man. The adhesive quality of the underside of the fronds increased in proportion to their appetite and was completely absent in those plants that had recently supped. The surface of the sides of the mounds seemed to be formed of a hard-packed earth or clay, but whether they had grown naturally or been constructed he could not say for sure—nor even if there was some internal connection uniting the mossy haven on top with the ravenous predators below. The size of the mounds varied widely from footstool dimensions to a few giants that measured ten feet in diameter and towered twenty feet in the air. Howard had decided not to approach the latter mounds on any account.

As near as he could judge, he had been walking due east, the direction from which both the dinosaur-man and the mysterious vehicle had come. When the sun stood at its zenith he stopped for lunch at a flat-topped outcropping that resembled richly patterned blue-green malachite. He drew his legs up and sat cross-legged to eat, the little crabs bobbing up out of the sand now and then to stare at him in mute frustration.

When he took the wad of brownish foodstuff from the pouch whose clasp was a tiny three-horned lizard head, Howard could find no evidence of the healthy bite he had taken from it that morning. The resinous substance was smooth all over and occupied the same space in his palm as it had before. Again he found that a small amount was enough to quickly satisfy his need for both food and water. He turned the stuff over in his hand, wondering uneasily whether it was honestly filling all the crevices where real food was needed—or merely expanding temporarily when it reached his stomach, thus tricking him into thinking starvation had been averted instead of just delayed. On that basis he took a few extra bites before replacing the lump in its pouch, its greasy surface already bubbling quietly around his toothmarks.

With the aid of his Timex Howard managed to arrive at a climbable bed-mound well before night was scheduled to make its sudden appearance. That evening he lay awake for over an hour, listening to a strange, hollow whistling that he had at first taken to be the wind scouring the nearby pocket valleys. If it was the wind then the wind had an appetite, for when it reached the base of his mound the sound grew louder and more rhythmic, keening and wailing eerily as if something was circling down there, waiting for him to leave his refuge.

Howard sat with his knees up and his arms wrapped tight around his legs, rocking slightly as he willed the mournful hunter to depart. Finally it vanished with a sound like the crack of a whip, and the night grew still. Howard wadded the dinosaur-man's garments into a thin pillow and forced himself to shut his eyes, knowing that dawn would be arriving in a few short hours.

As time passed he began to develop a routine, dividing the brief days into two-hour segments during which he performed rigorous physical exercises and kept himself occupied with particular lines of thought, hoping in this fashion to keep himself sane—if that was still an option—until he had outwalked the desert. He used the small notepad and pen he had found tucked into his shirt pocket to record sporadic notes on the local flora and fauna.

Howard now alternated night and day between his own clothes and the dinosaur-man's gray-green vest and shorts. He found the latter outfit to be cool and light-weight, well suited for daytime wear, while his jeans, shirt, and jacket provided the extra warmth needed during the cool desert nights.

It was late in the afternoon of the sixth local day of journeying when he saw another dust cloud. He was squatting near a tiny outcropping of quartz at the foot of that night's bed-mound, finishing off the three small bites of foodstuff he allowed himself for dinner. Through some process he was unable to fathom, the single lump of gray-brown resin regenerated itself when returned to its pouch after each meal. Now, seventy-two Boston hours after he had first begun ingesting it, the lump had only diminished slightly from its initial size. There were limits: he had discovered two days earlier that if he consumed more than a third of the substance at one time it was unable to completely replace the missing portion.

That the foodstuff was sustaining his life was undeniable. He still wondered if the process would continue indefinitely. He was losing weight—most noticeably in the vicinity of the small paunch he had been trying half-heartedly to exercise away for the past several years—but whether there were other less desirable effects he could not determine. His leg no longer ached; in fact, his strict regimen of brisk walking over the undulating desert for two hours every morning and afternoon had left him feeling healthier than he had in years. Still there were worrisome factors: periods of unexplained dizziness and nausea, as well as a certain drying and thickening of his skin, especially on the palms of his hands and the soles of his feet.

On the afternoon of the sixth day Howard was in the midst of a fishing expedition. Tired of the same taste in his mouth day after day—especially so far from the nearest toothbrush—he had resolved to snare one of the small landcrabs that haunted the shallow sand around the outcroppings. As he nibbled his rations he kept his eye on the ground in the neighborhood of his jacket, which he had spread in an arc around his feet and then buried to a depth of three or four inches in the fine sand.

He saw movement under the surface. One of the little predators had ventured into his trap. As he was reaching forward to yank up the ends of the jacket he was distracted by a blur of motion at the edge of his field of vision. He lifted his head. There, far to the east, hung a large dust cloud, the first evidence of sizable life he had seen in a local week. He leaned forward, shading his eyes with one hand and steadying himself against the ground with the other. Immediately he felt a stinging pain. He snatched his hand from the soft sand with a yelp. His neglected prey had surfaced long enough to clamp his fingers vigorously in its pincers before vanishing once more.

Shaking his hand briskly, Howard scuttled sideways in a low crouch, gauging the speed of the approaching unknown as he maneuvered himself out of sight behind the nearby red monolith, a recently fed eight-footer he had planned to scale after securing his dinner.

The rapid chaotic sunset was beginning, casting strange shadows and confusing shapes and distances. But Howard could see clearly enough to know that it was not the vehicle and passengers he had glimpsed six days before— nor was it moving at the same measured pace. Coming toward him was something long and dark and complicated-looking that traveled with a coiling, whiplike motion across the sand, puffs of dust obscuring much of its form even as they betrayed the great speed with which it crossed the desert.

Whether it had scented or sighted him he did not know. Perhaps it was only chance that kept the thing heading in his direction. Whatever the case, he was certain that the creature's path would bring it quite close to his bed-mound in the space of a very few minutes.

Howard carefully unwrapped the bright machete from its daytime storage place in his rolled-up shirt. Stuffing his other belongings loosely into his jacket, he tossed the bundle out of sight onto the top of the mound. Reluctant to make the climb unprotected, Howard tried clenching the curved sword in his teeth after the fashion of actors in old pirate movies, but the razor-sharp edge sliced the corners of his mouth immediately. With a curse worthy of an old pirate he launched the machete blade over the lip of the mound, grabbed a fistful of moss wool, and began hauling himself up to the top, his eyes behind him on the whipping, winding shape that was now no more than a hundred yards distant.

Turning back to the mound as he neared the top, he boosted his body forward and found himself staring face-to-face with a nightmare.

"Awp!" Howard cried, hanging frozen above the rim of the mound.

Round black eyes peered at him from a thin chalk-colored face that was partially hidden beneath a dark blue hood. Seconds later he recognized the garment as his own jacket and realized that it must have fallen square on the creature's head when he had flung it up moments earlier. The thing made no sound but stared out of cavernous eye sockets at Howard, who was still hanging a precarious four feet above the desert floor and whatever hunted there.

He could no longer see the sinuous thing that approached from below, but he could hear it all too clearly as it snapped and twisted close to the base of the mound. In the end it was the noise that pushed him into action, for above the cracking of its movements he heard the beginnings of a familiar high whistling wail that sent a cold chill crawling up his spine. He yanked his legs up and dove blindly forward into the middle of the nest, bumping the white-faced stranger to one side in the process. He rolled over and regained his balance, noticing with a sinking feeling that his machete was now held firmly in one of the creature's pale, oddly shaped hands.

The two sat and glowered at each other, Howard with

his heart pounding and his breath coming in little gasps, the skull-faced creature watching silently from the tent of the wayward jacket, a dozen or more white, wormlike fingers twining and tightening restlessly on the hilt of Howard's blade. The sky was darkening rapidly above the weird tableau, while below the keening whistle grew steadily more frenzied as something twisted and snapped in single-minded fury at the base of the bed-mound.

"So when's the next bus? Been waiting long?" Howard gave a tentative smile. "Here—friends?" His hands were shaking as he lifted them palms out from his sides and displayed them to his nestmate.

The creature swung its head loosely from side to side in an exaggerated pantomime of puzzlement, its thin neck extending on tightly coiled tendons beneath the chalk-white skin that reminded Howard of the spiraling cord on a telephone. Then it emitted a series of wheezes and croaks that seemed much too loud to have come from the skeletal body.

"Yeah, right, *gezundheit*," Howard muttered. "I hope you're interested in expanding yourself linguistically—I don't think my throat could survive tackling your language."

The creature croaked its comments again, gesturing with its thin shoulders and expressive neck while keeping both hands on the machete.

Howard shook his head. "Sorry, I must've missed that class. Hey, do you think we might set down the cleaver—"

He reared back as the creature suddenly sprang to life, hauling the machete above its head with surprising ease and swinging it down to strike a scant six inches from Howard's left side.

Howard threw himself to the right and twisted in place. He was about to hurl himself at the creature in hopes of disarming it before it could launch a second attack when something sinewy and dark fell twisting on the moss in front of him. Transparent liquid pumped sluggishly from the severed appendage. Was it tail, leg, or tentacle? Howard could not be sure as it continued to snap and jerk until the white-skinned creature caught it expertly on the flat of its blade and flipped it over the side of the

nest. At once the wailing, which had ceased momentarily
when the blade fell, resumed in full volume, then began
to recede gradually into the distance as the wounded thing
retreated from the mound.

Howard straightened slowly, gaping as the creature
carefully cleaned the blade on the thick moss at the lip
of the nest, reversed the machete in its worm-fingered
grip, and set it down between them. Leaning back with
a hollow croak, it regarded Howard expectantly from its
mournful deep-set eyes.

Howard reached forward hesitantly and lifted the
blade.

"Now I wish I did know your language, friend," he
said softly. "It'd be worth a sore throat to tell you how
grateful I am you were aiming for something other than
me." He thought for a moment, then replaced the machete on the moss. The creature wheezed in response,
gesturing to the blade. Then it lifted its arm palm-up and
mimed drawing the edge of the machete across its thin
forearm with the other hand.

Howard watched silently. The creature repeated the
motions several times as if to make sure it was being
understood, then reached out slowly and attempted to
perform the same pantomime above Howard's wrist.

Howard pulled his hand back and shook his head.

"If you're trying to tell me you want to slit your wrists
because you scared me, it's not necessary. If you mean
the two of us should become blood brothers instead of
killing each other, I appreciate the sentiment, but somehow I don't think I'm your type. Look, how about we
just curl up in our respective corners and discuss it in the
morning when I'm calmer and less apt to babble?" He
pointed first to the darkened sky and then to the soft
carpeting of the bed-mound. Then he settled back against
the moss and clasped his hands together under his cheek.
"See? Sleep. Do you sleep? You can keep the jacket if
you want—use it for a pillow."

The creature sat watching him without expression. Finally, as if making up its mind about something, it relaxed onto its own portion of the springy moss, drawing
its body into a tight circle and settling the skull-like head
on its bony knees, great black eyes staring out at him

from the enshrouding jacket till the darkness swallowed everything.

Howard listened to the faint rasp of breath from the other side of the nest, determined to stay awake until he could be sure the other had fallen asleep. But exhaustion soon pushed any misgivings out of his mind, and he lapsed into a fitful slumber.

CHAPTER IV

Language Lesson

HE WAS HAVING THAT DREAM AGAIN, WADING through sand drifts down endless corridors—only the drifts were deeper and thicker this time, clinging to his legs like quicksand. Each step was a monumental effort, and finally he could go no farther.

Howard opened his eyes to pale green morning light. It was still early, and the cool breeze brought him a spicy, pleasant scent that reminded him of cinnamon and nutmeg. Something white bobbed into view down by his chin, then disappeared.

He lifted his head and saw the creature from the previous night. It was hunched over in the vicinity of his lower legs, busily working at something with its peculiar hands. Stripped of the covering of his jacket, the chalky skull was knobby with small protrusions the size of bony knuckles.

"Good morning." Howard tried to lean forward but found his movements restricted. "Hey, what's going on?"

He craned his neck and saw that the clever wormlike fingers were making adjustments to narrow bands of fibrous material wrapped tightly around his thighs and ankles. He tried to sit up and discovered that his arms were also immobilized by tangles of the same material. From what he could see it looked to be some sort of living plant, with thick woody roots extending down into the tough moss beneath them.

"Hey, what's with the seat belt? You want to let me up?" He tried to suppress a growing sense of panic as he twisted and stretched unsuccessfully against his living prison.

The creature gave the bonds at Howard's ankles a final pat and turned to blink its hollow eyes at him. It moved toward his head and disappeared beyond the range of his vision. After a moment of silence Howard heard a small choked gasp.

The creature came into view once more, streams of red-orange fluid welling from a deep slice in the palm of one cupped hand, the many fingers writhing like a sea anemone's tentacles about the central wound.

"Jeez!" Howard tried to bend his arms. The springy moss offered no leverage, and the bonds seemed to grow tighter the harder he fought against them. "I thought we were buddies here."

The machete was in its other hand. Uttering what sounded like a croak of apology, the creature knelt at Howard's side and lowered the gleaming blade.

"Ow—dammit! Stop it!" Pain centered on the inside of his elbow as the creature sawed deliberately with the edge of the blade. Ignoring Howard's protests, which were increasing steadily in volume and outrage, it lifted the machete and pressed its wounded palm carefully over the sliced area. Then it held the hand there, boneless fingers clinging like a hydra's stinging cells to the sides of Howard's arm.

"You're some kind of Martian vampire, aren't you?" Howard struggled furiously against his fibrous bonds. "You're sucking all my blood into your system. Let me up—God! It hurts!"

The creature sat stolidly staring off at the orange-green horizon, crooning softly to itself.

Time stretched out endlessly. The mounting sun beat down on Howard's face until he felt as if his blood were beginning to boil in the relentless heat. Sweat beaded his forehead; it trickled down into his eyes and stung them.

Fever, he told himself. The thing had poisoned him with its orange blood. Maybe it ate that way, like a spider, trapping its prey and then injecting them with deadly venom before dining . . . His thoughts wandered into a confusion of grotesque images, and he closed his eyes.

When he came to with a start the sun was well past the zenith. He lay blinking for a few moments under the bright sky, then shaded his eyes and pushed himself up to a sitting position. His tormentor was nowhere to be seen.

The only trace of his bonds was a fine powdery substance on his arms and legs that evaporated into the breeze with his first movements. He touched the inside of his elbow gingerly and swore under his breath. Wrapped around the cut was a strip of cloth taken from his shirt, and the flesh above and below the bandaged area was swollen and tender.

Aside from the pain at his elbow he felt no ill effects from the bizarre assault. Perhaps the worst was yet to come. He wondered dazedly if he should open the wound and try to force out the alien blood but discarded the notion as impractical and extremely dangerous, as well as painful.

He heard a rustling from down below. Pale fingers appeared over the edge of the bed-mound, followed by the top of a knobby white dome. Howard looked around frantically for something to use as a weapon. Spying the hilt of the machete sticking out from under his crumpled jacket, he lunged for it, inhaling sharply at the pain in his left arm, then held the blade ready as the emaciated white face came into view.

"Hold it right there!" He brandished the machete, adding a few threatening sweeps in the air between them for good measure.

The creature paused, its small mouth rounded into a startled 0 beneath slitted nostrils.

"Fine—we understand each other. Now get the hell off my mound," Howard said through clenched teeth. "I want to see the back of your bumpy little skull by the time I count three. And don't even think about taking my jacket with you."

The creature freed one moplike hand from the moss and rubbed at a gaunt cheek.

"Actually," it croaked mildly, "I come bearing a gift

of much atoning for my unpleasant behaving in the early morning time of this day.''

Howard gaped.

''You speak English.'' He lowered the machete to his side. ''I don't believe it. The Martians know English.''

The creature stroked its scalp with a handful of writhing fingers. ''Actually, no. I could not wrap my mouth parts around your speech sounds without an extreme of discomfort. I am a Hant and speak my own tongue, called Neehant. Now, however, the parleybugs are industriously guiding us to a mutual comprehending.''

It was true. If Howard concentrated, he could hear the croaking gutturals as before. Only now they made sense. He shook his head.

''I don't get it. Why'd you try to carve me up? What's a parleybug?'' He eyed the moss around his feet for signs of infestation.

''The parleybugs have an extreme of smallness. They reside within, at home now atop the centers of speech in your brain organ where they may engage in beneficial renovations.'' The mop of white fingers divided into a network outlining a portion of the creature's knobby skull. ''Mandatory to share them with you through my body's blood, as you were clearly not of my battle-gang. Regrettable to conceive of no method for convincing you to partake of the parleyblood with willingness.'' The creature shifted slightly as it clung to the side of the nest and blinked complexly. ''It would be comfortable to squat on the mosstop in a few moments.''

''Yeah, sure.'' Howard set down the machete and moved away from the edge of the mound, his voice thoughtful. ''Come on up.''

The Hant entered the nest with a surprisingly agile somersault, landing on splayed feet and hunkering down in the moss with its thin arms hanging limply at its sides.

''So these little guys are in my head now?'' Howard was lightly patting his own scalp.

''Yes, affixed to the speech nodes, extending their complexity and function.''

''Uh, will I start growing bumps now?'' He scratched

tentatively at what felt like a small swelling above his right ear.

"Surely not." The Hant seemed mildly indignant at the suggestion. "These protuberances serve as organs of balance to the Hant. They have no connection to the helpful presence of parleybugs." Round eyes blinked sideways, then up-and-down. "Better to mourn the imminent loss of your minor fingers or prepare for the nose horn and tail you will soon be sprouting if you do not modify your diet."

"What are you talking about?" Howard rubbed the little finger of his left hand, where the gradually spreading patches of grayed and thickened skin were becoming most noticeable. "Do you know what's going on with my skin?"

For answer the Hant extended half a dozen fingers toward the food pouch that hung from Howard's belt.

"Evident you have been consuming Trull rations. Very clever foodstuff. Soon you are resembling deceased Trull well enough to deceive clutchmates of same."

"Oh, God, I knew there was something wrong with this stuff." Howard hastily opened the pouch and withdrew the wad of brown resin. With a shudder he lobbed the viscous ball out into the desert. "And I suppose you only carry Hant food in your lunch box."

Howard had noticed that the creature's robe and kilt were almost identical in cut and design to those the Trull had worn, but made from a softly shimmering pale blue fabric rather than the dull gray-green of the dead Trull's. About its own thin waist the Hant wore a twin to the adjustable mesh belt Howard had appropriated from the fallen Trull. Now he saw that the other's food pouch was embossed with a narrow white skull face instead of the three-horned lizard he bore on his own.

"Very right," the Hant intoned. "However, my gift of atoning will aid in preventing further distortion of your easily influenced morphology." From an inside pocket of its robe the Hant brought forth a thin, tightly rolled sheet of compressed black and orange particles.

Howard accepted the gift warily.

"I'm supposed to put this in my mouth, right?" He made a face. "There aren't any bugs in here, are there?

And can we be sure it's compatible with my metabolism?''

"Very sure,'' the Hant said patiently. "The Sunset People often partake of rockskin with no ill effects, and many deem it highly palatable, as well as nourishing.''

Howard tore off a piece and popped it into his mouth with a shrug. The rockskin proved to be a moisture-trapping species of lichen that surprised him with its pleasantly chewy consistency and sugary aftertaste.

"Not bad at all. Hey, thanks.'' Howard extended his hand, flinching only slightly under the clasp of a score of dry, white worms. "By the way, I'm Howard Bell, most recently of Boston. What do I call you?''

"Hawa'bel . . .'' The Hant essayed the foreign syllables with a grimace. Apparently the parleybugs drew the line at attempting to translate proper names for their hosts. "You honor me with the accepting of my gift. Having recently terminated a molt of some duration, I was extremely nameless when you found me. However, if you deem it appropriate I will now take up with gratitude the name you bestowed upon me at our first meeting here on the mosstop. I find 'Awp' to be a pleasing sound, resembling certain words of noble connotation in my Neehant tongue.''

"Awp it is, then.'' Howard grinned. "Pleased to meet you, Awp.''

"And I you,'' the Hant returned gravely, trying to mimic Howard's smile without noticeable success. "Until your face rose like a red moon at the mosstop I thought I was the last in the desert. And with the arriving of the slake I would have been less than that if not for your blade. But where is *Bossa'ta*? This is a Holding unfamiliar to me.''

"Beats me.'' Howard turned his eyes to the expanse of mound-dotted sand. "Tell me where here is first, then I'll see about locating Boston.''

Awp followed his gaze. "Here is the red desert of gold mosstops.''

Howard sighed. "Well, that makes everything clear. Seriously, Awp—where is this place? Do you know? There's a lot of red sand around—are we on Mars? Are you a Martian?''

The Hant shrugged with its face. "I am a Hant, but if Mars'sa is the name the Sunset People of Bossa'ta use for the desert of red mounds, then we are indeed in Mars'sa."

"Can't be." Howard shook his head. "My astronomy professor in high school said Mars had a day that was almost the same length as Earth's. Anyway, the sky wouldn't be green, would it? They've gotten pictures from the landers." He scratched his arm absently near the makeshift bandage and winced. "There's got to be an explanation other than the obvious one—my own insanity. Who are these Sunset People you've been mentioning?"

"They are your own people, Hawa'bel." The Hant squatted back on its heels to appraise Howard from deepset eyes. "Perhaps you have indeed been damaged in your reasoning. During the battle with the Trull, perhaps? Unless . . . When were you taken?"

"Taken? I just got here a few days ago, if that's what you mean."

"An extreme of oddness, to introduce a new warrior so near the end. The presence of the slake proves we are not long for this world . . . Hawa'bel, when you took the Trull's belt—as was your right after killing it—did you find it better stocked than your own?"

"My own? The only belt I brought was this." He pulled his jeans from the small mound of clothing near the edge of the nest and displayed a worn leather belt.

"*Rrreeee* . . . Tell me a thing, Hawa." The Hant was rocking with suppressed excitement as it spoke. "Are many taken from Bossa'ta, or are you the first in a long while?"

"I don't know." Howard lifted his palms helplessly. "I've never heard of anyone being 'taken' before—unless we're talking about UFOs or the Bermuda Triangle or something. But how could a UFO get inside the Matrix Building?"

"You are from outside the Holdings!" Awp's fingers wriggled against its flat cheeks, and the narrow head bobbed back and forth on its flexible neck. "The Travelers go seeking new stock after all. There will be much nonbelieving among the battle-gangs at Stillpoint. It was thought the Sunset People had finished their time . . . Much nonbelieving," it repeated. "Much deep inquiring."

"Yeah, well, I've got a little inquiring of my own to do if I ever—" Howard stopped abruptly, staring out over the edge of the mound with a startled expression. He rubbed his eyes with his hand, then blinked and looked again.

"What is it, Hawa'bel?" The Hant extended the coils of its neck several inches, peering along Howard's line of sight in perplexity. "What are you perceiving?"

"Don't you see it?" Howard gasped. "The water, the cliffs, those bird-things—where did all those birds come from? And that river, it's getting so loud . . ."

"You see dark cliffs, a river, a sky full of whisker-wings?" The Hant drew back from Howard with a croak of astonishment. "Keyholder," it wheezed softly, an unreadable expression on its alien face.

"What are you talking about? Don't you see it? Back and forth with the desert, like it's coming in and out of focus. Is it a mirage? But I can hear it, too. It's getting stronger . . ."

He felt the Hant's powerful fingers tighten on his arm; then he was being tugged vigorously to one side of the nest.

"Come, Hawa, we must descend! It is best to be on a low level when the Fade comes."

"Huh? Where are we going?" Howard allowed himself to be pulled over the rim of the mound to the surface of the desert, blinking and shaking his head at the crazy patchwork of images and sounds his confused senses were bringing him.

"Where is the water, Hawa? Where?" The Hant was shaking him, hands twined like vines about his neck. "Is it very near us? Are we beneath it?"

"No . . . about fifty feet over there. We're at the edge of some—"

Before he could finish his thought there came a moment of freezing darkness and absolute silence. Then the world was reborn in chaos.

CHAPTER V

Black and Blue

IT WAS LIKE BEING AT THE CENTER OF A THUN-
derclap that never ended.

Cliffs fell away in a sheer drop to an unknown depth
a scant two yards from where Howard and Awp lay
sprawled; at their backs towering black crags rose to
pierce the iron-colored clouds.

Howard lifted his head and watched uncomprehending
as his small bundle of clothes fluttered down the impossible chasm that yawned where a moment before the
sturdy bed-mound had stood. At his side, Awp prodded
his arm and pointed urgently to the machete, which had
landed at the very edge of the drop, a third of its length
protruding precariously over the uneven rim. Howard
scuttled over and retrieved the blade, then crawled back,
the hair standing erect on his nape and his eyes clenched
shut against the terrifying view.

They had fallen a short distance only—though from
where, Howard still could not fathom—onto a narrow
spit of black rock. On one side lay the chasm, while
fifteen feet to their left was another break in the land,
this one a rough channel through which blue-black water
coursed, foaming with a voice like thunder.

It was the noise that struck one—literally, Howard realized—for it felt as if a great hand were responsible for
both the ringing in his ears and the mad jumble of his
thoughts, a great hand striking over and over until it was

y

34

impossible to think of anything for long beyond the sheer pounding enormity of the noise.

Rising shakily to his feet, Howard looked out over a land of great extremes: terraced plateaus gouged by massive canyons that were themselves pierced by gigantic peaks. Sourceless rivers surged in a chaotic maze across the black terraces and plunged into many of the rifts, the combined reverberations of countless massive waterfalls creating the deafening roar that filled the world.

The sky was a deep ultramarine banked with tiers of gray-black clouds beneath a brilliant white sun. A multitude of dark, birdlike creatures flapped on huge wings among the towering peaks.

Howard stood reeling under the oppressive weight of land and sky and crashing noise. He spun around awkwardly when a fluttering pressure came and went at his shoulder. Awp was gesturing, mouthing something at him, the earnest croaking completely lost in the roar. Howard shook his head in exasperation and pointed to his ears.

The Hant seemed perplexed for a moment. Then its hands sought the sides of its own narrow head.

The Hant had no external ears, a pink-gray curlicue like the opening of a small seashell inset in their place on either side of the skull-like head. Now agile fingers probed the apertures, to return clutching puffs of bluish fluff that expanded rapidly into small ovals when removed from the twisty canals.

"I'm not going to eat that," Howard mouthed as clearly as he could.

The Hant ignored him, thin shoulders hunched as if in pain. It hurriedly pulled the two puffballs apart to form four, then reached forward to carefully insert the new ones into Howard's ears before replacing its own.

"—with few of the supplies necessary for basic surviving," Awp was saying as the pounding fury of the rushing water vanished abruptly and completely from Howard's ears. The earplugs themselves felt like small marshmallows: dry and soft.

"Wow. Unbelievable," Howard said, marveling at the clarity of his own words and those of the Hant, and at the utter absence of any background noise. "I've never heard of any ear filters this selective."

The Hant made its facial shrug. "The filterfluff has two functions: to prevent damage to the auditory mechanism, and to make speech sounds available for the use of the parleybugs. To all other sounds you are deafened while it sits in your ear holes."

The Hant scanned the near-vertical cliff wall that rose at one end of the narrow strip of black rock on which they stood.

"A time of great vulnerability," it commented. "We must strive for increased elevation." Its deep-set eyes seemed to grow paler, moving perceptibly closer to the surface of its face as it examined the jut of dark cliffs against the bright white sunlight.

"This place . . ." With the aural distraction removed, Howard turned himself in a slow circle for a better look at the fierce landscape. "Awp, old Hant, I've got a feeling we're not in Kansas anymore . . ."

"Kansa'sa, Mars'sa." The Hant grimaced its shrug. "You Sunset People are forever dwelling on names. Now the imperative is to reach Stillpoint before the next Fade—assuming capture can be avoided. We had luck once—more than luck. We cannot depend upon it a second time." Awp made its own slow scan of the landscape. "This place is the black-and-blue place, and I have only seen it twice before. Still, I have confidence that we may find a cave of good concealment on this rock face. We must occupy such a lair until nightfall."

"How do you plan to get us to Stillpoint from here? I thought you said it was back in the desert."

"It is everywhere, Hawa." The Hant uncoiled its neck in an impatient nod toward the towering cliff wall. "Now come—we ascend!"

The surface of the black cliffs was a wall of fractured planes that looked as if it might be capable of providing ample foot- and handholds. The cave Awp intended them to try for, however, was so far above their plateau that Howard could barely pick it out in the vast web of splintered shadows.

"Preferable I am rising first?" Awp asked at his side.

"I think you'd better." Howard nodded, eyeing the cliff

face dubiously. "I don't mind heights as a rule, but this . . . I wouldn't want you to be under me if I suddenly lost it. In fact, maybe I should just sit this one out. There must be some nice low caves around."

"There is a succulence of rockskin to be scraped and gathered on the way up, Hawa," the Hant coaxed. "Think of the feasting you will make when we have reached the cave of high destination."

"Appealing to my stomach at a time like this may not be the best strategy, Awp. Oh, hell—" Howard slapped the dust from his thighs with false enthusiasm. "Let's climb this thing."

According to Howard's battered Timex the ascent took them just over forty-five minutes.

About a third of the way up Howard's nose developed an uncontrollable itch, and he soon came to feel that he had been granted a rare insight into the true nature of Hell. Several feet above him the agile Hant scampered skyward—no doubt aided, Howard thought sourly, by its cranial balance bumps, and only held back, he suspected, by a touching unwillingness to desert its plodding companion.

Near the end of the climb they began to draw the attention of some of the great-winged creatures that flocked the higher peaks. For the last few minutes of their ascent the air was black with the dizzying sweep of wings, and weird, bewhiskered monkey faces danced around their heads.

"Curiosity only, Hawa," Awp assured him from above. "No danger so long as we are avoiding eye contact."

Finally the Hant wrapped its strong white fingers around his wrist and urged him up the last few feet to where it already squatted comfortably inside the jagged cave mouth.

"O praiseworthy Hawa! Good, quick climbing—the blood like a river rushes, *henh*?"

"Right. And the nose like a bastard itches." Howard dragged himself away from the cave opening, sat panting with his back against the sloping rock wall, and began to scratch the offending area furiously with both hands.

"Whew . . ." He lowered his arms cautiously.

"You're probably right about that rushing blood. I bet I've reopened my arm." He gingerly peeled away the double layer of cloth wrapped around his left elbow. To his amazement the wound had almost completely vanished, only a thin pinkish band left to mark where the Hant had initiated its unorthodox language instruction.

Awp examined the mark over his shoulder.

"In my body's blood live quick strong healants," it observed.

"I guess." Howard flexed the arm a few times, finding no trace of soreness. He followed the Hant to the cave mouth, wincing as his companion leaned out and extended its neck at impossible angles above the void.

"What are we looking for?" he asked, securing himself behind a sturdy rock tooth just inside the cave mouth.

"Those that look for us," Awp replied, scanning the eerily silent world of plateaus and waterfalls. "Nothing conclusive noted since the new world appeared, though I did believe I was catching sight of a patch of brown-red coloration several terraces over in the midst of our ascending."

"A large fox?" Howard suggested. "Some hikers with a new tent?"

"*Henh.*" The Hant bobbed its head in negation. "The Meticulous Victors wear that coloration. They know I am surviving the decimation of my battle-gang, and they were far from Stillpoint when the world Faded. It is not evident whether they shared our happy luck or plunged to their doom."

"Sounds like a nice careful bunch of guys, anyway," Howard mused, tapping the rock tooth with fingertips scraped raw by his recent climb. "Look, I know it's probably a bad time. I mean, I realize you're busy looking out for my safety as well as your own at the moment, but do you suppose you could reel your well-balanced head in here any time soon and answer a few questions for me?" He rocked slowly back and forth as he spoke. "Like, where the hell are we, for instance, what the hell are you, and how in the damned hell did we get here?"

The Hant drew its pale head halfway back into the cave and studied Howard thoughtfully.

"Your oaths convince me of your unfeigned and profound ignorance regarding our situation. That fact accepted, I am applauding your ability to face unfolding events with such an extreme of equanimity and good humor." Making a final scan of the outside, the Hant unsprung its neck and ducked back into the cave. "Now is perhaps a good time to attempt the mutual unravelment of these mysteries you enumerate. I may add to this list of questions, for you puzzle me greatly, as well." It lifted a writhing hand. "But first I am moved to present you with some rockskin as an emblem of my respect and friendship. Am I correct in believing that you did no gathering yourself on the upward way?"

"You are correct." Howard bowed his head, his mouth beginning to water at the thought of food. "I found my attention to be otherwise engaged."

"As I surmised. A moment of preparation, noble Hawa. Necessary to employ two flat rocks to encourage the appropriate consistency. The Wossil habitually stored such implements near the rear of the hollow." Awp moved past Howard into the shadowed portion of the cave. A moment later it was busily pounding strips of dark lichen, though with his ear filters in place Howard saw the activity only as a frantic mime.

He turned with a shake of his head and watched as the high white sun pierced the lowest level of clouds, sending rainbows arching in multichrome splendor around a score of nearby waterfalls.

Not such a terrible place with the volume turned down, he mused. Then a chunk of rock about the size of his fist vanished from the cave rim in front of him.

"Hey." He reached to examine the area with his fingers, felt strong heat, and withdrew his hand in wonder. Awp emerged from the interior of the cave carrying a newly formed sheet of rockskin.

"That's weird." Howard pointed to the gap in the stone. "Look what just happened."

"*Rrreeee!*" The Hant dropped the lichen and tugged at Howard's arm, backing into the cave. Two more gaps appeared suddenly in the rock, as if an invisible something had begun to nibble at their refuge. "The Victors have found us!"

"Oh, swell," Howard said. Then a brightly glowing

pellet arced into the cave and lodged in the rough ceiling, where it hung quivering like an incandescent insect. After a few seconds it was followed by another, then two more, then sudden blackness.

CHAPTER VI

The Redborn

HOWARD USUALLY WOKE UP ON SUMMER MORN-ings to the sound of his aunt conversing with Speedy, their overfed tortoise-shell tom. The aroma of toast and eggs and Canadian bacon would slowly fill his bedroom as he lay there listening to her coax the old warrior into accepting one more teaspoonful of Tempting Tuna. *Oh, all right*, he always imagined the unheard response, *but just to please you* . . . By the time his aunt came to the foot of the stairs to call him he was already in and out of the shower, toweling his close-cropped hair and pulling on shorts and a T-shirt.

"Mind the cat, now. Mr. Speedy doesn't need another knot in his tail," she would chide automatically as he bounded down the stairs and into the sunlit kitchen. "Where's that sister of yours? Sleeping the summer away, I tell you. Finish your juice and drink some of that milk. You want to grow up strong and tall, don't you?"

Speedy would leap up into his lap as soon as he sat down at the table. Clucking her tongue, his aunt would bring him a plateful of eggs, bowls of bright decanted jellies, and stacks of fragrant English muffins. Then he would dig in, the sound of the cat's contented purring growing louder and louder until it was like dining at the base of a waterfall.

Howard shifted position and the roar increased, droplets of cold spray making his face twitch. The sound persisted. It began to give him a headache. He fumbled at his left ear and opened his eyes.

Slabs of black rock towered against a brilliant deep blue sky, their fractured faces slick with spray from the crashing falls a few yards to his left. Figures the color of dried blood moved slowly on the other side of the water, unreadable shapes wavering through the fringes of the glassy torrent.

There was something wrong with his left ear. He probed with his forefinger and realized what had happened: one of the Hant's ear filters had come loose and fallen out during—

He blinked and wiped spray from his face as he came fully awake. During what? Why was he always waking up to situations he didn't understand?

He was on a higher plateau than the one on which they had originally appeared in this place. An even louder plateau, owing to the waterfall that crashed down the face of the cliff and plunged through a narrow flume in the center of the shelf of black rock.

His arms were bound at the wrist, crosswise on his chest, in the same fibrous, rootlike material Awp had employed the previous day in a previous world. By straining he could touch the side of his head with his hand. Taking a deep breath, he plucked the earplug from his right ear. Instantly the sound doubled in volume.

Clumsily he tore the blue fluff into roughly equal halves and stuffed the pieces hastily into his ears. Utter silence rewarded his efforts. Like the foodstuff, the filter material seemed to be infinitely divisible.

Sounds of speech began to creep into his awareness now that the background noise had been erased. Whoever was on the other side of the falls was having an argument, the strange voices rising sharply in both pitch and volume. Howard concentrated but could understand nothing of what was being said. Of course, he told himself, I haven't become blood brothers with these guys yet. He shuddered, imagining multiple repetitions of his first parleyblood ordeal. It seemed a rather high price to pay for some conversation.

There was a small croaking sound to his right. Howard

rolled over as far as he was able and saw with relief that the little Hant lay next to him, similarly bound.

Awp croaked again, eyes fluttering alarmingly, then lay still. After satisfying himself that the Hant was breathing regularly, Howard studied the gaunt features, noticing for the first time that his companion possessed several layers of eyelids, some closing vertically and others horizontally, the inner ones transparent while the outermost grew progressively more opaque. The round black eyes themselves were set a good inch and a half into the pale skull, giving the impression of either receding or moving closer to the surface of the face as lids of varying translucency opened and closed over them.

Several of the voices had climbed to a shout. Howard turned back toward the falls in time to witness a blurred scuffle through the curtain of water. Someone large was kicking someone much smaller, an unlucky individual who lay on the ground unable to escape or strike back, perhaps confined in bonds like his own. Howard caught a glimpse of blue garments and wondered if it could be another Hant, one more survivor of the defeated battle-gang Awp had mentioned earlier.

As if in response to his curiosity the figures vanished out of sight for a few moments, then reappeared abruptly on Howard's side of the falls.

Howard's skin tingled with gooseflesh as the half-dozen newcomers approached the place where he and Awp had been deposited. He counted eight of them—nine, if one included the motionless figure slung casually over the red-brown shoulder of one of the larger ones—and each seemed more grotesque than its comrades.

There were no Hants in the assembly, though there were two of the horned, dinosaurlike Trulls, as well as a long-necked, stoop-shouldered individual who also seemed to be of saurian stock but had an additional set of limbs between its arms and legs and a high, flexible crest of blue quills extending from its elongated snout to the nape of its scaly neck.

The creature that carried the limp, blue-clad burden also sported a pair of horns, but these were curved and more widely spaced than those borne by the Trulls. They were sheathed in silver filigree and capped with orna-

mental devices. The face that glowered below the horns
was broad and menacing, with yellow fangs and a flattened, upturned snout, the combined effect being that of
a perpetually enraged bull crossbred with a vampire bat.

Howard closed his eyes to slits and let his mouth fall
slack as the band of monsters drew near.

He felt hot breath on his face as he was examined by
a being that stood between three and four feet tall and
was covered with matted sheep's wool. Voices shrilled
and boomed above him for a few minutes, while he pon-
dered the parleybugs' herculean task in sorting out the
stew of conflicting languages. He saw a flash of color as
something sizable was unceremoniously dumped onto the
rock nearby. After another half minute the conversation
began to retreat in the direction of the falls.

Howard cautiously opened one eye and glanced to his
right. Beyond the unconscious Hant lay a second figure
clad in vest, robe, and kilt of shimmering blue.

With a grimace for the network of aches that seemed
to cover his entire surface area, Howard lifted his head
and shoulders to peer over the mound of Awp's body,
wishing momentarily for the little Hant's flexible neck.

The newcomer lay curled away from him, most of the
contorted body hidden by its garments, but as Howard
strained forward he felt a tingle of shock.

Clearly visible against the black rock at the edge of
the blue robe was a single hand. It was a strong hand,
slender and well-shaped, with calluses on the golden
palm. More importantly for Howard, it was a hand that
belonged unmistakably to a human being.

As he watched, the figure stirred, groaning as if the
movements caused great pain, and the hand disappeared
beneath the hem of blue material. Then, with a quiet
grunt of effort, the body turned slowly over to face him.

"Whoa," Howard said softly.

Eyelids parted slightly at the sound; then the dark gray
eyes widened further, seeming to focus on him for a few
seconds before closing again.

It was the most beautiful face he had ever seen.

Beneath the bruises and the dirt her skin shone a clear
ivory, flushed with rose and golden highlights. The hair

that fell loosely to her slender neck was a rich reddish gold that mocked the drab hue worn by their captors.

He winced at the scrapes and bruises that covered her face, arms, and legs, feeling a strange, unfamiliar ache growing in his stomach as he recalled what he had glimpsed through the falls of the hulking bull-bat's attack on her bound and defenseless body—partly bound, he noticed now, for her arms appeared to be free, though the long legs below the blue kilt were tightly held in fibrous shackles.

Howard watched her unconscious face for a long while, then turned onto his back and lay staring at the high blue sky.

Howard could not see his watch to gauge how time flowed in the Black and Blue World, but it was definitely moving more slowly for him than it had in the red desert. He glanced at the Hant from time to time and found himself craning his neck to observe the unknown woman even more often. Neither moved except as sleepers, sighing and stretching as best they could within their bonds.

Twice a Meticulous Victor returned to check on them, with Howard feigning sleep on both occasions. During the second visit Howard had the feeling that the injured woman was also awake, but when the shambling figure of the Trull departed she kept her eyes shut, her chest continuing to rise and fall in the measured rhythm of sleep.

Her face captivated him, and he returned to it more and more as the day wore on. He could not analyze why he found her features so compelling. Was it simply the undeniable pleasure of encountering another human being in this bizarre place? Under the grime and the fresh scrapes and cuts there was evidence of previous hardship: a small scar at the edge of her upper lip and another one crossing her cheekbone in a diagonal below the opposite eye. She had a strong chin and a straight nose beneath a high forehead. All told it was not a face that would be singled out as a model for sophisticated beauty in his own world, but it was compelling nonetheless—or perhaps for that very reason.

At one point as he turned from watching her to gaze

at the sky with its gathering clouds of iron, a fragment
of poetry he had learned in high school came into his
thoughts, and he murmured the words out loud:

> "Helen, thy beauty is to me
>   Like those Nicean barks of yore,
> That gently, o'er a perfumed sea,
>   The weary, wayworn wanderer bore,
>   To his own native shore."

He saw a flicker of movement and peered over to see
that she was awake and watching him, her eyes alert but
her face otherwise expressionless.

Howard cleared his throat.

"We haven't swapped any parleyblood," he said, "so
I know you can't understand me, but my name is Howard. Howard Bell." He tried to point to his chest with
his chin, then motioned toward the woman and lifted his
brows. "You—what's your name?" He repeated the exercise several times without result.

"Damn, I wish we could talk. I'd like to tell you a few
things—I'd like to *ask* you a few thousand things. I hate
what they did to you and the fact that you seem to be
stuck here with Awp and me. But I'm also glad that you're
here. I thought I was the only human being on this side
of the washroom door—not that I wouldn't have been
happy to run into you on the other side, believe me . . ."

Howard rambled on in a low whisper, passing the time
with ever more elaborate flights of fancy concerning himself and his taciturn observer. His stomach was beginning to rumble, and he spoke as much to keep his mind
off his hunger as to hold the attention of the woman. She
lay on her side watching him, her bruised cheek resting
on the back of one hand, and her dark gray eyes betraying
none of her thoughts though they continued to examine
him closely.

"And then after we've been together for a couple of
years and my book's sold a few hundred million copies
we can build this house out in the woods. We can set it
up so part of it straddles a river. I saw one like it in a
magazine once—sort of a contemporary, but with roots,
you know? The kids'll love it . . ."

"Hssssst!" Her face was stiff with alarm.

"Huh?" He followed her gaze over his shoulder and saw the approach of one of the Victors from the other side of the falls.

The woman gave him a glance full of urgent meaning, then carefully relaxed her body against the rock and allowed her eyes to drift half-closed. After a moment Howard followed her example.

The long-necked lizard-thing had come to check on them, its blue quills waving slightly in the damp breeze from the falls as it bent to inspect first Howard and then the still-sleeping Hant.

As Howard watched covertly the creature moved on to bend low over the woman, muttering to itself in a rapid singsong. Suddenly it gave an exclamation of surprise, then jerked viciously at the robe about her shoulders with its four clawed hands and began to haul her up from the rocky floor. The woman seemed only semiconscious, struggling feebly in the lizard's grasp. As Howard looked on in horror, the latter drew back one of its sinewy upper arms and prepared to strike her with its gleaming talons.

"No!" He bent his lower body clumsily and launched himself past the recumbent Awp, rolling the little Hant to one side with the force of his lunge. He landed between the woman and the six-limbed lizard, causing both of them to lose their balance.

As they fell apart Howard was surprised to see a thin blade of silver metal drop from the woman's right hand. She cried out in hoarse frustration as the lizard recovered first and kicked the dagger out of her reach. Turning, it thrust her roughly down onto the rock and swooped down to snatch up the wicked-looking blade. Holding the knife in two of its hands, their captor raised it high over its crested skull with a triumphant hoot. After stowing the weapon carefully inside its red-brown robe, the lizard-thing capered away to the other side of the falls.

"Are you all right?" Howard craned his neck anxiously toward the fallen woman. "I didn't—"

The woman twisted her body to face him once more. Blood was beginning to trickle from a split at the corner of her lip. Face dark with rage, she drew her head back and spat scarlet onto the black rock that separated them.

"Hawa?" Awp raised its pale head suddenly between Howard and the woman, blinked a succession of eyelids, and worked its round mouth cautiously. "Hawa, you still live—a blessing!" Slowly uncoiling its flexible neck, it spied the woman.

"The Redborn Alaiya! Now we are blessed beyond hope!" The small head spun back and forth between them like a pale balloon on a string. "You have already acquaintanced yourselves, I may assume, dear comrades?"

"Uh, not exactly, Awp," Howard said with a grimace. "I've been babbling, as usual, but your friend hasn't been in a very talkative mood—probably because she couldn't understand a word I was saying."

"But she understood your words with a certainty, noble companion," Awp declared. "As a fellow survivor of my battle-gang, the Redborn is naturally host to the same parleyblood as you and I."

"But wait, she and I never exchanged any blood," Howard protested. "I would have noticed, believe me."

"No need. The parleybugs in service to each team are like a family. They speak to one another through our words. Good clear communication, *henh*?"

"You've got to be kidding." Howard felt his face redden as the full import of certain recent events began to sink in.

"No humor was intended." The Hant lowered its head to the ground and intoned ceremoniously, "My new companion, Hawa'bel of Bossa'ta, I wish to effect your introduction to Alaiya, Redborn of the Sunset People, honored warrior and skilled comrade-in-battle."

"Pleased to meet you," Howard said with a tentative smile.

With eyes like shards of gray stone, the woman held his gaze for a long moment before turning to Awp.

"Wise and supple Hant," she said through tightly clenched teeth, her voice sounding husky and vibrant beneath the parleybugs' translation, "in worlds past it was often your custom to conceal selected useful items on the underside of your belt. Would we be favored by a quantity of unbinding salt sufficient to dissipate this tanglewood?"

"Indeed," the Hant replied with a puzzled sidelong glance at Howard. "But how—"

"My own hands remain unbound. The Victors' supplies are running low, and they thought me too well beaten to cause them further inconvenience. Recent events have no doubt supported this belief."

Reaching beneath the Hant's immobile body, Alaiya deftly unclasped and removed its belt. Turning the flexible mesh inside out, she extracted one of several flat pouches from its underside with a smile of grim triumph. Tearing open the pouch, she sprinkled part of the contents carefully over the knotty roots that bound her own legs, then began to empty the rest of the pouch onto the fibers that wrapped the Hant's thin arms and legs.

"Wait, Redborn," Awp protested. "We must spare a quantity for Hawa's bonds."

"Wise Hant, we must do no such thing," Alaiya replied calmly, upending the tiny bag over the last of the Hant's tanglewood. "This spineless mis-robe raved foul intimate notions to me as we lay bound, then interfered with my single opportunity to slit the long throat of one of these brown slakes, costing me my good knife Silversting in the process. If not for your own devious foresight we should surely have been doomed by his treacherous actions. Now you and I shall escape with our belts and our lives, make our way to Stillpoint before the Fading, and win ourselves berths on a new battle-gang."

Awp bobbed its head in weak confusion. "But, Redborn . . ."

"As you have named him friend, I am willing to grant the sorry mis-robe what is left of his life by allowing him to remain belted here among the Victors." She raised her palm as the Hant attempted to speak. "It is the more generous solution, I swear to you—for if this one were to accompany us on our journey I should only have to slay him for some new offense before too long."

The Hant turned to Howard with a look of baffled distress. "Hawa?"

"Slight error in judgment, Awp." Howard shrugged his shoulders inside the tight bonds. "Happens to the best of us on unknown worlds, right?"

The tanglewood had begun to gray and fall apart almost at once, as though the fibrous roots were being forced to age at a fantastic rate. In a minute Alaiya stood above them, helping to brush the crumbling remnants of the Hant's bonds from its cramped and shaking limbs. That done, she swept the still unsteady Awp up into her arms and turned resolutely toward the rock tumble that lay far to their right.

"Hawa, do not despair!" the Hant exhorted. "I do not abandon you!"

Then Alaiya trotted to the base of the strewn boulders and started to climb rapidly among the jagged crevices, the Hant cradled like an infant in her arms. Howard watched forlornly until the pair disappeared into a high gap in the rocks, leaving only a few black stones skittering down the face of the tumble to mark their passage.

Laying his head back on the cold rock, he stared at the bright sky and thought dark thoughts.

CHAPTER VII

Over the River

THE TRULLS WERE DEFINITELY THE WORST.

Howard figured it had something to do with the Trull insignia on the clasp of the belt he had been wearing when captured by the Meticulous Victors. When the belt was stripped from him after the departure of Awp and Alaiya, the two dinosaur-men had gone into a frenzy, tossing the ribbon of sturdy mesh back and forth while raising their beaks in piercing screams to the towering crags.

Were these brutal creatures indulging in an emotion as tender as grief? Howard found the notion dubious. Were they even capable of mourning the demise of a warrior from a rival gang—no matter its species? Again doubtful. More likely they simply resented the implication that a mere human could do away with one of their savage race. Whatever the reason, the black saurians took every opportunity to express their heartfelt antagonism toward the Victors' sole remaining captive. With the tacit approval of the bull-bat, the battle-gang's ostensible leader, the pair had assumed full responsibility for Howard's care and feeding shortly after the escape of the other prisoners, and things had gone pretty steadily downhill from that point on.

Howard did not much care anymore.

Days had passed since Alaiya had left him lying helpless on the black rock by the waterfall. After an initial beating that seemed designed to relieve the Victors' frustration at the escape of the others, Howard had been marched and prodded through the harsh landscape of the Black and Blue World for most of each day, as the battle-gang threaded its way through the maze of terraces and intersecting rivers.

Where they were heading he could only guess; without the exchange of parleyblood with this battle-gang Howard had been able to pick up no more than a few words of the several languages employed by the members of the team. These were limited to curses, commands, and the occasional interrogative. He felt fairly certain that their ultimate destination was the mysterious Stillpoint also sought by Awp and Alaiya. The fact that their trek was leading them in the same general direction as that taken by his erstwhile companions lent some credence to his theory.

At the time of his capture, Howard had eaten nothing but scraps of rockskin since before his arrival in the Black and Blue World. The limitations of that diet soon began to take their toll, and he found himself growing rapidly weaker as the days passed. When he tried to communicate his need to his captors he was at first ignored and later beaten for his audacity.

Finally, when his legs grew too rubbery to support him on the daily march, they had grudgingly put together a foul-tasting mixture composed of scrapings from several of the different forms of foodstuff carried by the battle-gang. Howard worked to master his gag reflex and hoped the noxious combination might at least serve to counteract the effects of ingesting a single variety, as he had no desire to even remotely resemble any of the Victors.

It was difficult to keep track of time. He had been checking his watch a few times each day for a while until one of the Trulls took a fancy to it and began wearing it fastened around its nasal horn. By that time he had been able to judge the length of the days on the Black and Blue World: about thirty hours from sunset to sunset, far longer than those he had passed in the red desert. By his calculations at least two and a half weeks had elapsed since his meeting by the waterfall with Alaiya the Redborn.

He could not get the warrior woman out of his mind.

Much of his waking time he spent rehearsing dialogues to be enacted in the unlikely event of a reunion. His desire to see her again—if only long enough to explicate his conduct on the day of their capture—alternated hourly with periods of sullen anger at her callous abandonment of him.

Aside from the constant but unimaginative brutality of the Trulls and an occasional outburst from one of the others, most of his captors treated him with indifference after the removal of his belt, as though he had at that moment ceased to exist as more than a troublesome animal in their eyes. The one exception to this was the little woolly creature. Sheepish, as Howard had dubbed the smallest of the Victors, seemed to display a furtive kindness toward him during the few instances when the rest of the battle-gang was occupied elsewhere.

Their journey took them along a generally ascending route, and the long days were spent either marching or climbing. The portion of the world that Howard had seen so far was largely uniform: rushing water, towering peaks, and black rock beneath a rich blue sky. There was little vegetation to break up the stern monotony of the landscape. The few small animals they encountered reacted with extreme fright to their approach, and the winged things that circled the peaks never came low enough for him to test Awp's warning by looking one in the eye.

Most nights they holed up in one of the caves that dotted the high cliff walls, with Howard usually flung by one Trull or another into the interior of the selected hostel to see whether it might already be inhabited. Sometimes a small animal would be crouching in the darkness. It would inevitably race out past Howard to the vast amusement of the battle-gang, whose members vied with one another at dispatching it in the most gruesome manner. Often these luckless tenants went on to become the Victors' dinner for that evening, though Howard was never invited to partake of such rich fare.

He was usually allowed to spend his nights in the rear of the cave with his arms unbound so that he could eat his meager rations. The team had apparently decided not to waste their remaining tanglewood on him, substituting tough leather cords to bind his wrists behind his back each morning. He took advantage of the evening hours to remove the filterfluff from his ears, finding the muted roar from outside preferable to the surreal world he occupied during the daylight hours: a silent place where the only sounds he could hear were the meaningless and unlovely exchanges of his captors. After several nights of experimenting, he found he was able to weaken the all-or-nothing effect of the filters by periodically thinning out certain thicker strands of the constantly regenerating fluff. From that point on he was able to pick up other noises in addition to the Victors' voices, though only if they were sufficiently loud or nearby.

One day after a particularly exhausting hike through the upward-climbing black plateaus, the battle-gang came up against a great wall of tumbled stone set squarely in the midst of the route they had been following. To judge by the freshly jagged look of the rocks the obstruction was the result of a fairly recent landslide. With a knot of ice in his stomach Howard wondered whether Awp and Alaiya lay crushed beneath the tons of rock and rubble, then resolutely banished the thought.

A map appeared for the first time: a small, oddly flickering circle of bright colors produced from one of the bulky packs most of the Victors carried in addition to their supply belts. A heated discussion took place among the more assertive members of the team, with Howard following as best he could on the strength of their gestures and the few words he had learned of each language. One faction seemed to be opting for an alteration in their course, favoring a circuitous route that would involve retracing their steps over the past few days. Their opponents proposed searching for a way through or over the wall of rubble in hopes that it did not continue on much farther.

Finally the bull-bat bellowed a halt to the discussion and barked an order to the gray-white sheep-creature that sent the little warrior scurrying. Rummaging through the pile of packs, Sheepish brought forth a small flat envelope, which it carried ceremoniously to the battle-gang's leader. It was rewarded by a cuff to its bowed head that sent it flying into the rubble at the base of the barrier, accompanied by appreciative laughter from its teammates. The bull-bat pried open the packet with its splayed fingers, then carefully removed a folded length of slick-looking material that gleamed strangely under the bright sun.

Howard watched in puzzlement as the bull-bat dropped the substance on the dusty ground, where it lay like a puddle of black liquid. Then, stepping daintily into the midst of the strange substance, it reached down with a grunt and began to draw it up slowly over its coarse-furred body and great horned head. The peculiar garment covered the massive form completely, stretching easily around the ornamented horns and sealing at the top, when the bull-bat pressed the open ends together and held them for a moment. Though the suit was solidly opaque from the outside, the bull-bat could apparently see out quite clearly, as it turned at once and began to mount the sliding slope of rocks and loam.

Moving like some bizarre shadow-shape, the black figure headed toward a slender crack situated several yards above the ground, through which a single narrow blade of sunlight shone. The climb on the dangerously shifting surface took about ten minutes. From his vantage point on the ground, Howard judged the width of the crack to be no more than that of a finger on one of the leader's pawlike hands. Expecting the bull-bat to peer as well as it could manage through the narrow opening, he was thoroughly dumbfounded by what occurred next.

The black-clad creature barely paused at the small fissure before it pressed confidently forward, its entire body sliding easily through the crack and out of sight on the other side. Howard wanted to rub his eyes, but his hands were confined behind him. Was it a trick of perspective? None of the others seemed impressed by the impossible feat—nor did they react moments later when their leader reappeared in the same fashion, its huge, black-wrapped skull popping out of the narrow slit like an inflating balloon, and the rest of the ponderous body flowing out behind it a second later. Did the creature have no bones under that leathery hide? Howard shook his head in wonderment.

Descending rapidly in a shower of stones to ground level, the bull-bat peeled off the strange garment and tossed it to Sheepish, who folded it with care and guided it back into the protective envelope.

The leader's findings were reported to the others in a series of snarls and grunts. From the reactions of those who had argued in favor of going ahead—as well as the muttered imprecations of their opponents—Howard deduced that the bull-bat had decided to scale the wall of rocks and rubble. Apparently it had observed enough from the other side of the crack to make up its mind about the feasibility of continuing along their present route.

Evening was coming, and a cave was selected near the top of a nearby cliff wall. Howard's arms were freed for the climb. He winced as the exertion quickly intensified the now-familiar pain of returning circulation.

The cave seemed deeper than most they had employed on the march, dwindling away from the broad ledge at the entrance to utter blackness at its far end. Howard tried to relax his body for the inevitable as the Trulls grabbed his tingling arms. The dinosaur-men were immensely strong, and he had learned from painful experience that a struggle would only inspire them to throw him farther into the shadowed recesses. Once Howard had seen a documentary on movie stuntmen. He concentrated on duplicating the loose-bodied roll he had watched professionals use to lessen the risk of serious injury.

Howard thought he caught a grimace of sympathy on Sheepish's blunt muzzle; then he was hoisted into the air and propelled forward, raucous laughter following him into the darkness.

He landed with bone-jarring impact near the back of the cave, his flailing right arm coming into contact with something soft and sparsely furred. He withdrew the arm instantly, waiting for a growl or the snap of fangs, but he heard instead a low, wavering moan.

"I'm really sorry," Howard said as he attempted to assess his body for broken bones. He struggled warily to a sitting position, his eyes straining to penetrate the dimness.

The creature he had struck seemed to understand his meaning if not the words, turning large, rheumy eyes on him in the half dark as it reached out with a wrinkled forelimb to pat his shoulder gently. It was small, smaller even than the diminutive Sheepish, and roughly human in shape, with a head that made Howard think of a turtle that had been reupholstered in worn brown velvet. He got the impression of great age as the thing blinked slowly at him, murmuring a few desultory phrases in a wistful contralto.

"Yeah, you and me both," Howard answered sadly, lightly clasping the sagging flesh of the extended forearm. The creature swung its head around at the noisy approach of the Victors, then darted a wild glance first at Howard and then at the rough cave wall that stood just behind them. Following the creature's gaze, he thought he noticed a slight depression in the surface of the wall as the Trull with the torch came near. It looked as if a narrow channel had been carefully chiseled into the naked rock. After another desperate glance at Howard, the creature seemed to make up its mind about something.

Crooning a final phrase in the direction of the wall, it gathered energy from some unknown source and launched itself forward past the lumbering Trulls, only to collapse with a forlorn ululation into the several waiting arms of the quilled lizard-thing that crouched a few paces beyond. The lizard gave a triumphant caw, then broke the creature's neck with a hollow cracking sound that echoed through the cave. Sickened, Howard looked off into the darkness.

That night he watched them devour the hapless creature.

First they charred its skinned body on a spit above the small, bright fire they had laid in the center of the cave. A similar fire was conjured up each night from a spot of bluish gel scooped sparingly from someone's belt pouch and daubed on the cave floor. The gel ignited into several hours' worth of leaping flames when spat upon by the nearest Victor.

The battle-gang tore into the blackened corpse with noisy gusto—all save Sheepish, who crept from the cave well before the start of the feast. Howard had decided the smallest member of the team was a vegetarian—or at least possessed of a more discriminating palate than its fellows—based on its consistent refusal to participate in

such repasts. From his seat in the back he could see the
little creature where it sat cross-legged on the broad ledge
staring up at the starry night.

The long evening dragged on as the battle-gang fell to
tale-telling and mutual insults. Finally the talk and rough
laughter dwindled, and they prepared to bed down. Howard was tossed his usual patchwork ball of foodstuff
scraps, which he downed as quickly as possible. He
moved closer to the rear of the cave and searched for a
spot on the floor where the bumps came close to matching his anatomy. In order to gain access to as much per-
ceptual input as possible, Howard had gotten into the
habit of removing the altered filterfluff entirely before
going to sleep. Prying the gauzy substance from his ears,
he settled down to the vast but distant roaring that raged
outside the cave like the death cry of a great beast.

Sometime near the end of the night he found himself
suddenly awake.

There was another noise, barely audible beneath the
roar of the waters. Howard lay on his back trying to de-
code the muffled groans and staccato barking sounds,
then crawled forward from his place near the rear wall.

The fire still burned on the rock floor at the center
of the cave. By its dancing light he saw the nearest Victor, the monstrous bull-bat, writhing and struggling on
the rough floor. He returned to his sleeping spot and
fumbled the filterfluff back into his ears, then watched
silently as the massive figure turned and clutched at its
brown-furred belly, its mouth stretching in a bellow that
seemed loud enough to wake the occupants of caves halfway around the Black and Blue World. Squinting past the
bull-bat, Howard could see that the others were indeed
awake and in a similar state, rolling from side to side in
apparent agony and adding their individual cries to the
cacophony.

Rising to his feet, Howard moved cautiously among
the spasming figures, his body tingling with excitement.

A flicker of movement drew his attention to something
huddled near the cave entrance. It was the little sheep
creature, watching him from wide liquid eyes as he approached. When he got within a few paces it suddenly

brandished a short dagger from behind its back and made a series of sharp squeals.

"Hey, no problem." Howard backed off slowly with palms raised. "I just want to get out of here. Then you can be king of the hill."

The little warrior made no response, but neither did it attempt to stop him as he began to move among the others, stooping gingerly to remove the mesh belt from each helplessly convulsing Victor. One of the warriors, a broad, flat-bodied creature that reminded him of an upright flounder with flexible arms and legs, had appropriated his machete, and Howard took the time to take it back, along with the warrior's scabbard, which he fastened to his own waist by means of an adjustable thong. Finally he reclaimed his watch from the Trull who had taken it and paused to strap it to his wrist. Since his bundle of clothing had fallen over the black cliff during his precipitous arrival in this world, the watch and his tattered Reeboks represented his only links to his previous existence, and he intended to hang on to both of them for as long as he was able.

He carried the armful of belts to the cave mouth. Sidling past a wary Sheepish, he laid them in a heap on the ledge. His original Trull belt was in the pile, and he considered reappropriating it, but after a moment he clasped the bull-bat's around his narrow waist instead, figuring that the team leader would probably be packing the most useful supplies.

He was about to begin his descent of the cliff face when something tugged at his memory. With a frown, he reentered the cave. Sheepish was busily searching through several of the Victors' packs in a corner removed from the furious stares of its fallen teammates.

Pausing to pluck a thin stick from a mound of rubble near the entrance, Howard spat lightly on the tip, then twisted up a quantity of the burning gel from the floor and walked to the back of the cave. While Sheepish craned its short neck to watch, he located the narrow channel in the rock wall and followed it curiously with his fingertips. When he applied pressure to one side of the cut a portion of the rough wall swung lightly inward on perfectly balanced hinges.

Howard waited a moment, his heart pounding, then thrust his makeshift torch ahead of him and stepped through the doorway.

He found himself in a small square room. Before him in the dimness sat a decidedly unusual object. Holding the blazing stick high, Howard tilted his head to one side, trying to interpret the unfamiliar lines and surfaces. In need of more space to examine the thing, he decided to attempt to drag it out into the main cave. It was surprisingly light, and he was able to heft it with ease.

The object was constructed mainly of polished wood and a smooth, ceramiclike material, with folded panels of lightweight fabric. Faceted stones dotted the wood with points of rich color, and fanciful beasts were depicted in faded dyes on the dusty fabric. Howard fiddled with the slender struts, discovering small fanlike shapes that opened outward and became rigid at a touch.

Some sort of gliding apparatus? Near the middle of the device sat a small ceramic housing. At its base ran a series of tiny toggles. Howard pressed one experimentally, and frowned at the lack of response. Thin, jointed stalks that had the look of steering rods depended from the housing, while straps formed a small harness on the underside.

Howard ran his hand down a carefully crafted shaft of wood that probably served as a rudder when one was airborne. He shook his head. The device seemed delicate and was plainly designed for a smaller passenger. He doubted that it could keep someone of his size and weight aloft for more than a few moments.

A shrill squeaking sound came from behind him. Howard glanced up from his reverie to see Sheepish backing toward the cave mouth. A few of the Victors were beginning to move more deliberately on the cave floor, with signs that they might be starting to regain control of their bodies once more.

Howard carried the device out onto the ledge, continuing to inspect it as best he could in the first wan light of dawn. It was a beautifully crafted object. There seemed to be only one way to insure himself a chance at further study, though it would doubtless make his climb down the cliff wall even more dangerous than it already prom-

ised to be. Making his decision with a shrug, he strapped
the device onto his back, gently bending pieces of the
flexible wood in several places to adjust for his girth. The
wing panels sat tightly contracted just above his shoulder
blades, with the small bulge of the ceramic housing between them, while the probable steering rods hung down
against his chest in easy reach of his hands.

He gathered up the belts and looped them about his
arms, then turned carefully and began to lower himself
from the ledge, feeling blindly for his first foothold. As
he was moving slowly downward to the next projection
he felt a sudden sharp pain just below his left shoulder.

"Ow! Damn!" Raising his head, he stared eye to eye
with Sheepish, while blood dripped from the dagger held
in the woolly creature's quivering paw.

Howard clutched at the rock ledge with one arm and
tried to bat at the little creature with his free hand.
Sheepish danced easily out of reach, squealing and chittering as it waved the bloody dagger. They both froze
when a hoarse scream sounded from within the cave.

Sheepish crept away from the edge and flattened its
plump body against the cliff wall at the side of the cave.
After a moment of silence the wicked-looking horns of
the bull-bat appeared at the cave mouth. The great head
shook groggily, then steadied as the bull-bat squinted in
disbelief toward Howard. Emerging onto the ledge, it
staggered toward him with a murderous cry.

Howard gauged his chances of making it to the ground
alive. Even if he could descend below the bull-bat's reach,
the ledge held several sizable boulders that could be used
to dislodge him quickly and surely from his precarious
position. Solid rock waited below at the end of a hundred-
foot drop.

With no alternatives in sight, Howard decided to shed
the cumbersome device and take his chances on the cliff
face. As he reached to slide his shoulder out of the confining harness straps a shaft of bright sunlight broke past
the peaks far to the east, bathing his back in its warming
radiance. He felt rather than heard the soft purr of energy
near the base of his neck as something came to life in
the small housing perched there.

Great jointed wings unfolded past his shoulders, then

dipped and rose sluggishly with a creaking sound in the cool morning air. A pause and they beat again, this time with enough force to tug at Howard's grip on the rock ledge. Then the sun climbed above the peak, and the world was flooded with light.

Before he knew what was happening his fingers were wrenched free of the ledge. He was out in the open air, struggling to jettison the encumbering belts while he grappled clumsily with the steering rods. The last belt dropped from his arm, and he yanked hard on the nearest rod even as the bull-bat stretched out a clawed hand and grazed the fragile left wing with its broad fingertips. The flight suit swerved in instant response, and Howard soared out above the channeled terraces with a cry of amazed delight.

He looked back as he glided away from the jagged cliff wall. Little Sheepish, bloody knife held high, had scampered past the reeling bull-bat, a bulging pack clutched under its arm as it crept to the edge of the ledge. Carefully stowing the knife in a sheath on its belt, it scooted over the rim of rock and started down the cliff face.

The bull-bat swayed indecisively, still staring in open-mouthed wonder at Howard's retreating figure. Finally turning its attention to its traitorous teammate, it roared, swiveled about on the ledge, and lumbered toward the nearest of several large boulders. Already several meters down from the ledge and climbing with a surprising agility, Sheepish gave a muted squeak.

"Good luck, little backstabber," Howard murmured. Then his erratic flight took him abruptly behind another peak, and he focused his full attention on the alien device that was bearing him, creaking and flapping, out of captivity.

Mastering the steering rods and the rudder was a relatively simple task for Howard, and he soon discovered that the small fan-shapes were used to provide additional maneuverability. Everything worked the way it should work, as in any well-constructed machine, and soon he was hovering over the broad river the Victors had been following for the past several days. Hanging like a faded moth far above the rushing current he found it easy to retrace in his mind the tortuous progress they had made over the last two weeks, his sense of pattern recognition sorting unerringly through a myriad of bends and twists. But where to go? he wondered, as the Black and Blue World spread out beneath him in all its harsh splendor.

He decided to make for the place where he and the Hant had first appeared when the red desert had faded out from under them. Perhaps there he might somehow find the means to return to his world, or at least to the desert of the bed-mounds—though both prospects seemed equally remote as he hung suspended in the high, cool air, his hair wild in the wind and the freedom of flight racing like a cold fire through his veins.

The day grew warmer as the sun rose, and the flying suit accelerated steadily, arcing like a swallow through the sky until Howard found ways of using the secondary rods hanging next to the main steering controls to adjust his speed. Solar energy was apparently readily stored by the machine; experimental swoops behind shadowing peaks had no noticeable effect on either height or speed.

Hours passed in flight, dreamlike. He was nearing the place where the Victors had captured him when he saw something odd out of the corner of his eye, a small flash of color that did not belong there.

He circled, pulse racing, and tried to spot it again.

Shadows fell on his face and arms, and suddenly there were black wings flapping in front of him. A pair of the high-flying creatures that haunted the topmost peaks had appeared, chittering curiously as they inspected him. Then Howard saw a flash of pale color and looked down to see a tiny figure waving both arms at him.

Something brushed his cheek. He lifted his eyes and found himself gazing into a wizened brown monkey face festooned with stiff black whiskers. Small bright eyes narrowed with fury as he stared dumbly. Howard raised his arms instinctively as the things attacked. He heard a crack and began to plummet earthward almost instantly, frantically working the steering rods as he tried to compensate for the damage.

There was something the matter with the left wing. Black rock rose toward him. At the last moment he was able to regain enough control to maneuver himself over a narrow stretch of water. As he neared the rushing river he saw that he was falling a scant fifty feet upriver from the crashing doom of one of the ubiquitous waterfalls.

He blacked out when he struck the water, all the air slammed out of his chest. He came to seconds later to find icy river water rushing into his mouth and nostrils. He coughed convulsively, straining to keep his head above water as the wild current seized him in its inexorable grip.

CHAPTER VIII

Through the Woods

MOMENTS LATER SOMETHING WARM BRUSHED against the back of his hand, clung for a moment, then fell away. Almost immediately it returned to clamp his left wrist in a grip of iron.

Howard opened his eyes and found himself held from behind with his back against the icy current. He felt himself being lifted slowly upward against the pull of the river; then, with a wrench that threatened to separate his left shoulder from its socket, he was hauled out of the water and dumped onto a slick, gleaming surface that he was sure had not been there moments before. His free arm slapped against a gelatinous mass that shone bright green above the dark water into which it protruded like an unnatural excrescence from the rocky shore. He knuckled the water from his eyes.

Bending over him with boots solidly planted in the rubbery green gel was Alaiya, Redborn of the Sunset People.

"Hurry," she cried as he stared up at her. Her face was pale with exertion, and she gestured urgently toward the nearby shore of black rock. "My powderbridge cannot last much longer in this current."

Howard tried to stand erect on the slippery surface, but his movements were hampered by the cumbersome flying suit. Alaiya reached out as if to tear it from his

65

back, but he raised his palm, warding her away as he fell once more to his knees.

"Don't wreck it," he said, panting. "It's valuable!"

Taking a deep breath, Alaiya reached down to clutch him about his waist and heave him to his feet; then she half dragged, half carried him to the shore. Shoving him past her onto the bank, she leaped to join him just as the slimy green mass began to come apart beneath her boots, flowing away in gleaming chunks toward the pounding falls.

Howard tried to speak again but found himself sputtering and choking around a portion of the river that seemed to be attempting to return to its origins by way of his mouth and nose. He turned away to spit cold water for a few moments, then reached back in a halfhearted attempt to free himself from the gouging lumps and sticks of the flying apparatus. Eventually he gave up and lay panting on his side next to Alaiya.

After her own breathing had calmed, his companion sat up and began to check methodically through the contents of her belt, apparently to make sure no water had entered the pouches. Howard noticed that one of the small pockets was half-full of a pale granular substance that sparkled greenly in the sunlight. He reached out a curious fingertip.

"Is that . . ."

"Powderbridge." Alaiya nodded toward the remnants of gel still clinging to the shore, moving the belt just beyond his reach as she continued her close inspection.

Howard was content to lie there watching her profile as she checked her various supplies with eyes, nose, and fingers. Finally she closed the last pouch and lifted her head.

"You came back for me," he said.

"So it would seem." She smoothed a strand of red-gold hair out of her eyes. "Finding you so quickly was unexpected, however. One moment all is calm, the next a bundle of sticks and cloth drops out of the air." She eyed him speculatively. "I am curious to know how you came to desert your newfound companions to challenge the whiskerwings for dominion of the skies."

Howard chuckled. "It wasn't easy." He told her briefly

of the long march with the Victors, of their discovery of the huge landslide, and of the decision to spend the night in the cave with the secret room. She raised her brows when he described the creature that had become his captors' dinner and the apparent consequences of their savage act.

"Wossil," she said thoughtfully. "The Victors must have deemed it an animal or they would never have eaten it." She rubbed her chin with a grimace. "So they pay the price for neglecting to familiarize themselves with this world. It is a law of the Keyholders that warriors may not devour one another, teammate or opponent, lest the offender be felled in turn by painful sickness."

"Warrior? That sad little creature?"

"Once the Wossil were counted among the battle-gangs, though it is said they never showed a true taste for combat and soon fell from favor with the Keyholders." She turned to scan the ragged peaks and canyons. "Truly I had thought them extinguished ages ago. Perhaps your rescuer was the last of its kind." She shifted her gaze to the flying suit still strapped to Howard's sprawled body. "It was also said that they wrought well in ancient times, though I have never before seen crafting of this quality pulled from one of the black caves."

Howard had begun carefully to undo the straps and fastenings that would enable him to slide out of the encumbering framework.

"So what do we do now?" he asked when he had freed himself of the device and sat cross-legged on the rock. "Those guys may still be crawling around here somewhere—they were already beginning to come around when I took off." He massaged his sore arms and legs. "And where's Awp? Is he all right?"

"I left the Hant in a high cave within sight of Stillpoint. It was entering an aftermolt and so could not travel back with me."

"How did you know where to look for me?"

"I was not sure how much ground the Victors might have covered by now." She rubbed flecks of green gel from her palm and looked around. "I decided to come back to this place to begin my tracking."

"But weren't the Victors headed toward Stillpoint, as well? Why didn't you just wait for us?"

Alaiya gave a small cold smile. "In point of fact the brown mis-robes were headed directly away from Stillpoint. I had snuck into their camp just before you and the Hant were brought down from your hiding place, for the purpose of tampering with the inner workings of their map. They caught me with my hand in the war chief's pack—that is why I was beaten so thoroughly by the cursed Dratzul itself." She rubbed her cheek where a yellowish bruise still showed faintly. "Truly I would have fought back properly against the great coward, never minding the tanglewood that held my legs, but I feared that might lead to the discovery of Silversting and the loss of my one chance to escape."

Howard felt his face grow hot. "I didn't know anything about the knife. I was just trying to keep him from hurting you."

"Yes." She regarded him soberly. "So the Hant surmised. Though you bear the semblance of a man of my race, only one who was truly ignorant of the ways of honor could pronounce so grave an insult to a warrior's very face." She shook her head. "The Hant insisted that you had acted stupidly rather than with malice—and it is persuasive like all of its dwindling race. Once convinced you were not of the Averoy—and of your profound ignorance regarding honorable and civilized conduct—I was bound to return here and undo the consequences of my anger."

"Yeah, we barbarians can sure get off on the wrong foot when we try to save somebody's life." Howard pulled himself to his feet and scanned the nearby cliffs as he tried unsuccessfully to stretch the aches from his legs and lower back. He released a deep breath and turned back to Alaiya. "Still, whatever the reason, I'm grateful that you came back. And now—assuming that you're willing to be seen traveling with an ignorant lowborn dog like myself—where do you suggest we go from here?"

"Toward Stillpoint, of course." Alaiya was already moving away from the river's edge. "Where else would one go among the Fading Worlds? Or is this more of the comradely humor the Hant said seldom leaves your speech? Such is always welcome among battlemates and can do much to brighten a grim situation so long as it does not become excessive—at which time it may achieve the opposite goal.''

"Oh, I'm a barrel of laughs, all right. Remind me to okay it with you first if I'm tempted to get really hilarious.'' Howard bent to gather up the flying suit, carefully folding and collapsing the device till it was the size of a small suitcase.

He lost his balance as he straightened.

"No, I can manage, thanks,'' he said stiffly as Alaiya offered her hand to steady him. "I've just got to retie my sneaks or I'll be tripping over my laces all the way down the black brick road to Stillpoint.''

Alaiya stood back, shaking her head at the bizarre juxtaposition of green vest and shorts above a pair of badly worn Reeboks. "A strange puzzle you are, Ahwerd. The Hant told me of your bravery—that you faced the Trull naked and unarmed and slew the beast with ease in the red desert.''

"Yeah, well.'' Howard thought he detected a flicker of grudging respect in the disquieting dark gray eyes. "The Hant wasn't there to see the incident, so he might have exaggerated things a bit.''

"It is true that left to my own assessment I would not have judged you other than a clumsy new-robe,'' Alaiya said matter-of-factly. "Still, the Hant has filled the days and nights with talk of your many virtues.''

Then God bless the Hant, Howard thought as he hefted the flying suit and followed the striding Redborn toward the nearest tumble of shattered rock.

After half an hour of steady walking, their route began to diverge from the path followed by Howard and the Victors, and soon they were heading in a completely different direction from that earlier trek.

Clusters of tall trees with shiny gray trunks began to appear in the pockets of dark soil that dotted the black terraces with increasing frequency. The land became gradually more level as many of the torrential rivers shrank into streams or went underground. Following Alaiya's example, Howard removed his ear filters, delighting in the quiet sounds of their footfalls and the chirp

of insects as the thunder of the waterfall region faded to
a distant growl. Soon they were surrounded by stands of
towering, gray-barked trees that swayed above miniature
valleys floored with a soft rose-red moss, and eventually
it was a true forest they walked through, with only an
occasional outcropping of black rock to remind them of
the noisy tumult of the steppes.

Alaiya set a brisk, measured pace that Howard found
no difficulty in matching after his weeks of marching under the prod of the Meticulous Victors. They walked
mostly in amiable silence, with Howard's thoughts divided between an appreciation of the growing beauty of
this part of the world and a bemused appraisal of the
changes that had taken place in his own body. Walking
through the serene wilderness, he had time to note the
muscles that now shifted smoothly beneath the sun-
bronzed skin of his legs and arms. Rubbing his belly
beneath the abbreviated green vest, he grinned to discover the tight bands that had surfaced to replace his
paunch. Alaiya caught him admiring himself, and he
blushed as she shook her head with an arched brow before doubling the pace of their leisurely jog, till they were
fairly sprinting across the carpet of rose-colored moss.

Howard was in for a less pleasant surprise when Alaiya
finally called a halt to their progress and motioned him
to a tree-shaded area beside a placid pond that was ringed
with nodding, flower-topped reeds. Before joining her at
the base of the stand of gray trees that towered above
them in the brilliant sky, Howard knelt at the pond's edge,
sweeping the reeds aside as he bent his head for a much-
needed drink of cool water.

"Good God . . ." He flinched back from the creature
that confronted him in the water's calm mirror, shook his
head in disbelief, and looked again.

"What is it?" Alaiya knelt beside him, hand at her
belt. "What did you see?"

"Are you kidding? It's the Werewolf of Boston. Jeez,
why didn't somebody tell me?" He stared incredulously
at the shaggy, bearded, sunburnt visage framed in matted
tangles of dark shoulder-length hair—then looked at the
exquisite face that now swam beside it in the water.

"The Amazon Princess meets the Shaggy Man. I can't believe you let me leave the house looking like this . . ."

"What are you trying to express?" Alaiya turned from the water to frown at him. "You are not happy with your appearance? Do warriors not go bearded on your world?"

"Not this warrior." He used his fingers to comb twigs from the area of his right temple. "I tried a mustache when I was nineteen, but a group of thoughtful friends were nice enough to ridicule me till I shaved it off."

Alaiya got to her feet and beckoned to Howard to follow her to a flat black rock some distance from the pond. She sat on the rock and motioned for him to sit on the lower ground. Then she removed her vest and began searching through the half-dozen pockets sewn into its inner lining.

"Here." She held up a small flat case made from two seashells. One edge of the lid overlapped the container with serrated teeth. "You would like to remove some of the hair on your head, correct?" She leaned forward when Howard failed to respond. "Are your parleybugs asleep? I said, do you want some of your hair taken away?"

"Um, yeah." Howard cleared his throat and looked off into the trees. "I've never had a haircut from a shirtless barber, that's all. No problem."

Alaiya leaned back. "My attire disturbs you?"

"Are you kidding? I was taught to be respectful of different cultures. Anything you want me to take off?"

Alaiya used the machete to hack off the longest part of Howard's beard, then applied a small amount of the sweet-smelling salve from the shell case, rubbing it deep into the remaining hairs.

"Is it your custom to remove the brows and lashes as well?" she asked, white-smeared hands poised before his face.

"No, thanks." Howard scratched at his chin and was amazed as clumps of hair came away in his fingers. Bringing him back to the edge of the pond, Alaiya carefully wiped away the remainder of his beard as she laved his face in the cold water, then had him lower his head so that she could wash his long hair.

She was hesitant about trimming his hair after she had

used the shell to comb it free of most of its tangles, informing him that among the Sunset People—or Averoy, as she called her own race—it was common for men of fighting age to grow their hair until it could be drawn back and tied in a queue. From her discarded vest she extracted a six-inch length of leather thong.

"Whatever you think," Howard said with a shrug. "You're the one who has to look at me."

Alaiya massaged a scented powder into his hair and then rinsed it a second time in the pond. He regretted the moment when she finally withdrew her hands and pronounced the job done, but he bent dutifully to view himself beyond the reeds.

"You do not approve? Is it not how you prefer to appear?" she asked when he made no response.

"It's not that." Howard straightened and rubbed his chin slowly. "It'll just take a little getting used to." He glanced back into the water and felt the back of his head. "Tarzan with a ponytail. If my sister could see me now!"

Alaiya moved closer to him, handing him the small pouch that held the cleansing powder. "My turn," she said.

"My pleasure." Howard followed the same routine of washing, then applying the powder and working it into the scalp before a final rinse. When Alaiya raised her head he allowed his hands to linger on her shoulders.

She looked back at him. "You are not finished?"

He shrugged. "I thought you might want a back rub. Your neck feels a little tense, and I used to be really good at this."

"All right." She made a gesture with her hand that he was beginning to recognize as her own people's version of a shrug.

Closing her eyes, Alaiya tilted her head forward as Howard skillfully massaged her neck and shoulders. When his hands moved downward along her spine, she arched her back and murmured appreciatively.

"You have a sister," she said as he continued to work on her back and sides.

"Yeah, Annie—Anne." Howard was surprised at her interest. "Haven't seen each other in years, though."

"She is not here in the Fading Worlds? Does she remain in your Holding?"

He shook his head. "She's in California, as far as I
know, with a cat and a roommate. Claire." He made a
face. "That's the roommate, not the cat. I always liked
her cat . . . We turned into two different people, I guess.
I was the English major, the quiet older brother who never
knew what he wanted. She seemed to have her career
plans all worked out by the time she was twelve. ROTC
in college, then a bunch of computer courses when she
was in the service. She got a hotshot job with some up-
and-coming corporation in California. We just didn't see
eye to eye about anything at that point. Later she chucked
it all and ended up in San Francisco writing interactive
programs for children's educational software. By then we
were down to birthday cards and the odd phone call.
Really, I haven't heard from her in over a year. And
now . . ."

"I find myself believing more and more in the Hant's
theories," Alaiya said in the silence that followed. "Ahwerd, where are you from?"

He dropped his hands and sat back with a sigh.
"Alaiya, I'm from Massachusetts, America, the World—
but what any of that means in relation to sitting next
to you on a bunch of reddish moss by the side of this
pool . . ."

"Tell me about your world, Ahwerd," she prompted
softly. "And keep doing that to my back."

"Well, let me see." He went back to kneading her
shoulders again. "Where should I start?" He began to
talk about Earth and about his life there, trying to orga-
nize his thoughts as he spoke but feeling overwhelmed
by the scope of the topic. In the end it was pure stream
of consciousness, and he found himself describing ran-
dom memories as they entered his thoughts.

"And in the summers we'd go to Maryland and visit
my Grandmother Bell—that was my aunt's mother—and
she'd take us all down to Baltimore on the train. A lot of
people still used the train back then. We used to go to
this pet store, and we always brought something back up
north with us, a turtle or a hamster or something. It drove
my aunt crazy, but my grandmother only had us for

a few weeks so she tended to let us get whatever we wanted . . .''

He looked down at Alaiya's upturned face and debated whether to follow a sudden impulse. As he was lowering his head her eyes flicked open.

"Yes?"

"Oh—well, I thought I might be boring you. Does what I've been saying make any sense to you?"

"Some. It convinces me that you are of the Averoy in appearance only, that you come from a free world and no Holding." She paused and pursed her lips. "Either that or you are a great liar or a madman."

Howard laughed. "Yeah, we shouldn't rule out either of those."

"How were you brought here? Do you remember?"

"Sure. I walked through a door into what I thought was the executive washroom of the Matrix Building. There was an angry Trull and a mess of red-orange sand waiting for me on the other side. I thought it was a dream or a nightmare or something for a while, but if it is I seem to be stuck in it." He recounted as coherently as he was able the events following his arrival in the red desert and ending with their meeting by the waterfall.

"Perhaps it was an error," Alaiya mused. "Perhaps somehow a Traveler opened a passage for itself and you fell through. I have never heard of this before."

They were both silent for a while.

"So what about you?" Howard said at last. "I gather you know why you're here."

"Of course." She shifted position to face him. "I was born on Noss Averatu, which is the Holding where the Sunset People live. When it was seen that I was Redborn, my training was begun, and on the day that I left my girlhood the Travelers appeared and I was taken to Stillpoint. I was chosen by my first battle-gang not long after that and soon entered the Fading Worlds as a warrior."

She turned her left forearm wrist-up and pointed to the first of the three small emblems tattooed there like pieces of an unfinished bracelet.

"The Howling Miscreants—not a very successful team," she said with a rueful smile. "But I fought well, returning many belts to Stillpoint, and soon, after I had

proven my worth, I was able to move to a more presti-
gious team. As Turns passed there were offers from other,
more famous battle-gangs, and last Round I joined the
Ferocious Rulebenders. We were a mighty team, ruthless
and clever—undefeated till we were ambushed in the red
desert this past Turn. The Hant and I suspect some
treachery there. We believe the Dratzul made a pact with
a Traveler to gain unlawful information on our whereabouts for the Meticulous Victors.''

"I love those names," Howard said with a grin. "It
reminds me of a club I started when I was about six. We
called ourselves the Breakneck Boys, and we were going
to solve crime and unravel mysteries. God, I haven't
thought about that in years—I wonder if anyone ever
found our clubhouse under the porch?''

"This was an initiation organization for young males
on your world?" Alaiya asked.

"No, actually, there were only seven of us, and three
were girls. We just liked the sound of Breakneck Boys.
It wasn't till a few years later that we learned we weren't
supposed to get along like that and started another club
for boys only. The Atomic Bravos, we called it—no girls
allowed. My sister hated it." He shook his head in rec-
ollection. "We even had our own secret password: 'Gone
fission.' Get it?''

"On Noss Averatu we had secret societies for the children, though segregation was based on clan affiliation
rather than gender and there was mandatory dissolution
at the end of every year." She found the shell comb in
the moss and began to draw it slowly through her long
hair. "Once I was deemed Redborn I no longer had time
to participate.''

Howard reached out his hand and drew the back of his
knuckles down the shining red-gold strands. "This is why
they called you Redborn, right?''

Alaiya quirked her lips in a crooked smile that empha-
sized the small scar. "The Redborn are those of each
generation who are judged to be born for battle and chosen while still children to be trained in the spilling of
blood.''

"Ah. Sorry." He withdrew his hand slowly.

"For what? That I am a warrior? I have fulfilled the

promise of my early years, spilling much blood in a rainbow of colors.'' Her expression was unreadable. ''When you are a child in the Holding you do not know about the other colors—you think all blood will flow red like your own . . .''

''How do they get your people, Alaiya? Doors that don't lead where they're supposed to, like with me?''

She wrinkled her nose in a small sniff—apparently the equivalent of a headshake among the Averoy.

''Stories say that our original home was a place of great beauty, a vast field of flowers where the Averoy lived in tranquil plenty. Then many thousands of Rounds ago the first Travelers appeared, monstrous creatures like dark holes in the air, that were themselves a bridge between two distant places. They served the Keyholders, never-seen demons that spoke and acted through them. It is said that they feigned friendship at first, but when the Averoy refused to bow to their will the Keyholders employed the Travelers to wreak great destruction. Thousands died. Finally there was a treaty, and a group of men and women were chosen to go with the Travelers under the condition that the Keyholders would never return to our world.

''They were taken to another place far from home, a harsh world that the Keyholders called a Holding, and left to struggle for life. We called it Noss Averatu, the Holding of the Averoy. Many of those men and women died soon after coming to the Holding, life was so difficult there for them. None of them ever returned to their home world, nor have any of their descendants.

''The survivors of the original settling bred and grew strong. At certain intervals the Travelers came to inspect the young, culling the fiercest from those just entering adulthood. To Stillpoint they were taken to learn the warrior's game. So it has been for countless Rounds, until my parents' parents' time when the Averoy began to lose favor with the Keyholders. It was felt our stock was too capricious—and too often rebellious, refusing to fight for the glory of our masters. And this is true: given the choice we will seek to crush the unseen Keyholders before we attack an opposing battle-gang.'' She twirled a tuft of rosy moss between thumb and forefinger. ''And so we feel their wrath—or their indifference—and are almost never chosen for the Fading Worlds. Now we have become what they name us—a Sunset People, destined to dwindle and die here at the end of our long day.''

Howard sat with his knees bent in front of him and his hands folded around his legs. "Do you ever see your family? Brothers, sisters, folks?"

"It is through successful performance as a warrior that we earn the eventual right to return to the Holding of our birth. My brothers were not chosen for the Fading Worlds, and they remain—if they still live—with others of my clan on Noss Averatu. Here there is only my mate.''

"Your—" Howard coughed. "You have a mate?"

"Omber Oss, who fights for the Gold Schemers.'' She bent her head to peer absently into the water, where small shapes swam and darted. "He is to join the Rulebenders if he survives the Round, and then we will fight together as is proper.''

"I see.'' Howard studied the nearby stand of trees while his fingers tugged at sprigs of the rosy moss. "Congratulations. Good luck to both of you.''

Alaiya gave him an odd look, then rose and stood surveying the quiet pond with arms crossed at her breast.

"We must try to capture a water creature or two.'' She drew her vest on and began to relace the leather ties. "They have a good taste and will provide some dietary supplements lacking in the foodstuff.'' Alaiya had shared her own small mound of sustenance with Howard at the beginning of the walk. Though he was grateful, he was disappointed when the foodstuff designed for humans turned out to be no tastier than that meant for other races.

"Yeah, sure.'' He stood up and looked around for some means of constructing fishing apparatus. Suddenly he clutched his head and swayed at the edge of the pond.

"What is it? Are you all right?'' Alaiya stood at his side, supporting him while she studied his face with concern.

"Yeah, I just had the weirdest dizzy feeling—like I was on a rollercoaster for a few seconds. Now it's—"

"Ahwerd!'' Alaiya pointed past him to an open area

among the tree clusters, pulling him around with her other hand on his shoulder.

"What on earth . . ." Howard blinked at the strange patch of darkness that hung above the rose-red moss in a rippling, ragged oval, half again as tall as a man. It was like a sheet of absolute blackness suspended in the cool forest air, shimmering at its outer perimeter with a border of silvery light that hurt his eyes.

"Traveler—we must run!" Alaiya tugged at his arm, turning to gather their supplies from the base of the nearby trees. She turned back to where Howard stood rooted in wonderment. "Come! There is no time."

"But . . ." As he stumbled backward, he felt something pulling at his attention, a mesmerizing force that made him want to stand still and stare. Something moved inside that black circle . . .

"Take your eyes away!" He felt Alaiya's hand on his arm again; then her fingers gripped the sides of his face and her gray eyes bored into his own. He shook his head and began to run haltingly at her side, resisting with all his will the urge to stop and look back.

Alaiya led them into a more heavily wooded area, leaping like an antelope over fallen trunks and darting skillfully past bushes laden with wicked-looking thorns as she ushered Howard along. Suddenly an eerie whistling sound pierced the growing gloom of the forest, a hollow, piteous howl that was soon joined by a second, then a third. Something large began to whip and slide through the underbrush at their backs.

"Slakes," Alaiya gasped as they increased their mad dash through the shadowy woods. The trees above them towered into invisibility, with gray branches so tightly knit at their crowns that no sunlight could penetrate. Alaiya plunged deliberately into the dark heart of the forest, and Howard stumbled blindly at her side as the wan slices of light visible at the edge of the wood grew fainter.

"Alaiya—I can't see," he said, panting. "I'm going to trip—"

"Wait then . . . Here—" came her strained voice at his side. Turning, he was astonished to see Alaiya shimmering with a cold, ghostly light as she ran next to him. The radiance, which seemed to pour directly from her skin and hair, was enough to illuminate the forest floor for a few feet in front of them.

"You never told me—you glowed in the dark," Howard gasped.

Branches cracked behind them, and the eerie wails suddenly doubled in volume.

"Run!" Alaiya cried, leaping a small brook and pulling ahead into the enfolding darkness.

Howard ran.

CHAPTER IX

In Grandmother's House

IF THE FEW HOURS HOWARD HAD SPENT IN FLIGHT above the black canyons of this world had seemed dreamlike, the long minutes that passed while he ran stumbling through the dark wood were the essence of a nightmare. Ahead of him flitted the pale figure of Alaiya, glowing like a ghostly candle as she led him through the black gloom. The ground beneath him was treacherous, the soft moss cobbled with rocks and littered with fallen branches, so that he could not allow his concentration to falter for an instant lest he fall sprawling in the darkness. Behind them something else came quickly through the trees, a snapping, sliding pursuer that voiced its eagerness to close the gap between them with an eerie, plaintive wail that sent icy ripples crawling up Howard's spine.

Howard glanced back for some sign of that which followed them and in that instant almost tripped over a twisted gray trunk that lay before him. He jumped frantically to clear the log, then veered abruptly to one side to avoid colliding with Alaiya, who stood wide-eyed in his path. He lurched to an awkward stop seconds before crashing into the shimmering figure.

"What—" He struggled to control his ragged breathing.

"A choice." Alaiya moved so that the radiance from her skin illuminated the small clearing in which they found themselves. Two paths diverged into the darkness

from the clearing's edge. "I say left—do you agree?"
She started in that direction.

"Fine—no!" Howard stopped and stood staring after
her retreating figure. "The slakes will go left. We have
to take the right—hurry!"

"How—"

"I have no idea. Come on!"

Alaiya retraced her steps and plunged down the right-
hand path, the ghostly glow shining ahead of her like a
pale beacon. Howard followed, his heart pounding in his
throat while his thoughts tried to outrace his steps. The
rough trail seemed to be leading upward through the dark
woods, as though they were climbing a ridge. Soon the
sounds of their pursuit had dwindled to a far-off wail,
and at some point Howard realized that even that had
ceased. By tacit agreement they slowed their pace to a
steady hike.

"You were right." Alaiya studied him over her shoulder as she pulled her way up through vines and small
trees. The expression on her luminous face was guarded.
"Ahwerd, what told you this was the way to follow?"

He shook his head. "I don't know. It was just a feeling, a tug in this direction." He squinted past her into
the shadows ahead. "What's this?"

Something solid loomed in front of them behind a
tangle of vines and leafy branches, a gray expanse that
filled their path. At first Howard thought it was the bole
of a great tree; then he realized that there was something
deliberate in the shape and curve of the thing, an archi-
tecture that he could only glimpse in the pale radiance.

"Is it a wall?" Alaiya raised her arms, casting the soft
glow higher into the twisted vines and branches that partially concealed the structure. There were darker patches
in the gray, the lowest set about twice their height above
the upward-sloping ground. Niches? Windows?

Howard started to reply, then caught his breath.

"Listen." He touched Alaiya's arm and pointed to one
of the dark areas. There was a quiet scrabbling sound;
then something perched there above them. He caught a
musty odor drifting down, as if someone had opened the
door to the cellar in a long-abandoned building.

"Is there only one?" Alaiya whispered. They moved closer together, linking hands.

There was a low cough from above, then a creaking sound followed by silence. Alaiya pulled her hand free and laid her fingers against his arm.

"Give me your sword."

He slowly lifted the machete from its scabbard and passed it to her in the dimness. "Is it an animal?" he asked close to her ear.

A series of coughs made them both start; then a dry voice like the rustling of dead leaves came from above their heads.

"Good . . . question . . ." Another dry cough. *"Ee-yena . . . Wait . . ."*

Howard raised his brows at Alaiya, who was frowning in puzzlement. "Did you understand that?" she asked.

"I got all but the third word. Why—didn't you?"

Her frown deepened. "The third word was all I could understand. It said 'wait.' Other than that it was gibberish."

"No." He squinted up at the barely visible shape. "It was English. Was that other word—*eeyeena?*—was that word in your language?"

She nodded. "Its pronunciation was better than yours."

More movement came from above. They scanned the dark wall to find another shadow-shape barely visible in a higher niche.

"Now . . . is better," husked the creature that had spoken first, while the newcomer rasped a phrase that Howard could not understand.

He exchanged glances with Alaiya. "Could you . . ."

"Yes. The second one spoke Averant. And that one?" She used the machete to indicate the lower niche.

He nodded. "English."

"Yes . . ." came the soft leaf-rustle voice from above. *"Tsaa . . ."* the other voice said simultaneously.

"Is better . . . only need . . . two throat . . . two tongue . . . to speak you both . . ." Coughing erupted from the original speaker, and the other fell silent until it had finished. "Complicated sound," it continued.

"Bad for simple throat . . . more time . . . make better."

"Who are you?" Alaiya asked. "Are you Wossil?"

"Not Wossil," came the dry whisper, while its soft echo said, "Wossil *kaati.*" They heard creaking as the second creature shifted position in its niche. "Made Wossil . . . made before-Wossil . . . upright brown-fur live in treetop . . . Wossil live in cave . . . Wossil talker . . . gone, all talker gone . . . must use upright brown-fur, throat simple, not good talker . . ."

The dry voice grew clearer as it spoke, though the painful rasp of words made Howard wince in sympathy.

"You're doing fine for the first time," he said. "Both of you."

A rattling sound that could have been laughter came in reply from the dark niches. "Is not both, is one . . . one made before-Wossil, one made Wossil . . . now one talk to you, use two throat, two tongue, two upright brown-fur . . ."

"That would make her grandmother to the Wossil, right?" Howard whispered to Alaiya. "She created their ancestors, and then she made them."

Again the protracted rattling. "Good thought, good understanding. I make upright brown-fur first, not perfect. Keep some. Change most, make big, send to live in cave. Is Wossil, is better. I stay forest, sleep long. Now wake up, find other come in my world like breaking, like small sharp point, bring many strange, kill my Wossil. Last one dead, you darkhair there, you see . . ."

"Yes," Howard said. "In the cave. How did you know?"

"My Wossil see, I see. I make eye, throat, leg, tongue. I use eye, throat, leg, tongue. Is fair."

"The Wossil helped me to escape my enemies. It gave me a flying device. I wanted to thank it for that."

"Is welcome," the dry voice said.

There was another round of convulsive coughing, this time from the creature that was speaking Averant, and as before the other waited patiently till its partner had recovered.

"Is hard speaking . . . throat hurt," it said at last. "Are hungry? Darkhair, brightskin eat, can rest two throat, give water."

"Sure," Howard said. "That would be great."

"Can climb past vine near brightskin speaker . . . around, inside."

"I guess she means we go toward the one who speaks Averant," Howard said. "Shall we?"

Alaiya shook her head and moved to follow Howard. "This is so strange," she said as they squeezed through a tight network of intersecting vines. "I feel like I must be dreaming."

"What, you find it hard to accept that we've been talking to the God of the Wossils, the grandmother of intelligent life on the Black and Blue World?" Howard reached back to cuff her playfully on the shoulder. "Come on, loosen up. We're about to get lunch."

There was a small opening at the end of the corridor of vines. They had to hunker low and squeeze sideways one at a time in order to get through it. Inside, the radiance from Alaiya's body showed them the outlines of a small circular enclosure set at an angle like a floorless, roofless tower on the sloping ground.

Creaking and rustling from above informed them that the two speakers were turning in their niches to face inward, while more small shapes appeared at the top of the gray wall at the back of the structure where the ground was the highest and the wall correspondingly lower.

"Look, these must be the waiters, dressed in their charming native garb, come to take our order," Howard whispered to Alaiya. "If today's special turns out to be rockskin I suggest we take our business elsewhere."

"I've never met anyone who enjoyed vexing the parleybugs as much as you do," she replied with a shake of her head that left dancing afterimages in the darkness between them. "Does everyone speak with so little substance where you come from?"

"Only those who practice every day," Howard replied, squinting in the dimness at a low mound set near the center of the moss floor. "Come on—if you insist on acting like a flashlight I'm going to have to start using you as one." He slipped his arm through Alaiya's and brought her with him as he approached the object. Upon close inspection it appeared to be a covered well or cistern made of the same gray material as the enclosure.

"I wonder if this is our table?" Howard mused. "Think we can see the floor show from here?" Just then one of the small creatures left the far wall and ambled toward them. Reaching the gray mound, it climbed up onto the lid and sat facing them, a diminutive version of the old Wossil Howard had met briefly in the cave by the landslide. Its body was covered with short brown fur, and it wore intricate circlets of plaited grasses around its wrists and neck.

A brief spate of coughing signaled that those who sat in the niches were preparing to comment.

"Is not table," the one who spoke English said. "Is myself."

"That—that's you?" Howard looked back at the little creature that sat scratching itself and blinking.

"Imperfect understanding." The rattling noise echoed hollowly inside the gray walls. "Inside, underneath stone top is myself . . . warm and dry in a bed of leaves, safe from rain. This upright brown-fur I bring for nearer eye, to see two guest in my house . . ."

"I get it." Howard nodded. "You're looking at us through this little guy while you use his cousins up there to talk."

"Is right, but two throat tired . . . Is food come, you eat, talk later . . ."

More of the little creatures came into view, each with its grass circlets and each carrying a handful of purplish berry-size objects that they brought to the well and deposited there near the feet of the upright brown-fur who squatted there.

Howard picked up a few and sniffed at them. "What do you think? Fruit? Nuts? Hors d'oeuvres?" He shrugged at Alaiya, then popped them in his mouth. "Not bad. A little of each."

Alaiya followed suit, chewing thoughtfully. "I have not seen such on this world before. Perhaps they are only native to this part of the forest."

"Yeah, or maybe Grandmother Wossil whipped them

up for us special,'' Howard said around a second mouthful as rattling laughter came from above.

"Is only grow here in nightwood," the creatures croaked from their niches in both languages. "Eat now . . . stop question, question, force me talk to you!"

Howard winked at Alaiya, and they slowly devoured the rest of the nut-berries in silence. When they had finished Howard moved to the base of the wall where the speakers sat, and craned his neck.

"Thank you for the food. Do you mind if we look around now? Don't hurt yourself answering—just cough once for no and twice for yes."

A single cough came from each inhabited niche, then a barely suppressed chorus of rattling laughter.

"I think she likes me," Howard said to Alaiya. "Hey, your bulb's going out."

"It doesn't last long without more exposure to sunlight," Alaiya said, looking down at the dimming light coming from her arms. "It comes from a bioluminescent one can purchase as a food supplement. I should try to conserve the energy in case we have to run again." The pale radiance obediently faded further.

Howard shook his head. "I think that is so neat," he said.

After obtaining permission in the form of two more coughs and a rattle, they lit a small torch using spittle and a pinch of firejelly from Alaiya's belt. Soon two more upright brown-furs entered the enclosure, carefully carrying between them a stretched skin filled with water. After Alaiya and Howard had helped themselves to several handfuls, the two folded the skin and climbed up the vine-covered front wall, bringing it to first one speaker's niche and then the other.

"Is better," their host said after each of its throats had drunk. Both voices had lost the painful rasp. "Now can talk, talk, talk with darkhair and used-to-be-brighterskin."

"You sound different," Howard said. "This must be great water."

"No, no, is change two throat, make more complex. Easy talk now, fit your word shape better."

"You modified the structure of their throats in five minutes?" Howard asked incredulously.

"Easy work, small change," the speakers declared. "You want I add three tail, make eye on back of head, take longer, maybe whole day."

"In by nine, out by five, huh? That's something."

"How long have you been here?" Alaiya asked. "Where did you come from?"

"Here whole time, long time. Sleep most. Wake up, make thing, change thing, back to sleep. Dry down here under stone top, warm, No rain, no wind, no bad smell—"

The voices halted abruptly. Then the half-dozen small creatures around them in the enclosure raised their heads and began to hiss softly in the direction of the front wall. Howard felt the hairs rise at the back of his neck.

"Something going on here we should know about?" he asked.

"Is other one follow you, is come close now my house," the speakers said.

"The Traveler?" Alaiya began to glow more brightly again, tapping the flat of Howard's machete in the palm of her hand as she looked to the front wall.

"Is noisy long dripping bad smell first. Come very careless through tree, make my upright brown-fur nervous. Wait . . ." The voices grew distracted. "I forget where put . . ."

"Ahwerd, we need to get out of here." Alaiya bit her lower lip, considering the gray wall that surrounded them. "We could defend the doorway for a while, but it will soon find a way over the back wall."

A far-off wailing had begun to reach them through the woods.

"We have to start running again, I guess," Howard said. "Oh, well, it was nice while it lasted. I wonder if these little guys will be okay." He walked to the stone-covered cistern and waved his hand in front of the blankly staring little creature. "Excuse me, but we've gotta go. Will your brown-furs be safe here?"

"Wait, wait, look for something . . ." came the reply from above. "Made long time ago, put somewhere, hole in ground with big rock to cover, keep warm . . ."

"No, really, we've got to take off. Do you know if it's all three of them coming?" He winced at the familiar whip-crack sounds beginning to be audible beyond the front wall.

"Is only one nearby. Other still not catch up, poke through wood, drip bad smell on my moss . . . Ha! There!" The voices rose in triumph. "Is found, deep under, not far. Can bring up, show you."

"Ahwerd, we must leave now if we—" Alaiya froze as a vast crashing came from the direction of the back wall. It sounded as if part of a mountainside were collapsing as dust began to fill the air around them.

"Hey—" Howard covered his mouth and nose with his palm, pulling Alaiya back toward the wall where the speakers sat.

"Yes, much dust, very noisy. Make big, put deep, not easy bring up." The ground shook as something huge loomed beyond the back wall, extended over their heads, and crashed again on the other side of the front wall. There was a strong odor of earth and age. The mammoth sounds continued to shake the ground, moving off down the trail Howard and Alaiya had followed. "See? Is careful walk, step over my house very easy. Good big eye to look through. I find bad dripper quick . . . Ha!"

The thudding noises were replaced by a convulsive thrashing not far from them. There was the sound of tree trunks splitting and a high-pitched whistle that drove like a needle into their heads. Then something went whipping and crashing off into the distance.

"Threw away," the speakers said with a note of satisfaction in the silence that followed. "Dead thing, go drip bad smell other end of wood . . . Now put away."

Ground tremors signaled the return of the massive shape. As it passed over the wall, Howard squinted upward but could make out no more than a great pale outline against the darker background. The sound of digging on a grand scale came from the direction of the far wall, as dust rose again to sparkle in an aurora around Alaiya's dimly glowing body.

"Is made good," the speakers said while stone grated loudly beyond the wall. "Big simple sometimes better than complex small. Now put back, keep dry, use again other time.''

"Yeah—" Howard sneezed twice. "That's good workmanship, when it starts right up like that. I can see you do a quality job."

"I think stay awake now, make more. Maybe make Wossil again. Push out other come like breaking in my world, clean up sharp point, throw away big blur."

"Big blur?" repeated Howard. "What's that, the Traveler? Is he still out there?"

"That tiny sharp thing, you call Traveler. Big blur other, near brightskin leave child in cave. Make more thing, time soon big blur throw away."

"Child in cave?" Howard frowned in puzzlement.

"Maybe she means the Hant," Alaiya said. "Maybe we are all children to her."

"Are you talking about a little skinny guy with a kind of springy neck?" Howard asked.

"Yes, that old baby," the voices affirmed. "Brightskin leave in cave. Upright brown-fur nearby, I see. Not like look there, cover eye, big blur hurt. Soon throw away."

"She must be referring to Stillpoint," Alaiya said suddenly. "Before the Fade, when it is not wholly in the world. You will throw away Stillpoint?"

"Soon," the speakers promised. "Now need more throat, need change, talk to tiny sharp thing."

"The Traveler's coming." Alaiya clutched Howard's arm. "If it gets in here it will capture us instantly and take us from this world."

"Other noisy dripper go back inside sharp thing now," the speakers reported. "I pull tiny sharp here, I scold now." A small upright brown-fur crossed the enclosure and climbed up the front wall to a third niche, where it squatted, creaking and rustling, in a bed of dry leaves.

Howard felt a wave of nausea pass over him. He clutched his forehead and looked at Alaiya. "I think it's here."

"Yes, stinky sharp black thing here now," the speakers said above them. A third voice had joined them, barking harsh gutturals beneath the English and Averant utterances. "Sharp language, too. Stinky."

"You have learned the language of the Keyholders?" There was awe in Alaiya's face. "No one has done that."

"It comes close, I poke inside, learn word, same you," came the triple reply. "Now I tell you, sharp stinky, leave my wood. I sleep, you kill my Wossil. Now I wake up, you leave, not touch my upright brown-fur. You drip bad smell my wood, maybe I come follow you someday, come into your world like breaking."

There was a moment of silence; then Howard felt his skin crawl as something from beyond the wall responded with the same rough gutturals in a strange, hollow voice that brushed at the edges of his memory. Abruptly the sound ceased as if cut off in mid-sentence. The nausea and dizziness terminated at the same moment.

"Ha! I tired of listening," the original two speakers said. "I push tiny sharp thing, go back out of my world. Soon I throw away big blur."

"Wait," said Alaiya. "We need Stillpoint. You must not throw it away now."

Laughter rattled through the darkness.

"You say soon, mean sun up, down few time. I say soon, mean different. Plenty time."

"We have to be taking off, anyway," Howard said. "We left our friend in that cave near the big blur, and we've got to go make sure he's all right." He squinted up at the trio of small shapes in their dark niches. "We want to thank you for the food and for saving our skins from the slake and the Traveler."

"Is welcome. Come back, talk again, I show you new thing, after-Wossil. Is great-grandchild, right?" Amusement rattled through the voices. "Now I tell you, go through my wood, is safe. Outside, near cave, cannot help, not yet. Need make more thing first, more eye, more leg, more throat."

"We are grateful for your help," Alaiya said. "We can make the journey to Stillpoint in a few days, and once there we will be in no more danger."

"Right," Howard said. "As long as those stinky sharp guys don't come after us again."

"Is hint," the voices from above said. "Push out tiny guest, little talker, sharp thing cannot find so easy."

"Tiny guest?"

"Is here, inside." Movement drew their attention to an upright brown-fur squatting near the small torch they had stuck in the ground by the cistern. As they watched it scratched repeatedly at the top of its head, blinking vapidly.

"Inside . . ." Howard put his hand to his own head. "You mean the parleybugs, don't you? The Travelers can track us somehow through the parleybugs in our blood. Damn!" Howard turned to Alaiya. "Is there a cure for these things?"

"After we get to Stillpoint we can try to purchase some purge pods," she said. "Until then there is nothing we can do."

"It might not be so terrible to be rid of these termites," Howard mused. "Then we could learn each other's language for real and have a normal conversation. Sometimes when we talk I feel like I'm in the middle of a badly dubbed movie."

Their host brought them enough nut-berries to last for several meals. They said their farewells and squeezed out of the tiny doorway, stopping at the base of the outer wall before turning to retrace their steps.

"Thanks again," Howard called to the three who squatted above. "If we can ever return the favor, just drop us a line."

"Come back other time," the voices said. "Is enjoy talking with you. Much laughter."

"You bet," Howard said. Then they set off down the dark slope, Alaiya glowing softly to light their way while Howard tried unsuccessfully to hum the tunes from several hymns he had learned years earlier during a brief stay in Sunday school.

CHAPTER X

To the Cave

ALAIYA LED THEM UNERRINGLY THROUGH THE nightwood. It felt strange to see the slivers of light beginning to appear as they reached the edge of the shadowed portion of the forest, as though they were summoning the dawn of a new day.

They stepped from the woods not far from the small pond, and Howard was relieved to see that the Traveler and its servants had left his flight suit where he had set it down hours earlier, in the rose moss at the side of a black outcropping.

It would have been pleasant to resume their interrupted idyll at the side of the pond, but Alaiya insisted they push on toward Stillpoint. Howard agreed, especially considering the possibility of another visit from the Traveler.

"Where's your map?" he asked her as he shouldered the folded flying machine and strapped it to his back. "Don't you ever get lost?"

"Not when I am heading for Stillpoint," she replied. "Nor do any of the Averoy." She closed her eyes, lifted her right hand, and pointed. "There. You do not feel it?"

"Not a thing." They started to walk briskly through the mossy meadows, keeping the nightwood on their right.

"You know," Howard said after they had walked for several minutes, "I realize the Travelers are the bad guys—and I fully support your decision to take off when it appeared—but don't you sort of work for those guys? I mean, why would it have been after you?''

"When the Hant and I came within sight of Stillpoint there was only a short time left in this Turn. When the Turn is over, five local days remain for the battle-gangs to return to Stillpoint. It is best to arrive early, however, for during those five days the slakes are loosed to cleanse the world for the next Turn and all stragglers are fair game. Because the Hant and I did not approach Stillpoint when we first arrived we are seen as outlaws. Once we join the encampment we will be safe, but until that time . . ." She raised her eyebrows and made the hand gesture that served her as a shrug.

"So you guys were on time, but you decided not to go in because of me? And by coming back you've put yourself in all this danger." He looked at the ground. "Alaiya, I don't know what to say."

"That does not usually prevent you from speaking," she responded, picking up the pace as she smiled back at him. "Come, Ahwerd—storm clouds threaten up ahead, and we must find a secure resting place by nightfall."

Rain began to fall lightly a half hour later, and soon they found themselves in the midst of a torrential downpour. They had left most of the trees behind them and jogged squinting through meadows filled with slippery moss and patches of reddish, ankle-high grass. Once they caught sight of a distant object moving rapidly through the curtains of rain. Alaiya identified it as a motorized transport. Howard remembered the flat vehicle he had glimpsed on the Red Desert World.

"Will they see us?" he asked as they stood shielding their eyes in the direction of the fast-moving shape. "Should we be waving, or running for cover?"

"They may well see us, but they will probably not approach." She wiped rain-soaked strands of hair back from her cheekbones and frowned. "I cannot get a clear look at the insignia but it appears to be the Howling Miscreants—or what is left of them. They are not so bold as to risk loss of time by challenging us—especially if they have recognized me."

As Alaiya had predicted, the transport soon increased its speed and moved out of sight.

The storm abated gradually, the air becoming colder in its aftermath until they had to run to keep warm, while lightning strobed silently behind the tall black mountains toward which Alaiya led them.

By sunset they had reached the foothills, a sprawl of coal-colored boulders rusty with moss and lichen. Howard used his machete to scrape off a small quantity of rockskin, which he proudly presented to Alaiya after mauling it between two flat stones. After eyeing the substance dubiously, she bit off a small portion, then spat it out into her palm. "Not ripe," she explained curtly, then set about the business of establishing a small camp for them in the hollow between two great mounds of rock.

Howard sat with his legs dangling off the edge of one of the boulders, watching the sun sink in a glory of gold and purple in the west. I'm becoming a collector of different sunsets, he told himself, smiling at the oddness of it. I wonder how many more I'll see before this is all over.

He forced himself to choke down a few fragments of the mangled rockskin, sourly noting Alaiya's small smile as she glanced up from her work.

"Need a hand?" he called.

"I can manage," she replied with a sniff, then straightened and carefully swung her head from side to side. "This is negative for you, correct?"

"Yeah, right, very good." He grinned and turned his attention back to the sunset. After a few moments he removed the belt from around his waist and stared down at the tiny bull-bat head that formed its clasp. Laying the belt across his lap, he narrowed his eyes in the fading light at the row of small pouches, recognizing firejelly, filterfluff, and tanglewood, but little else. He turned the belt over. On its inner surface was a clip with a small square of shiny material the thickness of a book of matches. Howard removed it from the belt and held it up to the last rays of sunlight. It was dimly translucent and sparkled in planes like mica.

"Ahwerd." Alaiya beckoned from below. "We should

eat now before we sleep. First some foodstuff and then a few of the nut-berries.''

"Nice job,'' he said when he reached the ground. Alaiya had cleared the area between the rocks and woven branches together with strands of tough red grass, raising up a partial wall to serve as a windbreak during the night. She had also started a small fire with firejelly at the base of some black outcroppings, where it would not be readily visible.

"I've got some of that, too, if you run low,'' he offered.

"I have sufficient, thank you. Here—'' She handed him the ball of foodstuff, and he took a small bite. "More?'' she asked.

"No, thanks. You actually think this tastes better than my rockskin?'' He chewed quickly and swallowed with a grimace. "Oh, hey, what's this stuff? I found it in my new belt.''

"New?'' Alaiya peered at his waist in the flickering light from the small fire. "You have the Dratzul's belt!'' she exclaimed, laughing with delight. "Oh, Ahwerd, the mis-robe is well repaid for the beating he gave me.'' Her expression altered, and she tilted her head to the side. "Ahwerd, why do you stare at me so oddly?''

"It's nothing,'' he said. "Just that I haven't seen you laugh like that before and . . .'' He blew air out of his cheeks and fumbled the small square from his vest pocket. "What did you say this was?''

Alaiya accepted the object and held it near the fire. She raised her head with a laugh.

"The nullification of my recent work here,'' she said. Turning to the windbreak she had painstakingly constructed, she began to kick it outward, scattering the branches with a rueful smile. When she was finished she returned to Howard's side and held up the shiny square.

"Naturally the leader would be carrying this. Watch now . . .'' First she used her fingernail to make a small vee in one edge of the object; then, holding it at arm's length, she grasped two opposing corners and snapped it sharply in the middle, rotated it to the two remaining corners and repeated the deed, then tossed the tiny tablet to the ground and stepped back. With a sliding, sparkling motion, the thing began to enlarge, planes moving and shifting like a crystal growing under time-lapse photography, till a faceted dome that was perhaps six feet tall at its crown sat before them in front of the rocks. The small notch Alaiya had made was now a low doorway.

Howard stood open-mouthed. "It's a tent," he said. "I've been carrying a tent around in my belt."

"Shelterstone," Alaiya corrected, retrieving the small flat rock on which she had started her campfire and carrying it inside the structure. Faint orange light shone through the cloudy crystalline walls. Arranging her pack and supplies against one corner of the shelter, she sat herself cross-legged in front of the fire and motioned for Howard to join her on the moss.

"Now let us see what other prizes you have filched from the Victors," she said, holding out her hands for his belt. "You thieve as well as a Trilbit, it seems, in addition to your other gifts."

"You would have been really impressed if I hadn't had to drop the other seven belts I'd collected off the side of the cliff," he commented, bending with her to inspect the transparent pouches.

"Yes, that would have been a feat worth recounting in the Stillpoint taverns," she acknowledged. "How one unarmed man managed to deprive an entire battle-gang of its belts." She checked quickly through the contents of the belt and pursed her lips. "Nothing else of note. Your powderbridge is depleted, but you have plenty of firejelly. The tanglewood is low, and filterfluff we won't be needing . . . It seems the shelterstone is the most valuable find." She resealed the last pouch and offered him the belt with a sigh. "A pity, as I had heard the Victors carried an amoeba suit—though I would not expect to find it here anyway. Still, the shelter is a great boon. It will magnify and retain the heat from our little fire—do you notice that it is already warming in here? Without that we would have been forced to find other methods for generating heat during the night."

"Yeah, that would have been awful." With a small sigh of resignation, Howard stretched out on his back on the other side of the fire. "Wake me up when the good cartoons come on, okay?" He clasped his hands behind his head and watched the dance of orange firelight in the faceted dome until he fell asleep.

Rising at dawn, they ate a breakfast of foodstuff and nut-berries before gathering their belongings. Howard was looking forward to watching their shelter shrink back to tablet size, but Alaiya informed him that the shelter-stone could be used only once and must be left behind to dissolve into harmless chemicals before the next Turn. They set off on a twisting path into the mountains, threading their way upward along a series of gradually ascending passes. When they reached the other side two hours later, Howard realized that they were standing on the inner edge of a vast craterlike depression that was bordered on all sides by a rim of black crags.

Alaiya directed his attention to the sawtooth peaks that marked the opposite wall of the crater.

"There lies the final barrier between us and Still-point," she announced, the wind whipping her hair into a red-gold nimbus about her face. "And there on the outer wall will we find the Hant, hopefully fully recovered from its aftermolt and ready to accompany us down to the encampment."

"Great," Howard said. "I'm looking forward to seeing old Awp again. He and I—" He paused with a frown. "Or should I be saying 'it and I'? You've known Awp longer than I have—is he male, female, or uncommitted?"

"I cannot say for certain. That race has a complicated method of reproduction." Alaiya seated herself out of the wind in a small alcove in the rock and began to braid her hair. "I once asked the Hant itself about its gender status. It thought for a minute and then said that it could not remember, adding that it had been so long since it or any other Hant of its acquaintance had reproduced, that it was no longer quite sure how they went about it. Their lifespans are unusually protracted, you see."

"I guess." Howard squatted at her side. "Still—there are some things you just don't forget how to do."

"It did tell me that it was fairly sure the process required the participation of eight or more individuals, rather than the five or six that were sufficient to most races," Alaiya said. "It seemed almost embarrassed when I said we Averoy managed to accomplish the business with only two. I think it considered our approach simplistic but was too polite to tell me so."

Howard laughed. "That sounds like Awp."

"I am still not used to thinking of it by that name," Alaiya admitted. "But the Hant has great admiration for your naming abilities. It has even been referring to the Red Desert World by the name you called it—*Kansa'sa*, was it?"

Howard grinned. "Kansas," he said.

"At any rate, you should know that it is a great honor for the Hant to have accepted the designation you bestowed upon it. For most of their lives they are nameless, but occasionally they will take one on to commemorate a significant event. Usually they slough it off during a subsequent molt and become simply 'the Hant' again."

"Must make it interesting at Hant family reunions," Howard said, digging his dwindling hoard of nut-berries out of his vest pocket and offering half to Alaiya. "I suppose they all learn to answer to 'hey you!' pretty quickly. But how do you know who you're talking about if you've got more than one of them in your battle-gang?"

"There are so few Hants left that it never becomes a problem. No one knows how many there are in total, or if there is a Hant Holding somewhere. As I said, they live very long lives and were among the first to fight for the Keyholders on the Fading Worlds. It is a great advantage to have a Hant on one's battle-gang. If you can keep it interested in the world, it will prove a most useful teammate."

"Interested in the world?"

"According to the Hant—to Awp—boredom is the reason the majority of them end their lives. A Hant is very difficult to kill, you see, and most of those still in existence have been around for thousands of Rounds. Sometimes one will simply lose interest and decide to enter its final molt." She looked away, drawing the long braid absently through her fingers. "I saw it happen once after a battle on the World of Whirling Air, a long time ago. It is a very strange feeling, a very strange thing to witness—as if a mountain or a river had renounced its existence in your presence.'' She released the braid, pushed to her feet. ''Speaking of mountains, we had best keep on if we want to reach them before another sunset.''

As they descended they gradually entered another zone of flat plateaus set amid peaks and jagged canyons. The vegetation grew sparser as waterfalls began to appear in the cliffsides, sluicing past them in foaming torrents. To Howard's relief, the noise was not so great as to require the use of filterfluff.

It took them three hours to cross the black-terraced floor of the crater with its intersecting network of rivers. Alaiya gave a wide berth to the center of the basin, where the many rivers converged for a final crashing, spectacular plunge through curtains of spray into the bowels of the planet.

''It looks like somebody's pulled the plug on the world's largest bathtub,'' Howard commented as they paused to survey the great circular waterfall from their distant vantage point. ''Where does it all go?''

''I have heard tales of vast underground seas,'' Alaiya replied. ''If we had headed deeper into the canyon where the Victors held us, you would have seen a much larger riverfall. There are many such on this world.''

A final trek through the outer ring of mountain peaks saw them descending toward a break in the rock wall from which Alaiya promised Stillpoint would be readily visible.

Howard found that it required all of his concentration to place one foot in front of the other without being swept away in a shower of stones as they made their way down the narrow channel between two monolithic rocks. So he was unprepared when Alaiya tapped him on the arm as he caught up with her after a particularly harrowing several minutes.

''What do you think?'' she asked over her shoulder.

''About what?'' He was feeling vaguely annoyed as he stood there waiting for her to move, eager to get the dangerous descent over with.

''About Stillpoint,'' she said, flattening against the rock wall to make way for him in the narrow passage. ''I thought you saw it as we started down. We're there.''

His jaw dropped as he stumbled past her and looked

out over the plain of rose-red moss that stretched below
them. Alaiya had told him little about the actual appearance of the place they had been seeking. As Howard beheld their destination he realized that nothing she could
have said would have prepared him for the reality of Stillpoint.

Or rather the unreality of it.

"Whoa," Howard breathed finally. "Talk about your
Emerald City . . ."

"Hard green?" Alaiya looked from Stillpoint to Howard. "I do not understand. Does it seem hard to you?"

"Just a figure of speech. My God, it almost does hurt
the eyes . . ."

Pale yellow towers, amethyst minarets, silver amphi-
theaters, filigreed domes in a hundred rich hues, airy
walkways, and soaring golden thoroughfares: all shimmered with a vast pulsation, real one moment, almost
vanishing the next. As his eyes strove to drink in every
detail, Howard felt sure that at times he could glimpse
the rose moss of the plain through the towering ivory
walls. Prismatic as a tear on an eyelash, the city called
Stillpoint beckoned to him in the afternoon sunlight, radiating beauty, grandeur, and sanctuary till his throat almost ached with longing.

"It's magnificent," he said softly.

Alaiya was gnawing thoughtfully on a fingernail, her
gray eyes on Howard's face as he turned to her.

"It is the place where slaves are kept when they have
been taken from their homes, the place where warriors
are taught to kill for the sport of unseen masters." She
gave him a light slap on the cheek, then nodded toward
the path where it continued down below. "Dream time
is over, Ahwerd. We must go down this way to reach the
cave where the Hant awaits us."

It was a short climb down, no more than fifteen minutes, with faceted black rockface sun-warmed and solid
on their left and Stillpoint shimmering a thousand ethe-
real colors on their right.

Howard flexed his hand as they neared the cave mouth,
grinning to find himself actually looking forward to the
mop-fingered, sea-anemone handshake Awp would give
him. There was a lot of news to tell the Hant, and several

questions Howard needed to ask it. One question in particular.

The path, which was really only a narrowing ledge of rock near its end, vanished completely several yards before the cave opening, and he and Alaiya pulled themselves up like spider monkeys from one small foothold to the next. A crust of rock like the heavy brow of a Cyclops shielded the cave from sunlight. Howard was relieved to see that no signs of habitation were visible from the outside.

"Noble Hant, I have returned with your remarkable friend," Alaiya said as she pulled herself up over the lip and disappeared into darkness. Howard followed moments later, squinting as he crawled over the edge.

"Alaiya? Awp?" He felt for the rough wall and rose tentatively to his feet. The cave was larger than it had seemed from the outside, with just enough room for him to stand up straight. "Anybody near a light switch?"

"Ahwerd." Alaiya's face glowed suddenly in front of him.

He started nervously, then laughed. "Right, the woman with the incandescent smile. You certainly got your money's worth with that food supplement." He touched her shoulder, trying to peer past her into the gloom. "So where's my buddy?"

"Ahwerd." Alaiya was not smiling. She turned and extended her arm, spilling light farther into the cave. Something that looked like a long, low slab of black rock sat on the empty floor. Next to it was a supply pack that Howard recognized as Awp's.

"I cannot believe it," Alaiya said softly at his side. "How could this have happened?"

"What? Where is he? He's not here?" He squeezed past her, searching the small cave in the dim light.

"It is here, Ahwerd." Alaiya cupped his elbow with her hand, her radiance increasing gradually. "Do you remember our discussion, so few minutes ago?"

"What? About his name, about whether he was male or female?" He sank to the low slab of rock and shook his head in frustration. He patted the rock at his side and motioned to Alaiya. "Please tell me what's going on here."

"I had thought it was intrigued by you, more interested than ever in going on." Alaiya stared down at him but came no closer. "I was wrong. It is quickly done, the final molt, and once begun there is no turning back."

"The final molt? You mean he's . . . gone? Dead?" He looked around the empty cave, gestured to the small pack. "How do you know this? Did he leave a note?"

"It has not gone yet, Howard." Alaiya said the words distinctly, as though speaking to a child. "The final molt is a slow process, lasting several days. While it lies in the overskin, the Hant looks back on its long life as its body systems shut themselves down and its tissues begin to dissolve. Soon memories and dreams and thoughts all merge, and then there is nothing."

"Overskin? What is that? Where is it?"

"Beneath you," Alaiya said quietly. "You are sitting on it."

"What?" Howard leaped to his feet, bumping his head sharply against the rough ceiling. "Oh, my God!" He stared at the long bar of rock and rubbed the back of his head. "Awp is in there—he's dying in there right now? We've got to get him out!" He looked wildly about for something to use as a tool. "Will anything dissolve it? It looks like it's made out of solid rock. What about that stuff you used to melt the tanglewood?"

"Ahwerd, we cannot open the overskin. The Hant uses body secretions to manipulate the materials at hand, in this case the rock of the cave floor." She indicated the area around the base of the overskin, where the black rock had a fused, glassy appearance. "Even if we should be able to penetrate the covering, it is too late. Awp explained the flow of events to me. Once inside, it is as good as dead. Destroying the overskin would only hasten the process, denying it the comfort of its memories and dreams."

"No, it doesn't make any sense." Howard knelt at the side of the coffin-shaped rock and pounded with his fist on its unyielding surface. "Awp, you idiot—come out of there! I need to talk to you. Why are you doing this?" He laid his ear against the slab for a long moment, then raised his head and looked up at Alaiya, his eyes bright with moisture. "I didn't even know he was depressed.

He seemed to have such a cheerful outlook. Awp, you jerk!'' He gave the slab a final blow and pushed wearily to his feet. ''You didn't even say good-bye.''

''They are a different people, Ahwerd.'' Alaiya put her arm around his shoulder and stared down at the silent object. ''When life is so long, one sees things differently, makes different choices.''

He shook his head in the gloom. ''This wasn't the right one for him to make, Alaiya. It just wasn't.'' He stood looking down for a few more moments, then turned from the slab with a sigh. ''So what do we do now? Just leave him here? This is a lousy place to end up, some little cave on a world that wasn't even your own.''

''It is said that the Keyholders will occasionally return a fallen warrior to his Holding after death,'' Alaiya said thoughtfully. ''True, the Hant did not die in battle, but it was a clever warrior and served them well for so many Rounds. Perhaps . . .''

''How do we go about arranging for that? I'd like to do it if we could.''

''First we must go down and join the encampment. Then I will make inquiries at the Gate. There will no doubt be a fee of some sort.'' She tapped a finger on her chin. ''There is a chance.''

''Let's do it, then.'' Howard bent to gather up the Hant's supplies and followed Alaiya to the cave mouth. As he turned to climb down over the edge he narrowed his eyes for a final look at the rock encasement. He could see nothing in the darkness.

''You jerk,'' he said softly, and climbed down to the first foothold.

CHAPTER XI

The Big Blur

IT WAS ABOUT HALF A MILE FROM THE BASE OF the crater's outer wall to the encampment that sat like a ragged beggar before the shimmering Gate of Stillpoint. Howard had not even noticed the small collection of vehicles and canvas tents when he had looked out upon the plain from the high peak. Even now, approached on their own level, they seemed pathetically insignificant in contrast to the pulsing beauty of the city.

When Howard and Alaiya were halfway to the encampment, one of the long low transports rumbled to life. Moments later, it came skimming toward them over the plain, its black skirt billowing as it rode above the moss on a cushion of air.

"Is this trouble?" Howard reached for his machete.

Alaiya sniffed in negation. "Only for them if they try to attack us. No acts of aggression are permitted within sight of the city. No, it is most likely curiosity and the opportunity to taunt us that brings these riders out."

"Alaiya!" An amplified voice boomed at them as a long-necked figure in yellow vest and kilt waved from the front of the bucking transport. "You return after all—and in the company of a Skirmisher! My eyes are wide. You realize it is too late to kill him, yes?"

"That is Kattalpin, an Attercack of the Gold Schemers," Alaiya said to Howard. "He takes you for one of the Punitive Skirmishers, as you wear their green. Say nothing.'' Cupping her hands around her mouth, she shouted over the whistling throb of the approaching vehicle, ''Rest easy, Kattalpin, and come closer. We are well satisfied with fighting and will not overturn your riding toy. Tell me, who else has come back? Are any of the Victors here?''

With a hoot of laughter, the long-necked driver swung its vehicle to within a few yards of the two, raising a wind that blew in their faces and tugged at their clothing. Howard recognized Kattalpin as a member of the same lizardlike race as the six-limbed creature that had stolen Alaiya's dagger.

''With your assurance of safety I will dare to accompany you for a few moments,'' the Attercack called, the long strip of purple quills flexing smartly atop its narrow head. ''Of course I would never insult you, never, by offering to convey you the remaining distance. How would it look to our fellow warriors?'' It spread its upper set of arms while the lower continued to guide the transport. ''As to your request for information, only one of the Victors has come in so far—a Trilbit.'' It twisted its long neck to gaze back at the tents. ''The Howling Miscreants arrived yesterday, with only two losses—my eyes were wide, considering the level of skill usually present on that team. Perhaps they spent the Turn in a cave somewhere, yes?—playing *daspka* and stabbing at shadows. My own battle-gang fought well against the Cyclone, winning three belts and losing none, but we were late in getting back, and slakes claimed two of our number high in the peaks to the east, while another was separated from us during the attack and has not yet reappeared.''

''Is Oss—''

''He is our missing teammate,'' the Attercack said. ''We expect to see him before the Gate opens. You Sunset People are a resilient folk, yes?'' The lizard-thing revved the motor and shot suddenly ahead of them, its amplified words returning in its wake: ''Come to our tent after you've bathed and fed. There's to be a tale-tell at sundown. The Skirmisher can come, as well, if you think it won't faint when the talk gets bloody.''

Raucous hooting diminished into the distance with the transport.

"Friend of yours?" Howard asked.

"There is no friendship across teams," Alaiya replied. "But Kattalpin fights well and makes no excuses for his mistakes."

"So I'm a Skirmisher now, huh?" Howard drew his machete and made a few experimental flourishes in the air.

"Not something to boast about, Ahwerd." Alaiya took the blade gently from his hand and returned it smoothly to the scabbard at his belt. "The Skirmishers are one of the weakest of the battle-gangs—if indeed any of them have survived this Turn to continue the team designation."

"Figures," Howard said. "So what's this tale-tell tonight, and do we have to go to it?"

"It would be useful. All surviving team members will gather at one tent and relate their experiences of the Turn just passed. It is known that the Keyholders often enjoy listening to the boasting. Sometimes one attends the tale-tell in person. If that should be true tonight it would permit us to inquire directly about the disposition of the Hant's remains."

Howard nodded. "Alaiya, there's something I have to ask you. I was going to discuss it with Awp before . . ." He gestured to the cliff wall behind them. "You call them Keyholders, right? Is this just like a figure of speech, like Key to the City or something, or do they really have keys?"

"The Key is what enables the Keyholder to move from one world to another, Ahwerd."

"What about those Traveler things? Do they carry Keys, too?"

"No, the Travelers are something different, a strange form of life that is like a living doorway from one place to the next. We do not even know if they are intelligent. But the Key . . ." She raised her hand in an unconscious grasping motion. "It is what makes the Keyholders masters, what allows them to move at will among us while we must await the Fade and go where their whims deposit us."

"The reason I ask is that—well—I thought I might have had a Key myself at one point."

"You had a Key?" Alaiya stopped him with her arm across his chest and stood staring into his eyes, all color draining from her face.

"Wait, wait—let me explain. First you have to tell me: Exactly what does a Keyholder's Key look like?"

"It is like a ring of this size." Alaiya overlapped the thumbs and forefingers of both hands to form a circle, her voice shaking with emotion. "From a distance it looks like a single piece of silver metal, but upon close inspection it is seen to consist of three rings, one fitting inside the other. It is said that there are small markings on each ring and that the Keyholder manipulates them somehow when it chooses the world into which it will pass. This is the extent of my knowledge of them—though there are persons in Stillpoint more learned in Keylore. Still, I know of no one who has touched a Key, and very few who have ever seen one. Warriors died to gain the small information I have just recounted—Ahwerd, *do you have a Key?*"

"No, see, I thought—but mine was nothing like that. It was shaped like a regular key, to start with—you know, long and with little bumps. And it was gold, not silver. But it was with me when I came here, so at first . . ."

"Perhaps you should tell me the tale of your coming here in greater detail," Alaiya said carefully.

Howard told her of his search for the executive washroom in the Matrix Building, of the key he had slipped from the custodian's key ring, and how he had been using it to open a perfectly ordinary-looking door when he found himself facedown in the sands of the red desert.

"Where is it?" Alaiya asked when he had finished. "Do you carry it with you at this moment?"

"That's just it," Howard said. "That's what makes the whole discussion moot. The key was in my jacket pocket, and my jacket was in a bundle of my clothing sitting on the top of a bed-mound, and the whole thing went over the edge of one of those million-foot chasms when Awp and I Faded into this world. So it's gone, whatever it was."

Alaiya's shoulders slumped, and some of the fierceness

went out of her expression. "Come," she said quietly, beginning to walk again. "We must reach the tents."

"I should have mentioned it before," Howard said. "At first I had no idea it was significant, and by the time I started hearing all the talk about Keyholders it was too late, the thing was long gone."

"No, it is not your fault. You are a stranger here and cannot be expected to know what is meaningful and what is not—nor, for that matter, who may be trusted with your confidences. For my part, I could have questioned you more closely concerning the manner of your coming to the Fading Worlds, but I confess when you first gave me the tale I judged it half confusion and half fantasy. Since that time I have learned that I was wrong."

They walked on in silence for several paces.

"Hey," Howard said. "How come I understood that Cattlepin guy? He's from a different battle-gang, right?"

"It is the custom for battle-gang survivors to consume a speaking stew containing parleybugs from every team, soon after they arrive at Stillpoint. Kattalpin has done this, and so he now carries Ferocious Rulebender parleybugs among the rest. When he speaks, all of the bugs translate simultaneously into their various dialects. In our bodies, the Ferocious Rulebender parleybugs listen to their brothers and translate the thoughts back to us. Unlike a direct infusion of parleyblood, the effects of the stew are temporary, lasting just long enough for all to share in the tale-tell. Some element in the broth causes the bugs contained within it to expire after a few days."

Howard scratched at his temple.

"I don't get it," he said. "Why not just have one brand of parleybugs that everybody uses? Why go to all this trouble to keep folks from communicating?"

Alaiya arched an eyebrow.

"No doubt the Keyholders see little value in members of opposing teams being able to speak with one another. What would be the purpose, when one's only goal is to attack and kill?"

"Yeah, right." Howard nodded. "Who knows, if they did it my way, peace might break out." He sighed. "Is there anything else I should know before we join the group?"

"Hard to know what to tell you," Alaiya admitted. "I try to see my world through your new eyes, but I cannot truly imagine what will seem strange to you and what will be commonplace."

Howard chuckled. "Now that's a word that hasn't entered my mind for quite some time." He shaded his eyes in the direction of the city and laughed again. "Commonplace . . ."

As they neared the ragtag grouping of tents and vehicles a straggle of figures gathered to greet them, numbering perhaps sixty in all. Howard saw members of most of the races he could name and several that he could not. In addition to the Trulls and Attercacks, there were specimens of the flat-bodied creatures that reminded Howard most of giant flounders. There was a smaller, stockier version of the Dratzul that had led the Victors, snorting as it appraised them through squinting red eyes; Howard almost expected it to paw the ground as its gaze fell on his belt buckle. There were no Hants among those who watched their approach, but there were three more representatives of the Sunset People: a tall woman with ivory skin and hair cropped to a silver fuzz on her scalp; a large, bearded man sporting a fiery mane the color of Alaiya's; and a thin woman with dark, almost purplish skin under a cap of loose black curls. Howard thought he detected surprise in their eyes as they scrutinized him, but their faces remained impassive as he and Alaiya crossed the last several yards and entered the encampment.

Kattalpin approached with another member of its race, this one with quills that were yellow at the roots, shading through orange to crimson tips, like a small fire waving atop its skull. With what seemed to be mock courtesy the two presented the newcomers with a deep bowl of murky-looking fluid. Alaiya lifted the ladle and downed a generous helping of the gummy liquid, then passed it to Howard with a nod.

His stomach leaping in rebellion, Howard took a deep breath and steeled himself as he touched his lips to the spoon's crusted edge. Surprisingly, the speaking stew was bland to the point of tastelessness, and he was able to ingest a sizable portion with little difficulty.

"Welcome, Alaiya," a low voice purred at their backs. "What is this you have plucked from the mountainside?"

Howard turned to find himself nose to nose with the short-haired woman. Alaiya pulled him back with a hand on his shoulder and nodded toward the other woman with a small crooked smile.

"This is Arpenwole who fights for the Exacting Cyclone. She believes in a life of close inspection."

"Hi, there. I'm Howard Bell." He saluted with his index finger. "Nice to meet you."

"Ahwerdbel? But you must be of my clan, with that name. Southern Chain, perhaps?" Gray eyes, lighter than Alaiya's, swept his body. "And fighting for the Skirmishers? They had no Averoy among them."

"Perhaps you missed him during your last inspection," Alaiya said smoothly. "For indeed he wears their colors."

"Indeed. And clasps them with a Dratzul's belt." She studied Howard with eyes half-closed in speculation. "Impressive, Sermantry, is it not?"

The other two humans had joined them while Arpenwole investigated Howard. Alaiya introduced the redhaired man as Sermantry of the Well-Mannered Assault, while the dark-skinned woman, who was missing the lower portion of her right arm, was Kimmence, another member of the Cyclone.

"New from the Holding?" The large man scratched his beard, frowning. "We had thought you the last, Alaiya. How can this be?"

"Perhaps we will find out at the tale-tell tonight, eh?" Kimmence twirled a black curl at her left temple. "These two are tired and hungry and could use a washing, by the smell of them. Besides, it wins us no favor in our respective battle-gangs to come running whenever an Averoy appears at the Gate. Our interests are supposed to lie with our designated teams, not with others who happen to be of our own species."

"If the Keyholders truly believe they can teach that lesson to the Averoy, then they shall surely fall one day," Arpenwole purred, her eyebrows raised in wonderment at what was left of Howard's Reeboks.

"Dangerous thoughts," Sermantry rebuked her.

"Kimmence is right. We must disperse and await the tale-tell for further information."

"You Sunset People clot like blood in the sand," one of the tall flounder-folk rumbled as Alaiya led Howard toward a dilapidated tent set some distance from the others.

"And you Ga'Prenny taint it like stagnant pond water," Alaiya replied over her shoulder.

Half a dozen narrow slits opened on the flat creature's chest to emit a wheezing exhalation that Howard hoped was laughter.

"A former teammate of mine from the Dreadful Noise," Alaiya explained, holding open the tent flap. "Here—you might as well get started. I will see what further news can be gained by trading gossip with the Ga'Prenny."

Inside the heavily patched tent Howard was amazed to find what could only be a bathtub, set like a great golden shell on numerous tentaclelike legs and large enough to accommodate even the Dratzul. Various tall urns of liquid stood nearby; Howard found one that contained hot, scented water and used a small bucket to half fill the tub before he removed his sweat-stained, mud-caked clothing and levered himself gratefully into the bath.

He was thoroughly enjoying himself when Alaiya strode briskly into the tent several minutes later.

"Whoa—you guys aren't into knocking, huh?" Howard leaned over the edge of the tub but was chagrined to discover that his clothing lay beyond his reach.

"Knocking?" Alaiya frowned in puzzlement at the loose tent flap behind her. "I thought you might be in distress. What were those noises you were making before I entered the tent?"

"Joyful ones!" he answered with a smile. "I was singing every Top Forty tune I could remember, out of pure joy. Do you know how long I've been wanting a bath? If only we had some Mr. Bubble, everything would be perfect!"

Alaiya came and sat on the flared edge of the tub.

"I have learned a few things from the Ga'Prenny. Tomorrow is the last day of the after-Turn. At midday the city will be fully in the world, and the Gate will open.

Also, there is a rumor that a Keyholder will indeed be in attendance at the tale-tell tonight. This is favorable in terms of our request concerning the Hant's body, but problematic in another way.''

"How's that?'' Howard was attempting to preserve his modesty without seeming to do so, with decidedly mixed results.

Alaiya studied his face with concern. "Ahwerd, I believe the water is too hot. You have changed color.''

"No, no, I'm all right. This locker-room camaraderie takes a bit of getting used to, is all.'' He shook his head at her expression of bewilderment. "You're making me feel a little underdressed, that's all. I can handle it.''

"Ah, I see. This is some sort of competitive ritual on your world.'' Alaiya straightened and casually slipped out of her kilt and vest. "Now we are equals, and you may return to your normal coloration, correct?''

"I'll work on it,'' Howard muttered, blowing out his cheeks. "You were saying something about problems?''

"Yes, concerning the tale-tell. Ahwerd, I have also been less than candid with you about certain matters.'' She resumed her perch on the edge of the basin, stirring her ivory fingertips absently in the water as she spoke. "I told you that I fled the Traveler because I was out of sight of Stillpoint and so in danger. That is not entirely true. When the Turn is over the slakes are loosed to comb the world for survivors—but they are always left alone, to succeed or fail in their efforts. I have never before seen a Traveler itself sent hunting for stragglers, and I could find no reason why one should be pursuing me.''

"Are you saying—''

"I believed the Traveler was after you, Ahwerd—that is why I wanted us to flee.''

"After me.'' Howard rubbed his chin, staring at the side of the tent. "That's a sobering thought. But what have I ever done to the Travelers?''

"The Travelers are but instruments of their masters. You seem to have attracted the interest of the Keyholders.''

"But why?''

"Who can say? Their ways are alien to us, their motivations unknown. In truth, this was a question I had planned to put to the Hant, hoping that its greater experience might provide some clarification. But you are from another world, and as far as we know no Keyholder brought you here—nor did you pass through a Traveler.'' She lifted her brows at him. ''All in all, it might be best if you did not attend the tale-tell. Perhaps I will be able to uncover the reason behind the Traveler's attack if I go alone.''

''If you think so . . . But what about what Grandma Wossil said—about the parleybugs? If they can track us through the bugs in our blood, how come they haven't come for me already?''

Alaiya made her hand-shrug. ''Perhaps she was mistaken. Or perhaps they cannot find you this close to Stillpoint by that method. There are strange energies at work in this area—and they grow more powerful the closer Stillpoint comes to the world.''

''Well.'' Howard gave his own shrug. ''I guess I should be letting you have your turn at this.'' He scowled at the heap of filthy garments he had left on the ground. ''I really hate to get back into those rags. I don't suppose there's a Laundromat in town.''

Alaiya walked to an open chest at the other side of the tent and withdrew an armful of clothing, which she brought to the side of the tub and held up for Howard's inspection.

''This is the customary garb for warriors inside Stillpoint.'' All of the garments were of jet black with silver piping. ''Once the Turn is ended battle-gang affiliations are suspended.''

''Hey, lucky for me.'' Howard . climbed self-consciously from the golden shell and began to dry himself on a length of fluffy cloth hung nearby. ''Although I shouldn't have that much trouble fitting in. Arpenwole seemed to think I was her long-lost cousin or something.'' He selected loose-fitting thigh-length shorts and a vest from Alaiya's offering, then added a short pocketed cape. ''Do they have any footwear in that chest? My sneaks are about shot.''

''Arpenwole was jesting with you.'' Alaiya brought Howard a selection of boots and sandals. ''Of course she heard your outlandish tongue beneath the parleybugs' translation and knows you are not of the Holding. They are as surprised as I was to see an unknown Averoy dressed as a warrior.''

"Yeah, well, let's keep them guessing, at least until I figure out where I'm going to fit in around here. I don't suppose there's a crying need for fix-it men—or novelists.''

Alaiya bent to open a stopper on the bottom of the tub, then moved to refill the bucket at one of the tall urns.

"A skilled repairman might find employment in Stillpoint," she said. "I do not think the parleybugs did justice to your other occupation.'' She replaced the stopper, then poured steaming water into the tub and climbed over the side with a grateful sigh. "You are a scribe of some sort?''

"No, I write books—well, book, so far. A novel is fiction—like a made-up story about people, you know?''

"You invent tales rather than record them? To what purpose would one put such lies?''

Howard set his foot on the edge of the tub and began to lace up one of the sandals.

"It's not lies, really. It's entertainment, thrills, tragedy. You know, people get bored, they like to read about other lives, other people's problems.''

"Bored?'' Alaiya watched him with curiosity. "On your world there is time for boredom? How strange.''

"You know, you're right.'' Howard finished the other sandal and moved to sit on the lid of a chest. "I've been beaten, starved, and scared half to death here. I've flown through the sky, almost drowned in the rapids, and had lunch with the local god. But there's one thing I haven't been—and that's bored.''

"Nor have I,'' Alaiya said almost wistfully from the tub. "It is a luxury I sometimes dream about.''

When she had finished with her bath and dressed in the same black garments as Howard, they exited the bathing tent and headed for a rickety stall that had been erected near the center of the motley assortment of tents. There Alaiya traded tokens from her belt for a tattered tent of their own, as well as some rolls of rockskin that seemed to Howard's eyes to be no better prepared than the delicacies he had offered her the previous evening. The shopkeeper was a plump bird-thing with stubby quills in place of feathers and a sharp whistling voice that set Howard's teeth on edge as it haggled prices with Alaiya.

It was nearing sundown by the time they chose their site in a sparsely populated section of the encampment.

"So you want me to hang out here while you go to the hoedown, right?" He settled to the ground in front of the tent and cracked his knuckles restlessly. "I just hope I don't luxuriate in too much boredom before you get back. I didn't notice any magazines over at the commissary, did you?"

Alaiya sighed. "You can fill your time by inventing more incomprehensible conversation to devil the parley-bugs. Try to avoid speaking with passersby, especially if they wear green. I have not sighted any Punitive Skirmishers since our arrival, but it could be awkward if one comes here seeking its teammate and finds you instead."

"You got it, Cap'n." Howard touched his forehead. "Give my regrets to Cotterpin. Oh, and try for a doggie bag if they serve those little cocktail franks."

Alaiya shook her head and walked off in the direction of the Gold Schemers' tent. Howard brought the Wossil flying suit and their other supplies into the tent, then sat at the opening propped up against their packs and watched the sun send streamers of gold and indigo into the western sky.

He was beginning to doze off when he heard a small scrabbling sound at the rear of the tent, then quiet movement behind him.

Howard cursed himself for removing the machete from his belt. Slowly he moved his right arm behind him, feeling for the blade inside the tent door.

Something touched his shoulder.

CHAPTER XII

Night Flight

HOWARD LEANED TO THE RIGHT, AT THE SAME time reaching back to grab whatever was behind him and yank it forward over his opposite shoulder.

Strong fingers clutched at his ponytail, and he found himself crying out in pain as his head was pulled forward to follow the trajectory of the small body. His forehead collided with his right knee, and he saw stars for a few moments while something furry squealed and tried to jerk free of his grip.

"You!" As Howard's vision cleared in the fading light, he was amazed to find himself staring into the wide black eyes of the little sheep creature that he had last seen on the ledge outside the Victors' cave. He tightened his hold on the woolly wrist, and the creature's lips drew back in a grimace of pain.

"Come back for more knife practice, you little back-stabber?"

"No, no! Protest! Stab-not in back, only small cut in arm, healing fast, easy draw blood for talking."

"Say what?" Howard narrowed his eyes in suspicion.

"Truth! Only for talking, hope to see you again. Now at Gate, too late, both eat speaking stew. Sorry, sorry."

"Let me get this straight." Howard loosened his grip slightly on the tiny arm. "You jabbed me because you wanted to be able to talk to me if we ran into each other later?"

116

Sheepish wiggled its ears frantically. "Truth! Mix bloods, follow you, but slow, no wings. Must give up, come to Stillpoint. Surprise, you arrive also."

"Yeah, and here everybody understands everybody else, because of that soup, so there was no need to draw my blood. God, the way you guys learn each others' languages . . ." He shook his head. "I'd love to have the Berlitz franchise for this place." He released the other's wrist and sat back with his legs bent at the knees. "So what did you want to talk to me about, anyway? And how come you're not at the tall-tale?"

"Thankful! Hating my battle-gang—no honor! Happy they pay for eating little cave dweller. Tale-tell not important, hate bragging. But steal much, wanting share, seeming fair." Squeezing past Howard, it entered the tent and reemerged dragging a bulging sack.

"Yeah, you seemed to be doing a pretty thorough job of cleaning them out back there. You must be—what did they call it? The drill-bit?"

"Trilbit." The little warrior bowed deeply. "Thievery like art to my people, much admiring. Steal together, now sharing booty." It untied a leather thong and opened the sack.

"So what did you end up with? I had their belts, but I had to drop them when the bull-bat was after me. The Dratzul, I mean. Did any of those guys recover?"

"No knowledge. Watch your flight, decide you go back to capture-place, follow you there, give up. Have map—" It lifted the small circle of glowing colors from the sack. "Figure out broken, easy fix, find Stillpoint quick. Arrive, no Victors. Hoping all dead." It replaced the map and pulled forth a double handful of transparent packets. "Find most belts at foot of cliff. Cannot carry, take best things. Look: firejelly, shelterstone, nervenumb. You want, you take. More: nighteye, tanglewood." It dropped the packets into Howard's lap, then rummaged around in the sack. "Here: worth much. Inside Stillpoint, good trade." It brought forth the narrow envelope Howard remembered from the site of the avalanche.

"That's that weird black stuff the Dratzul put on before it squeezed through the crack in the rocks. I still can't figure that one out."

"Amoeba suit!" the Trilbit squeaked. "Dratzul's own. Rare, powerful tool, worth much. Trade in Stillpoint, give you half."

Howard raised his hands in protest. "Look, you don't have to split everything with me. You don't have to give me any of it. I didn't poison the Victors—it's not like you owe me something."

"Owe you for laugh-not when Victors kill animals for pleasure," the Trilbit replied, a grave expression on its sheeplike muzzle. "Owe you for bad beatings while I watch, for attack-not when those Victors lie helpless— for reminding that honor and kindness still walk in world."

"Yeah, well," Howard said. "I'm glad you looked me up. You can keep me company if you want while Alaiya's at the big meeting. Hey—" He was struck by a sudden thought. "You wouldn't happen to have a dagger in there—I think the Attercack was carrying it—about so long, made of bright silver metal?"

"Look: this one?" The Trilbit produced a long, cloth-wrapped object from the sack. Howard unwrapped it slowly and held the knife up to the dying light of the western sky.

"Yeah, that's the one! She's going to want to kiss us both for this, you know." He replaced the cloth with a broad smile. "I mean—if you don't mind my giving it back to its rightful owner."

"Yours to give," the Trilbit said with a chitter of pleasure. It leaned forward to test the air between them, its large nostrils expanding. "You smelling of Hant. Two captives escape by waterfall—those survive the Turn?"

"Well, Alaiya did. She came back and saved my life." Howard looked in the direction of the black cliffs, though he could not see Awp's resting place in the growing twilight. "But the Hant didn't make it." He described what they had found when they reached the cave.

"Regret. All Hant wise and strange. Wish to serve on battle-gang with one." The Trilbit wrinkled its muzzle. "Ending up with Dratzul instead."

"Yeah, life stinks sometimes." Howard stretched out his legs and settled back onto the packs. "So tell me about yourself. Let's have our own little tattle-tale. Oh, first of all: I'm Howard Bell.''

The Trilbit executed another low bow, then joined Howard on the ground, sitting cross-legged at his side.

"Honor, Ow-er-bel. Yam-ya-mosh that name I own."

"Pleased to meet you, Yam. So, where are you from and how'd you get drafted into this business?"

They passed the hours in stories of their homes, with Yam-ya-mosh detailing life on the Trilbit Holding, a mountainous world of dells and meadows and purple vegetation beneath a sky of amber clouds, and Howard telling of Earth and of his unexpected arrival on the world of red deserts.

"Strangeness and bafflement," the Trilbit squeaked at one point in Howard's story. "You look much like others of Averoy race to me. Perhaps your world longtime secret Holding with none of you knowing. But why coming for you now, when Sunset People in decline? Rumors saying Keyholders finish with this stock and soon will have Averoy unbred."

"Beats me. Alaiya can't figure it out either. Anyway, it was right after I met Awp that the Fade came and we were dumped into this world. I had no idea what was happening—lost all my clothes and everything, except for my tennis shoes.''

"Your items come-not with you?" the Trilbit asked. "Usually whatever one carries Fades to the next world."

"Yeah, but I wasn't carrying them. They were sitting on top of one of those moss-mounds and when . . ." Howard broke off and sat staring into the darkness. "Wait a second. If I wasn't touching them, how come my clothes even came into this world? It's not supposed to work that way, is it?"

"Certain those objects follow you to this Black and Blue World?"

"Yeah, I saw them. I watched the whole bundle drop over the edge of the cliff." He illustrated with a swoop of his hand in the air. "I wonder . . ."

"And this happen there loud river, near place those hated Victors first make capture?" The Trilbit's ears were twitching excitedly.

Howard nodded. "Right over the edge and a thousand miles to the next stop."

"Your belongings reside in dark-blue-color wrapping," Yam-ya-mosh said. "Color of daytime sky above this world."

Howard blinked. "How did you know that?"

"See that parcel, Ow-er-bel!" the Trilbit squeaked. "Follow you, remember? Reach that capture-place, search carefully. Look all around, look down, see something on jut of rock. Dark blue, hard to notice. Fingers itch for that, but too far, no hand-grabs, climb down impossible."

"So it's still there," Howard murmured. "I could get it back."

"Risky try," the Trilbit said. "For only clothes? Here many clothes, more inside Stillpoint, some dark blue. Will share."

"It's not the clothes, Yam. I've got to tell Alaiya about this. There was something else in that bundle." He told the Trilbit of his discussion with Alaiya concerning the mysterious golden key. "It's probably nothing more than a regular old key, still—"

Yam-ya-mosh rocked back on its haunches, considering.

"Tales saying clear only Keyholders have ability make use of Keys," it offered after a moment. "But perhaps you hold this for trade, barter favors from those Keyholders. But how retrieve dark blue parcel?"

"Hey, don't you remember?" Howard grinned at his companion through the darkness and tapped his chest. "This guy has wings! Of course, there's still a minor problem with the left one, but that shouldn't take long to iron out."

There was the sound of sudden footsteps in the night, and then a figure stood before them, glowing faintly.

"Ahwerd, what is *this* doing here? Do you not recognize one of your captors?" Alaiya took a menacing step toward the Trilbit, her hand raised.

"Hey, hold on." Howard rose to his feet. "This is my good pal, Yam-ya-mosh. He and I—" He paused, looked down. "He? Is that right?"

"Currently correct," the Trilbit confirmed. "Though who can say what next farrowing-change will bring?"

"Yeah, life's full of little uncertainties, isn't it?" Howard nodded sympathetically, then turned back to Alaiya. "Anyway, he's brought something for you."

He picked up the cloth-wrapped object and opened it dramatically, then rotated the dagger and handed it to her hilt first.

"Silversting," Alaiya breathed. "I had thought never to see my battlemate again. Quick-fingered Trilbit, I am most grateful and in your debt. Please do not hesitate to inform me if you should ever need someone killed."

"That's a lovely sentiment, Alaiya," Howard said. "But a nice card would probably do the trick just as well. Anyway, there's more. Yam has seen my stuff—you know, the stuff from Earth I thought I lost over the edge of the cliff. It got caught on the rocks partway down—I can go right back and get it!"

Alaiya's eyes grew wide, then narrowed again in her radiant face. "There is no time. Even if we were sure about the nature of . . . the object."

"You can say 'key' in front of Yam. He's cool—I already filled him in about it. He thinks we could hold the thing for ransom or something. And there's plenty of time. If I take off around dawn when everybody's still in their sleeping bags and fly nonstop, I can get back here before the Gate opens."

"The flying machine." Alaiya thought for a moment, then sighed. "It still cannot be done. Word came at the tale-tell. The Gate opens earlier than we had expected. You would have to leave in a few hours, in the heart of the night." She tilted her face to the star-speckled heavens. "This world has no moons, and the nights are very dark."

"Easy fix," the Trilbit piped from the moss at their feet. It held aloft one of the transparent packets it had filched from its former teammates. "Look: nighteye!"

"You mean I can see in the dark with that stuff?" Howard turned to Alaiya. "Does it work for us?"

The warrior woman nodded. "The world turns red as blood, but all can be seen clearly. But, Ahwerd—can you find the place?"

"No problem." Howard tapped his skull. "I might not have a built-in homing beacon for Stillpoint like you do, but I have a terrific memory for patterns, and once I've been somewhere I never forget how to get back." He folded his legs and returned to his place at the front of the tent, drawing Alaiya down next to him. "It's settled, then. The ship sails at midnight. Now let's relax for a little while and see what else Santa's brought us."

Howard experienced a few moments of extreme panic shortly before he left, when he suddenly remembered that the flying suit's sole source of power was apparently solar energy.

He had examined the machine thoroughly while repairing the damaged left wing, pondering the small series of toggles at the base of the motor housing where it sat just below the back of his neck. He recalled pressing the middle one without result while inspecting the device in the Wossil's cave. Later, when exposed to sunlight, it had activated itself. Then when he had crashed into the river after the whiskerwings attack, the switch must have been hit again. But how long did the suit retain the energy it absorbed while exposed to sunlight? Howard ran his fingers lightly along the series of small switches. Nearby sat Alaiya, providing light for his repair work while she discussed Keylore with little Yam.

Finally, unwilling to experiment while still among the tents, he had kept his doubts to himself and left his companions with a cheerful promise to return by dawn.

Please let there be one incredibly efficient storage battery in this thing, he prayed silently as he stood on the narrow ledge not far from the mouth of the cave where the Hant lay in its overskin. He pressed the central switch, then released the breath he had been holding in a sigh of relief as he felt an answering hum in the housing. A vibration passed the length of the flying suit as the great wings unfolded behind him and he soared into the night sky.

Alaiya had carefully daubed his eyes with grayish paste from the small packet some hours earlier. His vision had been blurry for several long minutes, but had gradually cleared and brightened till he could see every detail of the nocturnal world in sharp, red-bordered relief.

He circled high above the encampment, straining to pick out the tiny figures of Alaiya and Yam in the cluster of tents, then headed back toward the cliffs, not daring to remain longer than necessary in the sky near Stillpoint. Alaiya had mentioned the strange energies that were generated by the growing presence of the city, and he had no desire to test their effect on his flying mechanism.

He rose gracefully through the air as he approached the cliffs; then suddenly he was over them, and the interior of the crater spread out beneath him as the muted roar of waterfalls reached his ears.

He had noticed during his first flight that the suit gave off a measure of heat while in action; now he discovered that another of the toggles provided a means of regulating that output, channeling it in some fashion through the framework that surrounded him till he was flying quite comfortably in the chill night air.

It took him less than half an hour to cross the crater, the intersecting rivers spreading out below him in a ghostly cobweb of red and black geometrics. From the other side, he reckoned, another hour of steady flight should bring him to the place where he had first appeared in this world. He checked the pockets of his cape to make sure that he had a supply of filterfluff, yawned in a mouthful of cold, clean air, and allowed himself to drift into a watchful but meditative state for the rest of the journey.

Near the end of his flight Howard became aware of a vast cool shimmering in the sky ahead of him, apparently centering on the zone of great waterfalls and chasms that was his destination. It was an awesome display that reminded him of the northern lights back home, faint sparkling sheets of color that he seemed constantly to be approaching but never actually reached.

He began to scan the landscape, starting a long slow spiral downward when he recognized the peaks that had towered above the plateau where he had first appeared. He landed awkwardly at the center of the spit of black rock, stumbling forward for a few paces till he thumbed the activation toggle and the long wings retracted onto his shoulders. Water roared like an enraged beast all around him. He fumbled filterfluff from his cape and hastily divided it between his ears.

"That's better," he muttered, making his way carefully to the edge of the plateau. The flying suit kept him feeling slightly off-balance, and he struggled to compensate for the changes it wrought in his center of gravity. That awkwardness combined with his eerie night vision and the deafness brought on by the filterfluff to cast the whole experience into the realm of dreamlike fantasy, and Howard had to fight to keep his mind on the task that had brought him there.

The Trilbit had been unable to give him more than vague directions to the place where it had glimpsed his jacket. He paced slowly at the edge of the rock, straining to pick out one blot of darkness from all the rest, the nighteye limiting his color perception to shades of red on a black background.

There!—or was it just a trick of rock and shadow? Howard blinked to clear his eyes, then clucked his tongue in frustration as he was unable to locate the dark spot that had caught his attention. Glancing up, he froze when his distorted vision reported a flicker of movement on the cliff wall to his right. Or was that another illusion? He stared for several minutes in the direction of the motion, finding nothing and concluding finally that it must have been one of the high-flying whiskerwings.

There seemed to be no other choice but to employ the flying suit again. He had hoped to pinpoint the bundle from the relatively safe and stable surface of the plateau, then to fly down to retrieve it. Now it looked as though he would have to conduct the search itself in midair. He reactivated the flying suit and stepped off the edge of the rock as he rose slowly into the air. Dropping like a feather through the red-black night, he drifted in as close as he dared to the cliff wall, squinting at the chunks and clefts of faceted rock.

There were several places where the cliff jutted outward in protrusions such as the Trilbit had described. Howard began to investigate them one by one, trying to ignore the unpleasant possibility that wind or whiskerwing had dislodged his prey from its uncertain perch days earlier.

Howard was hovering several feet from the next-to-last jut of rock within sight of the cliff top when he narrowed his eyes with a small exclamation of hope and floated closer to the cliff face. He reached out toward the promising shape that lay half in shadow at the base of the jagged protrusion. When his fingers were a few inches from contact, the shape moved.

Howard cried out in shock as something long and sinuous shot out from the cliff face. Then the world went whirling, and he gasped for breath. It was as if a giant whip had wrapped itself around his midsection. He struggled in silent desperation, the coils tightening with each movement while he felt himself being drawn inexorably into the cliff wall. Through a haze of pain he saw that a cave mouth yawned just below the jut of rock, and that something large was shifting and coiling within it, pulling him downward with the massive black tentacle that circled his chest with bands of iron.

His left arm was trapped beneath the slake's coils. With his right, he thrashed frantically at the control switches. A surge of power hummed through the flying suit, and he felt himself rising for a few moments as the great wings churned the air. More of the hidden creature emerged from the cave mouth; then it stiffened and all upward movement halted. Howard was dimly aware of other activity somewhere above him as the downward pull began again. He channeled all of his concentration into forcing gasps of air into his constricted lungs, air that grew progressively warmer as gusts of foul breath reached him from below. He closed his eyes and fought to remain conscious.

He was struggling like a captive bird inches from the jagged cliff face when he felt a series of tremors rack the powerful tentacle. Forcing his eyes open he saw small figures scrambling along the rock protrusion above him, several of them dangling in a chain of their own bodies to within inches of his chest and the whiplike arm that bound him. Tiny paws rose and fell rhythmically, small objects glinting in their midst, and again the tentacle shuddered.

Howard jerked his head back as one of the little shapes

detached itself from the rock and dropped onto his chest, where it clung with one thin arm about his neck, the other tiny hand slashing away at the bands of flesh that crushed him. It seemed to be holding a small pointed object, like a claw or a spur. Howard drifted in a fog of pain, unable to focus clearly on what was occurring as an acrid stench filled the air about him.

Suddenly the tentacle gave a last convulsive squeeze and relaxed. Howard felt the heavy coils slough away as the flying suit carried him flapping madly upward into the night. He groped dazedly for the proper switch at the base of his neck. Tiny fingers were there before him, and the motion slowed and then reversed. As they dipped back down toward the chaos on the cliff face, the small creature that rode with him leaped abruptly into space, then returned before Howard realized what was happening, a soft bundle clasped in its arms.

They began to rise again.

"Sneaky, sneaky!" The rasping voice seemed to come from somewhere on the plateau above him, or perhaps he was just imagining it. "Hide that bad smell dripping in cave like surprise. Ha! I come with poison thorn, big surprise on them. Now take pretty wrapping, fly back quick your big blur."

Howard felt tiny arms wedge the bundle securely between his chest and one of the flying machine's straps. Small feet pushed against him, and then he was alone again, the dark plateau spinning away below him as he rose dizzily through the peaks. He turned the flying suit and headed out of the canyon, wincing with agony at every breath.

Dawn was just streaking the eastern sky as Howard topped the last wall of cliffs and began his gliding descent toward the city. Stillpoint shimmered before him like a complicated flower of glorious shape and hue, seeming to grow more substantial with each passing second. Below him on the plain of rose moss, half a dozen figures jogged toward the encampment, too far away for him to see them clearly. As he soared over their heads, hoping to pass unnoticed in the pale morning light, one of them raised its face and pointed upward with a faint cry. Howard outdistanced them with a burst of speed and descended quickly, landing with a stumbling impact that sent lances of pain streaking through his bruised chest and ribs.

CHAPTER XIII

A Turn of the Key

"AHWERD!" ALAIYA'S IVORY FACE APPEARED AT the tent opening.

"Hey, I made it." Howard tried to grin, then found himself collapsing forward into her arms as his legs buckled beneath him. Alaiya unfastened the straps and removed the flying suit, then lifted Howard gently and carried him to the tent.

"What are the neighbors going to think?" Howard murmured. "You know, you're a very strong person."

"What happened to you?" Alaiya deposited him carefully inside the tent and knelt at his side, her forehead creased with concern.

Howard attempted a shrug and clenched his eyes in pain.

"There was a slake waiting by my jacket. It tried to convince me to prolong my visit." He winced as Alaiya peeled off his vest and explored his aching ribs with her fingertips. "I got some help from . . . somebody." He rubbed his brow, then peered in surprise at the intricate bracelet of plaited grasses that circled his right wrist. "Hmm. The last couple of hours are pretty hazy."

"I do not think any bones are broken." Alaiya leaned back, dragging her supply pack from the shadows. She opened a small packet and squeezed a few droplets of brown liquid onto the ends of her fingers. "This is nervenumb,'' she explained, beginning to massage his chest. ''It should help.''

''Yeah, that's better.'' Howard closed his eyes as warmth spread through his torso, then abruptly opened them and raised his head. ''The bundle—my jacket! Did you—''

''It is just outside the tent. I left it with the flying suit.''

''We should bring it inside.'' He tried to rise to his elbows against her restraining hand. ''When I was coming in, there were people crossing the plain. They saw me.''

''Latecomers?'' Alaiya rose and left the tent, returning moments later with Howard's jacket. ''They have gone directly to the Gate. I could not identify the individuals from here, but I did see their color: red-brown.''

''Swell—the Miserable Victors. I hope they don't run into Sheepish—Yam, I mean.'' He looked around the interior of the tent. ''Where is he?''

''Gone back to his own tent for the night. We talked for several hours, and he wishes to ally himself with us. I told him to meet us here before the Gate opens. Perhaps he is still asleep.''

Howard had tied the sleeves of his jacket together weeks before to secure the bundle of clothes. Rolling onto his side to unfasten them, he noticed that the bottom of the bundle had worked loose at some point in the past. He spread the jacket wide and grimaced in disappointment.

''Underwear and one sock,'' he groaned. ''This doesn't look good. Jeez, the sock's even got a hole in it.''

''Where was the Key?'' Alaiya watched him anxiously.

''In one of these inside pockets.'' Howard fished cautiously in the jacket's lining. ''But I don't—ah!''

As Alaiya leaned closer he slowly drew his hand from the jacket and held the ornate golden key in the air between them. ''Bingo,'' he said.

''Is that one of your gods?'' Alaiya asked distractedly. ''If so, thank him for me, as well.'' She extended a tentative forefinger, then withdrew it nervously.

''You can touch it,'' Howard said. ''It's just a key to the men's room, I'm afraid.''

''Is it?'' Alaiya squinted at the three narrow bands that

clasped the shaft of the object. "To me it appears wonderful and strange, like nothing I have ever seen before."

Noises came from outside the tent. Alaiya shook her head as if to clear it.

"The Gate is opening," she said. "We must gather up our belongings and prepare to enter Stillpoint. Once inside the city we will search out a master of Keylore and determine the truth."

"Right." Howard got slowly to his feet. He slipped the golden key back into his jacket and retied the sleeves around his waist. Then he hefted one of the packs with a grunt and pushed open the tent flap. "Let's go."

Something struck him in the midsection like a cannonball as he stepped from the tent, knocking him heavily to the ground. Yam-ya-mosh tugged urgently at his arm.

"Up, up, Ow-er-bel! Quickly!" the little warrior squeaked.

"I can't believe you just did that," Howard gasped, clutching at his ribs. "Oof—I didn't think it was possible to hurt more than I already did."

"Sorry, sorry!" The Trilbit danced a jig of anxiety as Alaiya came from the tent. "But Victors here now, full of hate. I see them approach Gate, speak with Gate guards, point at this tent."

"Uh oh." Groaning, hanging onto Alaiya's arm, Howard got to his feet. Around them the survivors of the Turn were abandoning the encampment, packing up their ragged tents and hurrying toward the huge opening that had appeared in the seamless ivory wall. Howard had a tantalizing glimpse of graceful gardens and soaring structures; then a small group of warriors came around the side of one of the remaining tents and began to move purposefully in their direction. Leading them was the Dratzul, its mouth stretched in a snarl of rage, while rising slowly at the rear of the group . . .

Howard clutched his forehead suddenly and swayed against Alaiya. "Oh, no," he said. "Not again."

"Traveler!" Yam squeaked. "They send Traveler for us!"

"Not for us, for me," Howard said, fighting to stand erect. "Get out of here, you guys. I'll deal with these bozos."

"Ya-mosh, help Ahwerd to his flying machine,"
Alaiya said calmly. "We should be able to hold them off
while he makes his escape. Ahwerd, put on the suit! We
are warriors and best able to handle this."

"No way!" He pushed Alaiya's fingers from his arm.
"That thing'll swallow you both while the Dratzul stands
by laughing. Wait—" He bent to fumble with the jacket
at his waist, then grabbed the flying suit from Yam's
hands and straightened with a yelp.

"Ow! Ow! Maybe this'll stop them." Holding the Key
aloft with one hand and clutching the flying suit to his
chest with the other, he faced the black shape that hov-
ered several feet behind the menacing group. "You better tell your masters to call off their bull-bats, or I'll send
this little trinket flapping away into the stratosphere."
He jerked his thumb in the direction of the black cliffs
behind him. "And if Grandma Wossil gets her hands on
it you know you guys'll never get it back."

The Victors scattered as a hollow booming sound issued from the rippling oval of darkness; then the Traveler
began to glide slowly over the moss toward Howard.

"Well, so much for that strategy." Howard backed
away a few paces, then stopped. "Alaiya, Yam, grab my
arms." He turned to face the Traveler as his companions
drew close to his sides. "All right, here goes nothing.
Alaiya—pretend you just won a dream vacation. Where
would you most like to be right now?"

As Alaiya started to reply, the Traveler suddenly
swooped forward, plunging down at them like a cloak of
utter night.

Holding the narrow bands of the shaft in one hand,
Howard twisted the golden Key with all his might.

CHAPTER XIV

Field of Flowers

HOWARD STRUGGLED TO FIND "UP."

Soft things pressed against his arms and face and brushed his eyes, his nose, his mouth. He had fallen into a vat of feathers, and he was starting to suffocate.

When his foot touched the yielding ground he pushed off reflexively. The next thing he knew, he was shooting end over end through the close-packed material, finally bursting free for a confused instant of bright colors and whirling patterns. He managed a single convulsive intake of breath before plunging down below the surface again.

When he touched bottom the second time he forced himself to moderate his movements and discovered immediately that he could put his head above the strange medium simply by straightening up. He stood rocking from one foot to the other, breathing in as deeply as he dared without taxing his damaged ribs, and attempted to survey the landscape. The latter task was made more difficult by the fact that there was no land in sight.

Howard found himself bobbing neck-deep in a sea of flowers, a vast multicolored sweep of blossoms that stretched as far as the eye could see in every direction. A constant breeze sent rainbow undulations through the flowers, which made them appear to be following a great, gentle tide. The sky above was a deep lavender with clouds of brushed silver, and the air smelled strongly of fresh mint.

Howard's reverie was interrupted by a sudden thrashing noise; then Alaiya shot into the air several yards away, the look of shocked disorientation on her features mirroring what he had been feeling himself moments earlier. Alaiya's leap was more nearly vertical than Howard's, with the result that she was able to land more or less erect in the rippling flower sea.

"Stay where you are!" he called to her as she swayed among the blossoms. The vegetation was shallower at her landing place, rising barely past her waist. The resilient ground rose gradually beneath Howard's feet as he struggled through the soft feathery mass to her side.

"Have you seen Yam?" he asked as Alaiya reached automatically for his outstretched hand and pulled him the last few feet. "Did he come through with us?"

"I do not know." Alaiya brushed petals from her cheeks with a distracted look, then gazed in amazement at the dust of golden pollen on her palm. "I cannot believe . . ."

Just then Yam-ya-mosh erupted into the air not far from where Howard had landed, disappeared back into the blossoms, and shot up again almost immediately. Squeaking wildly, the woolly projectile bounced up and down repeatedly in the flower sea, a look of panicked bewilderment on the small face.

"Hey, hold on there!" Howard took a breath, then dove toward the spot where the Trilbit rose and fell like an animated yo-yo. There was a frantic thrashing beneath the surface, and he emerged moments later with the flailing warrior under his arm. With Alaiya's help, he hauled Yam ahead of him to a place where the Trilbit was able to stand on his own, chin-high in the close-packed petals.

"Unusual effect, isn't it?" Howard remarked. Yam gave him a rueful look, his breath coming in short pants as he tried futilely to comb pollen from the springy fur of his head.

"Flowers, Ow-er-bel!" Yam said in a tone of mystified indignation. "But buoyant, like salted water! How can this be?"

"You know, I don't think it's the flowers. Watch." Howard squatted next to Yam in the shallow area and propelled himself carefully upward, whooping with ex-

citement as he flew several yards straight up into the air.
He landed with his arms curved up, like an acrobat waiting for applause. "It must be the gravity that's different
here—you know, like on the moon."

Yam wrinkled his nose as if testing the air. "But how
can this be?" he said again. "Everywhere is the same pull
on these Fading Worlds, all matched with Stillpoint."

"Unless we have left the Fading Worlds, Yam-ya-
mosh," Alaiya said behind them in a rapt whisper, her
eyes bright as she continued to scan the endless vistas of
glorious color.

"Left the Fading Worlds?" The Trilbit was dubious.
"Where have we come, then? A Holding?"

"No, not a Holding." Alaiya turned to Howard with
something new and strange in her eyes. "Ahwerd—how
have you done this thing? What are you, truly?"

He shrugged, uneasy under the intensity of her gaze.
"I'm a fix-it man from Massachusetts, Alaiya. I have no
idea where we are or how we got to be here." He looked
down to find with relief that he still clutched the golden
Key in his hand. "I know it has something to do with
this, but beyond that . . ."

"You asked me where I would most wish to be, Ahwerd. Then you turned the Key and brought us to this
place." She rotated in a slow circle, bobbing up and
down slightly in the low gravity, her eyes glistening. "To
Field of Flowers you have brought us, to the ancient home
of my people, which no Averoy of the Holding has seen
for millennia."

"You're kidding," Howard said.

"From my mind you must have plucked the image
shaped through the ages by tales passed from parent to
child." She took a deep breath of the scented breeze. "I
never dreamed to see this place, and now you have
brought me here!"

"Yo. Alaiya." Howard waved his hand before the warrior woman's eyes. "This is me, Howard Carter Bell,
we're talking about. If you remember, I originally swiped
that key with a specific purpose in mind—and it wasn't
that I wanted to pick a cheap bouquet. I'm just as surprised to find myself here as I was the first time I turned
the thing."

"Ahwerd—"

"Look." He raised his palm. "You can believe what you want about this being the home of your ancestors—I hope it turns out to be true, if it makes you happy—but don't go all weird on me just now, okay? Remember, I spent the first ninety-nine percent of my life stuck on one world, so I'm kind of counting on you more experienced types to help me make sense of what's going on here. Okay?"

Alaiya watched him for a long moment, traces of a variety of emotions coming and going like cloud shadows on her ivory features. Finally, she seemed to reach a decision.

"I believe you, Ahwerdbel," she said with a smile and a shake of her head. "That it is you who have brought us to Field of Flowers I have no doubt. It is also plain to me, however, that you have no knowledge of the methods used to accomplish this feat. Perhaps we may uncover them together."

"Great." On a sudden impulse he held out his hand to her, palm up. After a moment's hesitation Alaiya placed her own hand on top of it. Howard turned to the Trilbit warrior.

"Is this jake with you, Yam? Come on—give us your hand. I always loved this part in the movies. Okay—all for one and once and for all!" He removed his hand and scratched behind his ear, dislodging a stem of tiny blue blossoms. "Now, my hearty musketeers—let's see what we can see."

It took almost half an hour of shuffling through the nearby deeps for Howard and Alaiya to locate their packs and the flying suit. Then the two returned to the shallows where Yam waited and pressed forward in that direction. They were apparently on a ridge of some sort, the blossoms rising no higher than knee-level for the two humans. The ground beneath the flower covering fell off gradually on either side. They soon realized that the flowers grew to approximately the same level over vast areas, no matter the depth of the soft land below, resulting in a more or less uniform surface that truly resembled a great, wind-shaped ocean.

"Is this supposed to go on forever?" Howard asked

Alaiya as they waded through the close-knit stems. "I mean, assuming this is your ancestors' homeland—was the whole thing just flowers?"

"No, there were great cities set upon smooth rock and surrounded by circles of farmland and tended forests." She surveyed the seemingly endless plain of blossoms. "The flowers lay in fields that marked the borders between the settled areas."

"Seems like a mighty big border." Howard peered at the softly curved horizon of blue-green, red, and gold beneath a lavender sky. "Distances are tricky here, because the flowers all blend into each other." He raised his eyes. "Maybe we can get our bearings if we try a slightly different perspective."

"The flying machine?"

Howard shrugged. "I don't know. With this funny gravity I'm a bit nervous about navigating up there. Actually, I was just going to try a little vertical jump."

Alaiya sniffed in negation. "Your ribs will not approve."

Howard stood still and ran his hands cautiously along his sides.

"No problem," he said after a moment. "That nerve-numb stuff is really terrific." He inhaled deeply, then grinned. "It's like there's nothing wrong at all."

"Nervenumb has no such abilities," Alaiya said with a frown. "It will quiet the surface pain for a short time, but continued exertion brings it back. And I saw your flesh—it was deeply bruised."

Howard opened his vest and peered down at his chest and stomach. "Well, there's not a mark on me now, and I feel great. Maybe they're using a new improved brand of nervenumb you haven't heard of yet. Anyway—here goes." He squatted down, then pushed off from the soft undersurface with all his strength, twisting to wave at his companions as he shot high into the air above them. He landed a short distance away, up to his armpits in soft petals. It took him a few seconds to slog through the feathery stems and rejoin Alaiya and Yam.

"Find an end to flowers?" the Trilbit queried as Howard dusted pollen from his shorts.

"Not yet. It just goes on and on. The jump was kind of fun, though."

Yam sneezed twice and shook his head mournfully. "Not fun for Trilbit to float in sea of flowers," the little warrior said. "Maybe good place for Sunset People, but not for my kind."

"Damn." Howard noticed for the first time the damp fur surrounding Yam's eyes and muzzle. "You're allergic to this place."

"Apparent truth," the other chittered sadly. "Making your report on persistence of current environment much bad luck for me."

Howard and Alaiya manufactured a makeshift pollen filter from the sock Howard had stuffed into his cloak pocket, securing it to the Trilbit's muzzle with the thong from Howard's short ponytail.

"Maybe we should just start running—or leaping," Howard proposed. "It seems like a more efficient way to travel than wading through this stuff, and the sooner we reach the end of it the better for Captain Sneeze here."

The small warrior bobbed his head hopefully, a strange apparition with his argyle face mask and gold-dusted wool.

With Howard carrying the flying suit and Alaiya cradling Yam in her arms, they set off in bounding strides that grew longer as they gained familiarity with the exercise. The ridge did not run in a straight line, and for a while they had to rely on guesswork to aim their leaps, often plunging in over their heads as they strayed from the shallows. Howard was first to notice the subtle patterns in size and coloration that were only visible from the air. Above the ridge of high ground the flowers tended to reds and oranges, while the deeper areas lay beneath smaller blooms of generally bluer hue. Once he had communicated his findings to Alaiya, they were able to triple their pace, bounding tirelessly through the multicolored sea toward an unknown destination.

Alaiya had made several purchases from the ramshackle stalls in the encampment outside of Stillpoint during Howard's flight to recover the Key. During a rest period after several hours of loping through the flower sea, she brought forth packages of what she rather disdainfully termed "recreational food."

"It is not possible to purchase the true healthy food-stuff without entering Stillpoint," she explained, slicing off portions of a fragrant loaf of fruit-filled bread. "While this will certainly curb our hunger until we locate a source of native food, it falls short of supplying us with the proper nutrients present in the victuals keyed to each race."

"This stuff is great!" Howard licked crumbs of deep-fried crust from his fingers. "I knew somebody must be selling junk food on the Fading Worlds." He stuffed the remainder of the pastry in his mouth and held out cupped hands. "More, please."

"Yes, I suspected this fare would be more to your taste." Alaiya pursed her lips in disapproval. "A warrior cannot fight for very long on sweets alone." She handed him another slice of the fruitbread, along with a small bowl of what looked like butterscotch tapioca.

"Maybe not, but he'll go down with a smile on his lips," Howard said. "Yam, take that sock off your face and join us for some dessert."

The little Trilbit picked disconsolately at his share of the food, his sense of taste all but nullified by the effects of the pollen.

"Were you a warrior on your own world, Ow-er-bel?" he asked when his muzzle was secured once more behind the protective filter.

"Not exactly, though the Breakneck Boys scared their share of dogs away from the neighborhood garbage cans on trash day."

"Do you wish instruction in how to fight?" Alaiya tapped the hilt of Howard's machete. "You should learn how to properly use this blade."

"Hey, why not?" Howard leaned back into the blossoms and sighed into the scented breeze. "Seems like we've got some time on our hands." A moment later he had straightened up again, a frown on his face. "Although there is something we haven't taken care of yet."

Alaiya nodded gravely. "The Hant."

"Yeah. Did you find out anything at the Attercack's party?"

"The Keyholder never made an appearance—probably just as well, considering our recent encounters with the Travelers. If they had identified me as being with you, they might have taken me then and there, before you had retrieved the Key. I did make inquiry among the battle-gangs present, and the general belief was that the Key-holders would probably agree to return the Hant's body to its Holding. There has always been great interest in Hants among the Keyholders."

"I wonder what that means," Howard mused. "You don't suppose they would've wanted to dissect old Awp or anything?"

"I do not know. At any rate, the option is no longer open to us. For whatever reason, the Keyholders have been searching for you, and now that you have demonstrated your ability to utilize a Key, they will be doubly zealous in their attempts to apprehend us."

"Sorry you got dragged into this, guys. Maybe if you told them I kidnapped you they'd take you back."

"Hate the Keyholders!" Yam sputtered indignantly inside his sock. "Now all are for each one, you said. Hateful to return to the Fading Worlds and become slave once more! Better to fight at your side and die in freedom."

"I feel the same way about you and Alaiya," Howard said. "Except I do have to go back—assuming the Key knows how to take me there." He lifted his brows in a mournful expression. "I can't leave Awp's body on the Black and Blue World for the Keyholders and their slakes."

"I will return with you, Ahwerd, once we have found land." Alaiya met his eyes with her dark gray gaze. "Perhaps it would be best for Ya-mosh to remain on Field of Flowers and establish a camp while we are gone."

Finishing their meal in sober silence, the three set forth once more, loping through the ocean of petals with gargantuan strides. For lack of a true destination they continued to follow the main ridge, which snaked generally forward while small tributaries wound away from its sides. After they had traveled for another hour Alaiya called their attention to a small cloud of objects hovering above the blossoms some distance to their right. Moving off on one of the smaller ridges, they slowed their pace and cautiously approached the phenomenon.

It was a flock of butterflies, giant pastel creatures with rounded wings wheeling and dipping silently above the flowers. Ranging in size from dinner plates to manhole covers, the insects reacted without fear to the travelers' approach. To Yam's consternation, his pollen-dusted wool seemed particularly attractive to the flock, and they made repeated gentle passes above the small warrior as he stood waist-deep between Alaiya and Howard.

"How many are there? About fifty?" Howard craned his neck as the flock gradually settled into a loose pattern that wove a canopy of bright colors above the three companions. "Funny we haven't run into any before this. At least they're not afraid of us—that's a good sign."

"Perhaps they are migrating." Alaiya plucked an orange-gold blossom and extended it at shoulder height. A butterfly the size of a small falcon came to hover above her hand almost at once, extending a delicate golden proboscis to probe at the flower's center. "I have heard of no such ornamental creatures in the tales of my people."

Howard squinted up at the declining sun through the wheeling shapes.

"They seemed to be heading west above this little ridge. Shall we tag along for a while? Maybe they'll lead us to some land."

They struck out at a slower pace, increasing their speed gradually when it became clear that the flock was not disturbed by their peculiar mode of transportation. Soon they had resumed their leaping run, the butterflies circling and dipping exuberantly among them.

"Look," Yam cried from his vantage point on Alaiya's shoulders. Ahead of them a small outcropping of purple rock rose in the shallows, the first solid material they had seen on this world. The three crowded around their find, marveling at its smooth, almost polished surface. The butterflies seemed reluctant to approach the rock, circling at some distance till their new companions had finished their investigation. Another hump of rock became visible shortly after they returned to their journey, and soon smooth formations of purple and lavender dotted the flower sea in their path, some of them bearing an almost sculpted look. They had started looking for a place to rest when they spotted an outcropping up ahead that seemed large enough to allow the three of them to stretch out upon its smooth surface. Racing past Alaiya with a shout of victory, Howard leaped to the side of the boulder and vaulted up into the center of the purple rock. He landed with an impact that left his teeth chattering in his skull.

"Ow. Jeez." He crawled slowly to his feet, rubbing his bruised tailbone. It felt as if he had on a suit made of lead. He moved to the edge of the smooth surface with a grunt and lowered himself carefully to a sitting position as Alaiya landed lightly in the flowers a few feet away.

"There's something wrong here," he said as she made her way to the rock's side.

Alaiya accepted his hand, knitted her brows in puzzlement as she and Yam struggled up over the edge to sprawl at his side.

"Pull is back," Yam squeaked. "Big change happen quickly."

"That's it, isn't it? The gravity's gone normal." Howard frowned, tipping his chin toward the flock of butterflies wheeling serenely several yards from the large rock. "But not for them."

He levered himself slowly down the side of the rock, released his grip on the edge and pushed away with his palms. Immediately he found himself floundering on his back among the blossoms like a beetle in a rain puddle, his weight reduced to a fraction once more. He righted himself and stood swaying amid the flower stems.

"The effect is limited to the stone itself, is it not?" Alaiya slid forward over the edge of the rock and joined Howard with a sigh of relief. She reached her hand out to graze the smooth purple stone as Yam dove into the flowers several paces to her left. "The heaviness extends a few inches from the side."

There were more rocks in the distance, and after a short rest they continued on their way, stopping to investigate each one they came to. It soon became clear that the pull of gravity around the rocks was close to that of Earth—or "Stillpoint normal," as Alaiya and Yam referred to it—while the lighter pull was confined to the

flowered areas. The rocks increased in both size and
number as they continued west, making it necessary for
them to slow their bounding pace lest a leap above one
of the heavy areas bring them crashing down to earth.
Finally they beheld a great plain of lavender stone rising
in front of them like an island from the sea of blossoms.

"At last." Alaiya's eyes shone with relief and anticipation as she stood swaying gently with her companions
several yards from the smooth shore.

"I almost hate to leave the flowers," Howard said.
"But I suppose if we stayed out here forever our muscles
would start to atrophy."

"More work for bodies," Yam agreed. "But maybe
Trilbit nose will function better on solid rock."

The narrow ridge of higher ground they had been following ended abruptly a few feet beyond where they
stood. Lifting Yam to his shoulders, Howard moved into
the blue-green area ahead, sinking at once to chin level.
Alaiya joined him, and they began to push through the
close-packed stems.

They were about thirty feet from the shore of lavender
stone when Yam leaned to one side and raised a small
hand to shade his eyes. "Peculiar thing . . ."

"What's that? You see something?" Howard tried to
follow the Trilbit's gaze, but the blossoms limited his
field of vision to a few feet.

"Something moving. Now gone."

"Perhaps it was the wind," Alaiya said.

"No, moved different direction from wind." The Trilbit's words came muffled from within the filter-mask.
"Like something under flowers . . . There!"

Following Yam's pointing finger, Alaiya propelled herself up out of the flowers, rising till the blossoms brushed
her ankles before sinking back into the ocean of vegetation.

"He is right. I saw it that time. Something moving
near where the flock is feeding."

The butterflies had declined to approach the island of
stone, hanging in a whirling hemisphere above the flowers some distance to the south.

Howard pushed himself and Yam up just in time to see

the flock scatter, the great-winged insects flapping outward from something thrashing in their midst.

"It's got one of them!" Howard cried as he sank back into the flowers. He pushed off again, Alaiya rising at his side.

A large butterfly fluttered in the grip of what appeared to be dozens of taut black threads. As they watched it was drawn struggling below the surface of petals. A moment later all motion ceased.

"What is it? Some sort of slake?"

"No!" Alaiya's denial was fierce. "Not here, not on Field of Flowers."

"Look!" Yam pointed to a spot midway between them and the place where the butterfly had been taken. "It comes this way!"

"Hurry up!" Howard turned and began to scramble through the soft material. "Hit the beach!"

It took long seconds of wading in nightmare slow-motion before they dragged themselves gasping from the flower sea onto the lavender stone. Gravity returned like a blanket of fatigue.

They pulled themselves up the gentle incline and huddled together several feet from the blossoms. There was no more movement visible beneath the surface. A good distance from the shore the butterflies had come together again. As the three watched, the flock began to move southward, keeping a course roughly parallel to the shore of stone.

"Well," Howard said after he had caught his breath. "It doesn't seem likely the thing'll follow us up here. Has either of you ever seen anything like it before?"

"Several Turns ago," Yam volunteered. "On the Sinking Swamp World. The Ga'Prenny called it a whip-slake, said it was cousin to slake used by Keyholders." He gave an apologetic look to Alaiya. "Smaller, but with many more graspers and a sting. Could be different, seemed same."

Alaiya said nothing, gazing resolutely ahead of them as they gathered up their scattered belongings and walked slowly up the smooth stone. The incline grew steeper for a few paces before abruptly leveling off. They pulled themselves over the edge onto a featureless plain of rock that descended gradually away from them for several miles. In the middle distance rose a curving purplish gray wall of forest.

Howard surveyed the barren terrain, then gestured toward the woods. "Looks like the place to go," Howard said. "Are we up for a walk?"

The minty smell that had dominated the flower sea gave way to a mixture of exotic and familiar spices as they moved inland. Yam removed the sock from his muzzle and tested the air warily.

Alaiya's spirits rose as they neared the wall of trees. "Beyond this forest will be a ring of farmland," she said. "And inside that a city."

"Great," Howard said heartily. "Let's look for a motel with one of those vibrating beds. I could use a good massage."

The forest grew from rich-smelling soil that seemed to occupy a vast crater in the smooth plain. Yam eyed the darkness between the trees as they approached the end of the lavender stone.

"Night comes," he observed. "Not easy to find way."

"How are we fixed for kilowatts?" Howard asked Alaiya, who stood staring into the woods with an expression of longing. "Were you able to recharge your batteries at the encampment?"

She closed her eyes in concentration for a moment, then opened them with a sniff and a shake of her head. "The bioluminescent has dissipated," she reported. "It is very expensive and unfortunately only available for purchase within the walls of Stillpoint."

"Hmm. Well, I know how eager you are to get to this city, but I think it might be a good idea to hang out here till morning, don't you? We can use the rest."

Alaiya assented. Howard daubed firejelly on the stone and spat it into crackling life while she and Yam collected fallen boughs and armfuls of large, soft needles for them to lie upon. They sat in a close circle in the lengthening shadows of the towering evergrays and spoke in hushed tones as Alaiya meted out more of the food she had purchased at the encampment.

Two great moons rose to cast silvery light upon them as the darkness deepened.

"It's a beautiful place," Howard said finally, stretching out on the needles. Yam was snoring softly at his side, pollen mask clutched in his small fingers.

Alaiya said nothing. She had positioned herself so that she faced the forest, her head propped up on an edge of the flying suit. Howard contented himself with watching the firelight dance in her dark gray eyes until his own lids grew heavy.

CHAPTER XV

The Body Snatchers

HOWARD STRETCHED LUXURIOUSLY, RELIVING the last portion of his dream, in which he had crawled off to sleep in a gigantic feather bed. The mild breeze tickled his face with strands of his own unbound hair, and he awoke to tantalizing fragrances.

"Tea?" he murmured, sniffing the spice-woven air.

He lifted his head and saw Yam sitting cross-legged next to a tiny fire over which a small pot hung suspended on a delicate wire frame. The Trilbit greeted him with a cheery wave.

"Fine dawning, Ow-er-bel. Wish some morning drink?"

Howard crawled yawning from his nest of evergray boughs. He rubbed his face, idly wondering whether the depilatory salve Alaiya had applied back by the pond on the Black and Blue World was permanent in its effects, or if he would ever again awaken to a stubbled chin. He wandered over to the fire, tilting his head back to inhale the delicious steam rising from the pot.

"Where on earth did this come from?" He squatted next to the diminutive warrior.

"From Trilbit Holding." Yam unfolded three small papery cups from his pack and poured golden liquid into one of them. "Here. Bigtassle tea, my people's great favorite drink for assistance in waking up."

Howard accepted the cup and sipped gratefully at the fragrant liquid.

"Unbelievable," he sighed a short while later. "I don't need to see the label to know there's caffeine in here."

"Have more." The Trilbit refilled Howard's cup and poured one for himself. "Plenty leaves in pack. This morning Alaiya find water pools in forest. Finally I can brew my tea."

"Where is Alaiya?" Howard scanned the empty plain of stone, then turned to the purple-gray forest behind him.

"In exploration. She is all eagerness to find the city of her people."

"I know." Howard drew designs on the lavender stone with a slender purple branch. "I hope she isn't disappointed."

Yam cocked his woolly head to one side. "You believe-not this is ancient home of Sunset People?"

Howard shrugged. "I don't know. I have no reason not to believe it. There's just a funny feeling to the place, like it hasn't been . . . used in a while."

Yam's nostrils narrowed in agreement. "Possible truth. Presence of whipslake kin in flower sea also disturbing."

"That's another thing." Howard plucked soft gray needles from the branch. "If this world hasn't been visited by the Keyholders since the first group of Averoy were taken to the Holding thousands of years ago, there shouldn't be anything like that here. And if the Keyholders've been around recently, I'm afraid Alaiya's not going to find things the way she expects them to be."

"Difficult to have-not expectations, Ow-er-bel. My life experience is more similar to Alaiya's, though you two are of the same race. You lived-not your whole life on a Holding, knowing your people's home was forever out of reach." Yam looked to the white sun rising over the lavender plain. "Here I feel her excitement, wonder how I would react to walk the ground of Trilbit home world."

"I know things haven't been easy for either of you." Howard squinted at the sunrise, rubbing his forehead. "You don't happen to know if a guy named Omber Oss turned up at the encampment last night, do you? He's another one of the Sunset People . . ." He paused to clear his throat. "And he's Alaiya's mate, as a matter of fact, so she's got that on her mind, as well."

The Trilbit turned to lay a branch on the small fire, releasing a ribbon of aromatic smoke into the air. "It is my understanding," he began, then fell silent as a flash of red-gold appeared between the trees and Alaiya stepped soundlessly from the forest's edge.

She joined them at the fire with a nod and a small smile, accepting a cup of bigtassle tea from Yam.

"Good morning," Howard said. "What have you found?"

"A forest, a beautiful forest. The trees go on and on, with deep round pools of water here and there that seem to be fed by underground streams."

"Any wildlife?"

"Brightly colored birds, green with black wings, blue with gray wings. Also some tree dwellers that remind me of the upright brown-furs, only much smaller. They have stick nests in the lower branches, and they hang from their tails beneath them and watch you walk by."

"Do you have any idea how far the woods extend?"

"No way to tell." Alaiya shrugged, a gesture Howard realized she had learned from him. "They might go on for miles, they might end just beyond the place where I turned back."

"I see." Howard nodded. "Well, I guess we should get going, then. Yam, how about a cup for the road?"

"Ahwerd." Alaiya set her hand on his shoulder. "You would prefer to return for the Hant's body before we go any farther, would you not?"

He looked into the forest for a long moment before he answered. "It's just that it may not be gone yet," he said finally. "I know we can't bring it back, but I'm afraid the Keyholders might figure out a way to break open its little coffin before it's done reminiscing. That would be awful."

"I agree with you." It was Alaiya's turn to scan the woods. "That is why I think we should go back to the Black and Blue World now, before we become too distracted by other matters."

"Are you sure you want to come along? You can stay here with Yam if you want. I can always catch up later."

"The Hant was my good comrade for many Turns. I will not desert it now." She rose to her feet and began to strap on her supply pack, inserting a few small branches from the ground before sealing it shut. "Besides, I do not think you will be able to free the overskin from the cave floor without some assistance."

"You may be right there." Howard also stood up. He dug the Key out of an inside pocket of the jacket, which he still wore tied around his waist. "Well, then . . . Yam, do you mind keeping an eye on the store for a little while? We should be back by this afternoon at the very latest."

"Content to remain," the Trilbit said. "No pollen reaching this far inland, and here seems a peaceful place, good choice for your comrade's final rest. I will spend the hours till your return in meditation, or perhaps I will find one of the forest pools and wash out my garments."

"Okay, fine. Hey—" He was struck by a sudden thought. "Are we going to have to do a transfusion or something in order to keep on understanding one another? I mean, that speaking stew should be wearing off soon, right?"

"Not necessary," Yam said. "I mixed your blood with mine back at the cave. You took blood from Hant, who was member of Ferocious Rulebenders along with Alaiya. All now carry parleybugs from Redborn's battle-gang."

"I get it. Well." Howard walked a few paces from the small fire and stood fingering the Key nervously as Alaiya came to stand by his side, her fingers lightly grasping his arm. "I'm not exactly sure what to do here," he said. "I mean, how does it know where we want to go? Do I tap my heels together three times or what?"

"What did you do the last time?" Alaiya asked. "You moved the rings on the shaft and then you turned the Key."

"Did I?" Howard looked blankly at the gleaming instrument. "I just remember giving it a sharp turn. Look— I've got an idea. Why don't you try it this time?"

"No!" Alaiya backed away slightly as Howard held out the Key. "I am no Keyholder."

Howard felt his face grow warm. "And you think I am?"

"I meant no insult." She gazed down at the golden

Key, then reached out her hand and grasped it hesitantly. "All right, I will try."

Howard laid his own hand on her trembling arm as she held the Key at arm's length from her body.

"To the Black and Blue World—now!" she said under her breath. "Please?" Her face averted, she held the shaft in her left hand and twisted the Key with her right.

After several seconds Alaiya opened her eyes and looked around at the purple-gray forest and the wide plain of lavender stone. Howard released the breath he had been holding.

"Okay, give it to me," he said with a sigh of resignation. His fingers moved upon the gleaming shaft for a few seconds; then he gave the Key a turn.

There was the snap of a wire cutter biting through metal, followed by a wave of intense cold and darkness.

Then the air grew slightly warmer, and the quality of the darkness changed somehow. Howard became aware of Alaiya's fingers biting into his arm.

"Did it work?" he whispered. There was a different smell to the air, as well.

"I think so. Perhaps we are inside the cave," she answered. Howard heard her fumbling at her belt for a few moments; then there was a scraping sound and a small torch blossomed between them.

They stood just inside the cave mouth, with blackness behind them. Howard stuck his head outside and peered up at the tiny stars that frosted the moonless sky. Easing back into the cave, he froze suddenly.

"Did you hear that?" he asked quietly.

"I heard only the wind," Alaiya replied. "We should hurry now."

Howard waited by the opening for another minute. Then he shook his head and made his way into the cave to where she knelt by the black overskin.

"Is there a chance somebody is looking for us? Could they be watching from the city?"

Alaiya lifted her head from her inspection of the rock-like slab and stared at the dark ceiling of the cave.

"Stillpoint is no longer near this world." She gave a sniff and lowered her eyes. "The Gate is closed."

"I wish I could do that." Howard narrowed his eyes

in concentration for a few seconds, then shook his head. "So the city's vanished completely? There's nothing left?"

"Only what the Wossil grandmother would call the big blur. Stillpoint never completely leaves any of the Fading Worlds."

Howard squatted by her side, running his hand lightly over the cold material of the overskin. It was smooth but faceted, like rock that had been melted and then fused into a new shape.

"I forgot how big this thing was," he said softly. "How the hell are we going to move it?"

"First we are going to try some of this." Alaiya brought a belt from her pack and turned it inside out.

Howard's eyes widened. "This is Awp's belt. Where did you get it?"

"It was with the supply pack the Hant left before sealing itself inside the overskin." She removed a small packet from the inner surface and set the belt on the cave floor. "This is a liquid we call eater. We must be careful that it does not touch our skin."

"Like Krazy Glue, huh? I once had a couple of fingers stuck to the side of my nose for an hour and a half." Howard watched over her shoulder as Alaiya brought the packet to the base of the overskin and pressed a shallow dimple in the transparent material. A thin stream of clear liquid shot onto the slab where the fused surface had melded with the rock of the cave. Steam rose hissing into the air. Lifting the small torch from where she had propped it against her pack, Alaiya stepped back.

"Whew, that really stinks," Howard said. "Is it working?"

Alaiya waited for the activity at the base of the slab to cease; then she went down on her hands and knees to peer at the treated area. She raised her head with a sigh.

"It is not strong enough. There is a tiny crack, but the weight of the overskin fuses it shut again even as it is made." She carefully replaced the packet in the Hant's belt and rocked back on her heels. "Perhaps I am wrong, Ahwerd, but I am assuming that the Key will not enable you to take an object like this with you simply by touching it."

"No, you're right," he said slowly. "I don't know why, but I'm sure it doesn't work that way . . ." He paused, groping for words. "The thing has to be . . . free, I think. That's why you and Yam come with me, but the ground under my feet stays put."

"As I suspected. Yet the eater did not free it. Without access to Stillpoint we cannot obtain a mountain gun, which I believe to be the only weapon capable of blasting the overskin from the rock floor." Alaiya was silent for a few moments, rubbing her chin between thumb and forefinger. Then she clicked her tongue and turned back to the pack. "There is one more chance. How is your nerve, Ahwerd—or more importantly, your stomach? Can you witness something truly bizarre, yet keep your mind on your task?"

"Witness something bizarre . . ." Howard pursed his lips. "Gosh, that would be different."

"I am not joking." Alaiya turned to him as she withdrew something from the pack, her face solemn in the flickering torchlight. "I know of no other way to separate the overskin from the cave floor, but my method will take concentration and trust on both our parts."

"Just tell me what you have in mind," Howard said. "If it's weirder than talking flounders, fires you start by spitting into jelly, and worlds with two kinds of gravity, I'll buy you dinner at the fanciest place in town."

Alaiya placed a long flat envelope on the rock floor between them and raised her eyes to Howard's face. "I am proposing to don the amoeba suit that Yam-ya-mosh stole from the Meticulous Victors. Then, as you squirt a line of eater around the base of the slab, I will insinuate my body into the tiny crack as it forms, flowing between the overskin and the cave floor until there is a complete separation. You will then grasp both myself and the overskin and bear us all safely to Field of Flowers."

"Do you suppose there's a pay phone nearby?" Howard craned his neck toward the shadows at the back of the cave. "You have to call these ritzy places pretty early if you expect to get a good table."

"You do not support my plan." Alaiya leaned back, her hand on the envelope. "Have you an alternative?"

"Look, I can't—you're going to go *under* the slab?"

Howard took a deep breath. "Are you sure this is safe? I mean, squeezing through a narrow opening is one thing—but we're talking microscopic! How does this suit work, anyway? I figured it must be something only Dratzuls could use."

"It works." Alaiya opened the envelope and slowly poured out the amoeba suit, which puddled like thick black ink on the rock floor. "None of the warrior races has come close to understanding Keyholder technology, though many have tried. Tests to analyze materials or devices purchased in Stillpoint routinely end in explosions that claim the lives of the experimenters. For the lucky there is merely punishment. Better to be like the Trulls or the other low-technology races and accept it all as sorcery, than waste our time in wondering how it works."

She lifted the shining black mass in her two hands and raised her eyebrows at Howard. "Will you help me put it on?"

Howard chewed his lower lip. "Maybe I should be wearing it. You probably have better aim with the eater stuff."

"You have no experience with the suit. Besides, it is difficult to manipulate objects from inside. You might not be able to operate the Key."

"You think you're smart, don't you?" Howard reached out his hand as Alaiya returned the suit to the cave floor and stepped gingerly into the center of the amorphous puddle. "Jeez, this stuff has a weird feel to it."

He helped her tuck her long hair down her back as she pulled the material up over her shoulders, stretching the remainder into a sort of cowl which she began to guide carefully up the back of her head. She stood blinking solemnly at him for a moment before drawing the edges together across her face to seal the suit. Howard leaned forward abruptly and planted a quick, lopsided kiss on her lips.

"For luck or something." Then he stepped back and watched her disappear beneath the slick black substance. Waving off his offers of assistance, Alaiya lowered herself clumsily to her knees. With a rubbery mittenlike hand, she gestured to the Hant's belt, then indicated where he should spray the corrosive on the overskin.

Although it was apparently possible to see while wearing the amoeba suit, Alaiya's ability to speak and to hear both seemed to be impaired. Howard watched, fascinated, as the featureless black humanoid knelt in an attitude resembling worship at the head of the overskin, using gestures to communicate her readiness to begin the procedure.

Removing the transparent packet from the Hant's belt, he placed his thumb over the small depression at one end and held the container away from his body as he had seen Alaiya do. At her signal he pointed the packet at a spot near the base of the slab and pressed.

Alaiya edged forward like a shadow as steam rose from the rocky surface. Howard moved to the side and continued spraying the stream of clear fluid, his breath becoming shallow as he watched Alaiya's black-clad hands probe and then slide into the tiny crack formed by the corrosive. Her arms slid in smoothly up to the shoulders; she paused, then pressed forward slowly. Suddenly her head bent backward at an impossible angle and slid out of sight.

Howard swallowed with difficulty as her body followed, passing under the slab in a series of rippling, snakelike movements. He had reached the far end of the overskin. Returning to the place where he had started, he began applying the eater to the other side of the faceted rock, trying not to watch as the powerful substance splattered harmlessly on the shiny material of the suit. Only Alaiya's legs remained at the head of the slab. It was difficult to follow their movement: slick black shadows gliding over faceted black planes.

When he had reached the foot of the slab once more he tossed the nearly empty packet into the shadows at the rear of the cave. Then he stood back against the cave wall, panting. Lifting the torch, he saw that the suit was almost completely lost beneath the slab. Only a few inches of black material remained. A flicker of reflected light brought him to the foot of the slab, where two flat black extrusions had begun to leak from the minute crack at that end. Hands? Then he saw that a thin ribbon of the material was pushing forth to form an irregular fringe all around the overskin.

"God . . ." Howard tried to picture Alaiya's body, flattened and formless beneath the crushing weight of the rocklike slab. "How am I . . ."

Near the foot of the slab a portion of the amoeba-suit material flapped limply, elongating itself outward from the crack.

Howard returned Awp's belt to Alaiya's pack, then strapped the pack to his own back. He knelt by the side of the slab, leaning forward so that the black projection rested upon the skin of his left forearm. His flesh crawled as the slick pseudopod tightened blindly about his wrist. Curling his other arm awkwardly around the overskin's cold facets, he brought his hands together to clutch the golden Key.

He tried to let his mind go blank, hoping that his hands would utilize whatever secret knowledge they seemed to possess and return them swiftly to the world of flowers. His brain buzzed with fear and concern for Alaiya.

"I don't . . ." Finally he twisted one of the bands savagely between his fingers, closed his eyes, and concentrated on the small campfire by the forest where they had left Yam. His fingers moved again, and he felt the Key turn in his hands. Then the now-familiar sensations of travel between two worlds enveloped him.

CHAPTER XVI

Whither Yam?

THE AIR WAS WARM AND SMELLED OF SPICES.

Howard found himself lying with his cheek pressed against the hard facets of the overskin. As he raised his head a wave of fatigue passed over him. He cradled his forehead in his hand and puffed air out through his cheeks.

The massive coffin shape of the overskin sat like a giant obsidian knife on the smooth lavender stone of the plain. At its base a strange, tattered-looking ruff of black material fluttered weakly in the scented breeze. Howard stared at it dumbly for a moment; then a shock of comprehension passed through him like an electric current, and he sprang to his feet.

"Oh, God, Alaiya!" He trembled above the slab, then dropped to kneel at its side on the hard stone. The slick black material of the amoeba suit slipped through his fingers like oiled plastic. In desperation he put his shoulder to the overskin and heaved, then drew back in horror as the slab began to rotate slightly on the shiny material beneath it. His heart pounded in his throat as he imagined Alaiya trapped in the distorted shape, a ton of rock grinding her into pulp inside the suit.

There was a ghost of movement from the base of the slab. As he watched, the amoeba suit withdrew slowly under the coffin shape. He leaped to the other side, where a vaguely human form was being extruded, expanding

156

with agonizing slowness in obscene parody of an inflating balloon.

Finally the grotesque figure rolled free of the overskin and lay motionless on the lavender stone.

Howard fell to the ground and set his ear against the slick black torso.

"Maybe sound can't get out at all," he muttered to himself, scanning the still form for other signs of life. "How do you get it off?" The suit fit the body like a second skin; Howard could find nothing resembling a seam.

"Alaiya!" He grasped the rubbery shoulders and shook the body, at first gently, then with rising panic. His fingertips began to sink slowly inward. "Alaiya, come out of there!"

He thought he felt a quiver of answering movement and tried to hold himself absolutely still, noting with some detached portion of his mind that his hands were continuing to tremble convulsively.

The shoulders moved again beneath his fingers. Then the right arm contracted slowly, the hand drifting through the air toward the black-shrouded head. The mittenlike palm tugged lazily at the face area, and suddenly a sliver of ivory skin gleamed beneath the featureless black.

Alaiya screamed—a muffled, gurgling sound.

Howard fumbled his thumbs into the small opening at the level of her cheekbones and tugged outward. The material came apart grudgingly, making a wet, tearing sound as it split open to her waist. Her body was bathed in sweat, and she shuddered uncontrollably as Howard peeled away the remainder of the suit and cradled her head in his lap.

"You're all right now," he whispered, smoothing damp hair back from her forehead. "Are you all right? Alaiya, what's the matter?"

She lay staring upward without speaking, her eyes glassy, her breathing ragged. Howard stroked her hair and murmured to her, willing her to recognize him. Finally her eyes seemed to focus, and she cleared her throat.

"Hard . . ." Her body was racked by a fit of coughing. She spat something black onto the ground, wiping her mouth with the back of a shaking hand. "Harder than I thought . . . to handle first time in the suit. Had no idea . . . the sensations . . . I was under there, I was under the rock, as if I had no bones in my body . . ." She squeezed Howard's arm, staring at her own fingers as if reassuring herself of their solidity.

"Are you in pain?"

"No, but it feels as though I have not been in my body for a while." She shook her head, unable to explain further. "I was afraid I would go mad in there."

"Well, it's all over now. You did it. We got back and we brought Awp's body with us." Howard's forehead creased in sudden consternation. "Wait a minute—what did you mean, 'first time'? You said you had experience in the suit."

Alaiya gave a crooked smile, shook her head weakly. "I said that you had no experience in it. We never discussed me." She pushed gently at his hands. "I should get up."

"Oh, no. You're going to lie here until I'm sure you're all right. God, what a stupid thing to do! I wonder if Yam has any more of that bugtussle tea . . ." Howard searched the immediate area with his eyes and frowned again. "Speaking of our small friend—this is the spot we left from, isn't it? I don't see any sign of the campfire—or of Yam."

Alaiya lifted her head.

"This is indeed the place," she confirmed. "There is the double trunk where I entered the forest a few hours ago." She squinted at the smooth purple bark. "But there are markings on it now that were not there this morning."

Howard pushed to his feet and examined the trunk. A crude arrow pointed into the woods.

"It's the right height for Yam," he said. "But doesn't it look like it's been there awhile?"

Alaiya studied the markings, propped up on her elbows.

"Yes, those are old cuts." She turned her head in a quick scan of the area. Aside from the faceted slab of the overskin, the plain of lavender stone was empty. "Where is Ya-mosh? Why did he not wait for us?"

"I don't know, but I don't like it. At any rate . . ."
He returned to her side with an armful of evergray
boughs, which he slid under her back and head. "You
aren't going anywhere but to sleep for a few hours. We'll
figure out what to do when you wake up."

"But we should—"

"Hey, I don't want to hear it. You lied to me, and now
you owe me one. Close your eyes. I'm going to see if I
can hunt up the flying machine and my pack, which also
seem to have vanished." He turned and began to walk
toward the forest, stepping around the black puddle of
the amoeba suit with an expression of distaste. "I'll be
back in a while with some fresh water," he said sternly
over his shoulder. "Don't. You. Move."

Howard wandered into the woods as far as he dared,
unwilling to leave Alaiya alone for more than a short
time. After collecting some water in the storage bag
folded into his belt, he retraced his steps with ease.

Alaiya was sitting propped up against the Hant's overskin, a wistful expression on her face.

"It almost seems that our friend is with us," she
mused. "Hard to imagine that the Hant is most likely
gone in body as well as spirit inside this black shell."
She accepted the water gratefully, eyeing his empty hands
as she drank. "You found no sign of the Trilbit or your
belongings?"

"Only a few more of those arrows pointing deeper into
the woods. Not one of them is freshly made, however,
so they can't be Yam's doing."

"Yet I combed those woods this morning and never
saw a marking."

"It was dark, you were excited." Howard shrugged.
"Who knows? I just can't figure out why Yam would take
off like this."

"We are both thinking the same thing, are we not?"
Alaiya stared somberly into the purple-gray forest.

"What, that he might not have gone voluntarily?"
Howard looked around unhappily. "I suppose we have
to consider the possibility."

"We must look for him." She made to rise from the
ground but sank back with a grunt as her legs spasmed

beneath her. "We will wait until tomorrow morning, if you do not object."

"This is weird." Howard had paced to the other side of the slab, and he bent over to examine something near the foot of the coffin shape. "There's a bunch of graffiti on Awp's overskin." He raised his head with a scowl. "Just when you think you've found a nice neighborhood . . ."

"What are you talking about?" Alaiya pushed to her feet with an effort and moved around the slab to stand next to him, bracing herself against the black surface.

"See there? It was too dark for us to notice it in the cave." Howard took her shoulders from behind and helped her to lean forward above the small, brightly painted characters. "What's it say—Keyholders go home? Maybe Grandma Wossil's got a few juvenile delinquents among her upright brown-furs."

"Ahwerd . . ." Alaiya leaned back with his help. "This is the warrior speech, a written language that is common to all battle-gangs—despite the Keyholders' attempts to suppress it."

"Fan mail from some Ga'Prenny?" He was struck by a sudden thought. "Or is it from Awp—like a farewell note? What does it say?"

"It is a message written by some of the warriors at the encampment. Of course . . ." She nodded to herself. "They saw us vanish when we were confronted by the Victors and the Traveler." She read the rest of the message, then lifted her eyes with a wondering look. "About half of them refused to enter the city after witnessing our disappearance. Instead they have fled into the black mountains, there to await our return."

"Our what?" Howard shook his head. "Has somebody been making campaign promises I can't fulfill?"

"I believe the other Averoy are leading them in this. Arpenwole has been on the edge of open defiance for some time, and the message says that Oss is among them." She pursed her lips in a thoughtful smile. "He is a born revolutionary and could incite the others to follow our cause with little trouble."

"I see." Howard looked off into the distance, his expression unreadable. "And what exactly is our cause?"

"Why, war against Stillpoint, the defeat of the Key-holders!" Alaiya laughed. "The message does not say, but it is not difficult to read their intentions."

Howard did not share her amusement. "And how are we supposed to find this little band of rebels, assuming we ever make it back there?"

"Ah, that is here in the final lines." She pointed to a double row of curving characters. "It is written in the old Averant script. Apparently they did not think it wise to share directions to their hiding places with anyone who happened to stumble into the cave."

Howard scratched at his chin, his eyes on the distant curve of the flower sea beyond the stone plain.

"Do you want to go back for them?" he asked.

"Ahwerd, we must find Yam-ya-mosh. Then, if you wish, you may utilize your Key to return us to the Black and Blue World."

"Okay. Sounds good. How long do you think they'll wait for us?"

"They have given a list of dates and places." She nodded to the flowing Averant script. "They will remain at each location for about a Turn, then move on to the next. It is a clever system, no doubt of Arpenwole's devising."

"Oh, Oss is just the rabble-rouser, huh? They have to rely on Arpenwole for the nuts and bolts?"

"Ahwerd, does this message disturb you?" Alaiya peered into his half-averted face. "Do you not wish to join with these others?"

"I'm sorry, Alaiya." He took in a deep breath and blew it out. "I guess I'm just tired. Maybe we should turn in now so we can get an early start in the morning."

Howard prepared two bed-nests of the soft evergray needles, positioning them several feet apart on one side of the black slab. Alaiya was silent as Howard helped her lie down. Then he stretched out on his own pile of bedding, his back turned toward her.

Howard lay awake for some time, unable to sleep. He was surprised when the sky began to darken after what had seemed like only a few hours. Finally he drifted off, his body's fatigue overruling the multiple concerns that warred for preeminence in his mind. He was indeed tired, he discovered. He wondered if transportation of the

Hant's overskin had been a more physically draining task than his previous experiences with the Key.

Alaiya rose early the next morning, waking Howard to announce her full recovery. After a modest breakfast, the two set out into the woods to search for Yam.

For want of other clues, they decided to follow the directional markers that had apparently been carved some time earlier into the purple bark, hoping that Yam had done the same. The forest was as beautiful as Alaiya had claimed, and Howard's mood soon lightened as the two walked in silence past the big-eyed stares of upside-down tree dwellers, while jewellike birds flitted above their heads through the canopy of silver-gray needles.

The waist-high arrows continued to appear at regular intervals. They followed the trail through the trees, stopping to rest around midday by one of the deep circular pools.

"I do not understand it." Alaiya divided a piece of fruitbread from her pack and handed half to Howard. "Something is different here. Do you feel it? This is the same forest I walked through yesterday, and yet it is not."

"Maybe the seasons are changing," Howard said. "It feels cooler today." He eyed the tall trees that surrounded the pool, chewing thoughtfully. "And the needles seem shinier than before, more silvery."

"Yes, I had thought it my imagination, or a trick of the light." She dipped her cupped palm in the cold, clear water of the spring and drank. "Something has changed in the short time we were gone."

They continued their journey for the rest of the long day, bedding down at sunset by an outcropping of smooth lavender stone.

The next day passed uneventfully, as did the one after that. Although they observed a variety of birds and small animals, they encountered nothing larger than the squirrel-size tree-hangers. Unhappy with the overly sweet fare in her pack, Alaiya caught and cooked small crustaceans that she found under flat rocks near the edges of the well-like pools. She and Howard spoke little as they made their way through the purple wood. Alaiya's eyes and ears were all for the new world unfolding around her, while Howard spent most of his waking moments mulling the events of the past few months. He was trailing several paces behind on the afternoon of the fourth day, lost in his thoughts, when Alaiya gave a glad cry and called his name.

"Look," she said when he caught up with her. "The end of the forest at last!"

Sunlight shone brightly beyond the last few trees in front of them as they quickened their step. In a few moments they walked out into a field of waving purple ground cover. Ancient, great-trunked trees dotted the meadow, their thin, twisting branches heavily cloaked in leaves of violet, maroon, and green. Teardrop-shaped fruit the size of plums hung in clusters of five from the boughs above their heads. Howard plucked one as they walked through the knee-high underbrush; it was deliciously fragrant, with an outer skin as clear and bright as an amethyst.

"What do you think?" He held it out to Alaiya. "Good to eat?"

"Undoubtedly, if this is the farmland of which the tales spoke." Her eyes shone in the sunlight. "Ahwerd, it is all coming true. Soon we will reach the city of my people that lies at the heart of this land."

"I hope so," he said. He sniffed the piece of fruit again, saliva gathering in his mouth, then tucked it reluctantly into his jacket pocket. "I think I'll wait till we can check with the farmer," he told Alaiya. "Just to be on the safe side."

"If you think it necessary." Alaiya gave her handshrug and moved on ahead of him. Howard sighed. It was obvious that she was bothered by his seeming lack of faith in her knowledge of this world. Catching up with her in a few paces, he made a point of drawing the small fruit from his pocket and taking a healthy bite. The flavor fulfilled the promise of the fruit's aroma, with the addition of a slightly tart aftertaste that reminded him of red wine.

The crudely incised arrows continued into the orchard meadow, guiding them from tree to tree through the rank undergrowth. The chill pools of the forested area were absent, in their place a network of narrow, canallike streams that lent credence to Alaiya's theory that the land had been used for farming. Whether that use had occurred within the last few centuries was another matter entirely, Howard thought as he waded through the knee-high purple grass.

They had walked for perhaps a mile when Howard stepped over a small embankment and found himself standing on a section of dark green paving, partially overgrown with leafy ground vines.

"Look what I've just stumbled onto," he called to Alaiya, who had left the trail for a few moments. He shaded his eyes and looked toward the west. The land rose gradually into a steep hill that was precisely bisected by the green roadway.

"The trees seem to run out here. I wonder if this road picks up the trail."

"We must assume so." Trembling with anticipation, Alaiya moved into the lead as they began the climb. The road had a peculiar spongy feel to it. Howard wondered how old it was.

Alaiya reached the top of the hill first. She stood with her head down, silhouetted against the lowering sun. Please don't let her be disappointed, Howard thought as he trudged up the last few feet to stand at her side.

A vast city filled the valley beneath them.

The outermost parts of it, including the towering walls, were of smooth purple stone. Bright metal shone from the roofs of the inner buildings in flashes of silver and copper and gold, while in the distant center a great interconnected structure of domes and towers rose gleaming into the violet sky of evening.

The emerald roadway ended at a gigantic gate in the curving wall of the city, perhaps another mile from where they stood. Through the thick underbrush they glimpsed another dark road on either side of the one they followed, which led to equally spaced portals in the towering walls. Symmetry argued that three more thoroughfares met three more gates beyond their view on the other side of the great valley. There was no traffic along any of the roads.

They started down, Howard scanning the countryside for signs of life while Alaiya's gray eyes devoured the grandeur that lay before them.

The sun was setting in earnest by the time they reached

level ground, its last rays streaming up behind the walls of the city. Howard became aware of colored lights starting to glow among the central towers, as distant and unreal as the stars. He narrowed his eyes, reminded of something as Alaiya strode confidently down the vine-choked road. He hung back for a moment, then forced himself to continue, unable to pinpoint the memory or why it had disturbed him.

A twilight unreality had begun to settle over the scene for Howard. They crossed the floor of the valley in silence.

A small door stood ajar at the base of one side of the massive gate. Howard's skin prickled. They exchanged a wordless glance and walked through, their footsteps falling soundlessly on a continuation of the smooth, slightly cushioned surface as they entered the city. On the other side of the portal ghostly light fell from high-set lamps whose nature Howard could not discern.

"This is the way Ya-mosh came," Alaiya said softly. "Look." An arrow had been heavily scratched on the flooring just inside the doorway. "And here." The wan light picked out four short lines of crude characters scratched at waist level onto a blank portion of the elaborately carved stone of the door.

"Warrior speech?" asked Howard.

Alaiya nodded. "It says, 'I Yam-ya-mosh/the Trilbit/ entered here.'" She frowned in the ghostlight from above. "There is a date underneath, but he has gotten it wrong." She straightened up, counting softly under her breath. "He has written here that he came into the city almost a full Turn from now."

"You mean a full Turn ago?"

"No." Alaiya looked at him in perplexity. "The date he has scratched here has not yet passed."

"Maybe he looked at his calendar upside down or something. Lord knows it's not the clearest arrangement I've ever run across."

During their trek from the nightwood on the Black and Blue World to the encampment outside of Stillpoint Howard had made an attempt to familiarize himself with the system used by the warriors to reckon time on the Fading Worlds. With the help of Alaiya and his faithful

Timex, he had ascertained that a Turn was roughly equal to forty-five Terrestrial days. Turns were gathered into Rounds, a Lesser Round containing seven Turns and a Greater one nine. When Alaiya began to detail the calculations necessary to account for the five local days allotted to each after-Turn, Howard threw up his hands in despair. "I can see why you don't bother to wear watches," he had said, at which point Alaiya informed him that all participating warriors were imbued with a 'time-sense' while on the Fading Worlds that did away with any need for such imprecise instruments.

"Perhaps his thoughts were not fully focused when he left the message," Alaiya said, turning from the door.

The light from above was too weak to be of any real assistance. Alaiya smeared firejelly on the tip of a branch from her pack and ignited it.

They stood in a courtyard just inside the outer walls. Ahead of them, the walls of featureless buildings bulked beyond the wavering circle of light. Directly in front of them a score of different-colored pathways radiated outward, most receding toward the buildings in the distance.

"Looks like Yam picked the center path," Howard said, stepping back to sight along the arrow scratched into the yielding pavement. "Shall we?"

After they had walked for a good ten minutes through increasing darkness, the crimson path abruptly turned into a narrow alley between two of the buildings. Oval doorways were set deep into the walls, alternating with circular windows of dark blue glass that swiveled open on a diagonal rod set into the stone. The walls themselves bore an intermittent mosaic of gleaming jewellike stones set at eye level in intricate raised patterns.

Some of the doors were locked shut; others yawned open to reveal empty rooms floored with dust.

"It is plain that no one has lived here for a very long time," Alaiya said quietly after they had searched the dozenth room with their torchlight.

"Maybe they've withdrawn to the center of the city," Howard suggested. He looked into the gloom ahead of them. "This alley looks like it goes on forever. What say we bed down in one of these rooms and take up our search again in the daylight?"

Alaiya agreed, and they spread their cloaks on the floor of the next open room. Howard swung open one of the cobalt-colored windows, conscious as he did so of a familiar, sweetish fragrance he had not noticed earlier. He watched regretfully as Alaiya lay down on the yielding floor, wishing he could make the city come alive for her with multitudes of welcoming Averoy. She extinguished the torch, and Howard closed his eyes.

CHAPTER XVII

Under the Dead City

THE CORRIDOR SEEMED TO GO ON FOREVER. AT some point Alaiya had allowed the torch to slip from nerveless fingers, and they had walked for a time in utter darkness. Then a faint light began to glow from damp greenish patches on the walls and ceilings. Howard was conscious of walking next to Alaiya, and of wanting to walk, and of little else inside the haze of sweet fragrance. Somewhere a tiny portion of his mind buzzed like a bee around a sleeping giant, trying to wake him, trying to tell him something. Alaiya marched at his side, her face slack in the greenish glow from the patches of luminous fungus. Turning to look at her, Howard was mildly surprised to see that small flowers had begun to sprout from her lips and eyes.

"Ahwerd!" She stood in front of him, pinning his arms to his sides, her feet firmly planted on the smooth walkway. Her face showed puzzled concern in the wavering torchlight from below. Howard looked dazedly to the right, where moments before she had been walking contentedly at his side, her face wreathed in blossoms.

"Oh," he said with an embarrassed grin. "I was dreaming. Sorry if I . . .'' He looked around. They were back in the alleyway, the wall markings unfamiliar. "What's going on?" he finished weakly.

"You left the room. I heard the door open and followed you out. You seemed to be asleep, but walked as if you knew where you were heading. You started to go faster. Your arms and legs were moving like parts of a machine.''

"Whew." Howard shook himself. "Totally bizarre. I haven't sleepwalked since I was six years old.''

"We may as well try another room.'' Alaiya pointed to the door on the opposite side of the alley and picked up the torch she had propped against the wall at their feet. "This time perhaps I shall sleep by the door.''

They stretched out in a small empty chamber similar to the first. Howard yawned hugely as he laid his cheek on his folded arm. His legs and arms ached.

The next thing he knew, Alaiya was bending over him, shaking him gently. The room was lit by a soft silver glow of moonlight from the alleyway.

"What?" He started to sit up. "Not again. Was I—''

Alaiya laid her hand on his chest and put a finger to her lips.

"Hssst. It was in the room for a few moments, then it left.''

"What was?'' Howard looked to the door, which they had shut behind them. It stood slightly ajar. He felt a chill flutter up his spine.

"I did not see it. I awoke when I heard a scraping sound near the doorway. When I raised my head something was sliding out through the door.''

Howard grimaced. "What do you mean 'sliding out'?''

Alaiya gave an Averoy shrug and followed it with an American one. "It sounded like something small being pulled across the floor. I went to the window and peered down the alleyway, but it was gone.''

Howard sat up with his arms clasped around his knees. He sniffed the air. "Do you smell something?''

Alaiya nodded. "I noticed it when I awoke. Sweet.''

"Hmm. It's still the middle of the night, you know. We'd be crazy to leave this room and go prowling around before sunrise.''

Alaiya watched him, saying nothing.

"On the other hand . . . you don't suppose it could have been Yam peeking in the door, do you? I don't know how well Trilbits see in the dark. Maybe he was startled when you moved and hightailed it out of here without stopping to see who we were."

"Possible," Alaiya agreed. "He had gotten a large amount of pollen from the flower sea in his fur and belongings, and that might account for the odor."

Howard groaned. "So what we're going to do is go prowling around in the middle of the night and see if we can track him down, right?"

"I have already strapped on my pack, and Silversting is in my hand." Alaiya smiled grimly as something flashed at her side in the moonlight. "Let us go to seek our friend."

They found the trail easily in the light of Alaiya's torch. It looked indeed as though something damp and narrow had been dragged along the path.

"One way or another, it looks like we're destined to find the end of this alleyway tonight," Howard commented.

After they had walked for a few minutes they noticed that the alley was beginning to slope gradually downward. At the same time the patterns of colored stone on the walls had changed from predominantly reddish tones to blues and blue-greens. After a while it was like walking down a ramp, and the intricate mosaic burned a fierce yellow-green in the torchlight as it ushered them into the earth.

A blank wall appeared at the end of the alleyway. When they reached it, they saw that the passage took a sharp turn to the right through a narrow doorway, doubling back on itself as it began to descend at an even steeper angle. The walls in that section were completely unadorned, and for the first time they walked with a low ceiling overhead.

Howard was reluctant to lose the silvery moonlight. "I don't know about you, but I'm not exactly overjoyed at the prospect of navigating an unfamiliar subway system in the middle of a power failure. I wish you still lit up." He gazed doubtfully at the small torch. "Any chance we'll be stranded in the dark in the next half hour or so?"

"Firejelly burns for a good long time," Alaiya said.

"It will be some hours before the flames even begin to devour the wood."

"Okeydokey. Down we go." Howard reached out a hand to brush the wall as they descended. It was clammy to the touch. They followed the passage for some time before it doubled back again, the downward climb becoming even steeper.

At the next turning point the corridor suddenly opened out into darkness.

"Bingo," Howard said softly. Alaiya repeated the word in reverent tones and raised the torch above her head.

They were standing at the entrance to a vast chamber, domed like an amphitheater with a ceiling that vanished into the shadows. They walked slowly into the huge room. It was divided in half, the far section of the chamber sunken to a level of fifteen or twenty feet below the other.

"Olympic-sized pool," Howard said as they crossed to the edge of the pit. A great crack halved the floor of the sunken area. He pointed to a black archway on the far side of the empty pit. "I wonder if the sauna's in there."

There was a narrow ledge running along the wall. They edged single file around the empty pool till they stood before the tall archway. Alaiya held out her torch to reveal a long ramp leading into a second chamber that was several feet lower than the first. The room was otherwise identical, although the floor of the second sunken area was intact. Several feet of odorous green-black scum concealed the bottom of the pool, and there were large lumps in the viscous material that Howard did not wish to inspect too closely.

"Let's hope one of those isn't the lifeguard," he murmured as they stood looking down.

Alaiya touched his arm at a faint noise, a strange slapping sound that seemed to be coming from beyond the pit. She lifted the torch.

"Oh, swell," Howard muttered. "Door number three."

They sidled around the edge of the foul-smelling pit. A faint glow emanated from the third portal.

"I feel like Goldilocks," Howard said as they stepped

through into a still lower chamber. "I just hope there's nobody sleeping in this bed."

The third room was dank and chill, the water pit on the opposite side of the room filled to the brim with something that glinted blackly in the torchlight. The odor that reached their nostrils as they stood on the ramp was nauseating.

Howard took the torch from Alaiya and stepped back into the archway, holding the light behind him into the second chamber as he peered forward into the third. Most of the curved walls and ceiling were covered with irregular patches of something that glowed with a sickly greenish radiance.

"What is it, a fungus or something?" he asked softly.

There was a swishing, gurgling sound from somewhere in the darkness. Howard thrust the torch into the room in time to see ripples spreading slowly across the pool of turgid black liquid. Oily wavelets slapped rhythmically against stone.

Howard and Alaiya exchanged glances and moved forward cautiously. As he stepped from the ramp, Howard's foot struck something that felt like a tree root. He lowered the torch. The floor was crisscrossed by a tangled network of moist gray ropes, as if a vast fisherman's net had been spread out to dry. They stepped carefully toward the stinking water pit.

"Hey." Howard pointed with the torch. "At least we're in time for the log-rolling competition."

Something large lay half-submerged near the back of the great pool. It resembled a partly rotted tree trunk, its gnarled and knotty surface partially covered by patches of the same pale fungus that glowed faintly above them.

Alaiya took the torch from him and held it forward.

"There is no door on the other side," she said. "This is the last chamber."

"Thank God," Howard murmured. The stench from whatever filled the water pit was making it difficult to breathe. "Let's retrace our steps and find some decent air. If we want, we can always check this place out again tomorrow."

He led the way back toward the doorway to the second chamber, Alaiya scanning the room behind them as she followed him with the torch. Howard squinted at the tall archway as they neared it. Was something obscuring his vision? He blinked and wiped his eyes, but the obstruction remained, strands of something moist that reflected the light from the torch. At first he thought he was looking into the adjoining room; then he realized that something was hanging over the doorway itself. Cobwebs? An ornamental curtain?

"Alaiya, do you remember passing through—"

A sound came from the water behind them. Again they heard the slapping, louder this time, as a series of oily waves reached the stone. A puff of foul-smelling air blew over them.

Then there was another noise, not from the water: the slightest of sliding sounds, now somewhere to the left of them, now in front, then all around them.

"Come on," he whispered, taking Alaiya's arm as he quickened his pace toward the doorway.

The curtain of gray strands was stirring softly as they moved toward it. There was something strange about the motion. Howard thought of scores of snakes, flexing and twisting as they hung by their tails in the darkness. He froze.

"There's something alive in the doorway," he whispered urgently.

Alaiya brought the torch up. "There is something behind us, as well," she said through clenched teeth. "It must have come out of the water pit. Wait, now it is over there . . ."

She reached into her belt.

"Here is the last of my firejelly," she said quietly, smearing another dab on the shaft of the branch. She spat softly on it, and light flared.

Gray, ropy tendrils were moving quietly everywhere on the damp floor, like a thousand serpents writhing blindly about their feet.

"The whole place is alive." Howard clutched Alaiya to his side. "Look at the ceiling."

The ragged, glowing patches had begun to move, descending slowly toward the floor along the curved walls.

Howard swallowed. "God, I think it's all one thing. We've got to get out of here."

Alaiya cried out suddenly and jumped to one side. She

reached down and stabbed viciously with her dagger at something that was beginning to coil around her ankle. Instantly the floor around them erupted into a frenzy of snapping, flexing tendrils.

"We have to keep moving!" she cried as a second whiplike appendage snapped around her leg. "Use your sword!"

Howard danced from one foot to the other, swinging his machete in the dimness. "Let's try for the door! They don't look so strong there."

Hopping and leaping through the coiling web of tendrils, they headed for the doorway. The living curtain of gray whips stretched eagerly toward them, seeming to sense their approach. A few feet from the archway Howard heard Alaiya gasp.

He looked back to see her body alive with gray snakes. She was sawing furiously at them with her dagger. As quickly as she severed one of them, new ones rose to wrap themselves around her.

She dropped to one knee with a curse. A large tendril had fastened itself tightly around her lower leg. Slowly it began to drag her backward toward the water pit as other tendrils coiled about her neck and arms. The smack of heavy waves against stone increased as something huge shifted in the pool.

"Keep chopping—I'm coming!" Howard made his way back through the writhing madness that covered the floor.

The light of the torch she still held in one hand illuminated the water pit. A second twisted shape was rising slowly through the water, closer to the center of the room than the first. Floating just above the waterline, it split open lengthwise to reveal a dripping maw coated with glowing fungus.

At the rear of the pool the first shape had also come to life. Howard stared at the ridge of gnarled and twisted hide upon which great filmy eyes were now opening—dozens of them set in a row like toads perching on a trunk of rotted wood. The sucking mouth dipped slightly into the foul liquid; yards behind it, the eyes rocked in response. A bloated, barrel-shaped hump of flesh became momentarily visible between the two, then sank sluggishly back below the surface. Tendrils like gray ca-

bles flexed and shuddered from dozens of wartlike protrusions just beneath the gaping mouth of the nearer
section.

Howard swayed at Alaiya's side, slicing with the machete at the mass of wriggling tendrils.

"I think they're going for the heat!" he shouted. "Get
rid of the torch!"

With a grunt Alaiya bent back her arm and hurled the
torch at the gaping mouth in the pool. They watched as
the rear section flinched its bulk away from the flaming
trail, the row of eyes closing convulsively. The torch
struck the tough hide above the huge mouth, bouncing
off harmlessly into the water where the firejelly flared for
a few moments before dispersing.

"The eyes are afraid of the fire," Alaiya observed.

Howard knelt at her side, slashing unsuccessfully at
the thick cable that held her leg, unable to strike with
full force in the dim light cast by the creeping fungus for
fear of hitting Alaiya. Now that the torch was gone, more
of the things were beginning to pay attention to him. He
swore as powerful tendrils coiled about his sword arm.
Alaiya inched closer to the water pit, her teeth clenched
in pain as a dozen more tendrils tightened like wires on
her limbs.

"I have some firejelly left." Howard strained upward
against the tendrils, fumbling with the packets at his belt.
"Hold on—I'm going to try something."

Slicing at a small tentacle that bound his leg, he loped
to the rim of the pool and began to edge along the narrow
lip toward the ridge of eyes. Tendrils raced through the
black liquid like water snakes, rising to strike at him.
Shielding his face with his arm, he tore open a packet
and sprinkled half the contents in a wide arc on the water
in front of the eye ridge. Flames spread instantly across
the surface of the pool. The eye section heaved upward
and fell with a resounding splash, dividing the sheet of
fire into floating pockets of flame that were quickly carried away on waves of oily black.

"Damn!" Howard stuffed the packet back into his belt
and raced back to where a grimly struggling Alaiya was
being borne slowly across the floor toward the water pit,
her body almost completely shrouded in squirming ten-

tacles. ''The fire won't stick long enough to hurt the thing—it just floats away!'' He began to slash at her living bonds.

''Ahwerd, you must leave—'' Alaiya gasped for breath. ''You cannot help me, but you may yet escape.'' The thick gray cable around her leg gave a sudden jerk, and she slid across the floor. A few yards away, the creature's mouth yawned hungrily at the lip of the water pit, luminous drool sluicing from its jaws as it awaited its prey.

''Shut up and give me your belt!'' Howard severed a small tendril from about her waist and bent to pry apart the ornate fastening.

''What are you doing?'' Alaiya stared at him in shock. ''You would take my belt, after all that has happened?''

''I know what I'm doing—I think,'' he grunted, freeing the belt at last and pulling it from her body. ''Just keep fighting!''

He returned to the far side of the pool, squinting and cursing as he fumbled through the contents of the unfamiliar belt.

''Ah!'' Clutching a packet of pale green powder, he leaped forward onto the ledge, coming as near to the floating ridge of eyes as he could. A mass of snapping tendrils pursued him as the gnarled ridge of flesh drifted away in the dark liquid.

Great clouded eyes blinked impassively at him. He tore open the packet and hurled it into the water pit directly in front of the ridge. Instantly a mass of green gel blossomed in the filthy water, expanding furiously outward as it separated the two sections of the creature. For a second the tendrils that clasped Alaiya faltered as a green wall grew in front of the eyes. Then the eye ridge suddenly dove forward beneath the encroaching wall, surfacing seconds later in the middle of the sticky green mass. The cords tightened around Alaiya once again, starting to pull her body the last few feet to the edge of the pool.

With a shout of desperation, Howard leaped from the ledge, slogging out onto the slippery powderbridge. When he was close enough to touch the ridge of eyes, now smeared with clinging gel, he drew a half-empty packet from his own belt. Ripping it open, he threw it down inches from the center of the twisted mound of flesh, turned, and ran stumbling to the edge of the heaving bridge. The eye-thing made a second lunge forward, and foul liquid splashed onto the powderbridge.

The green gel ignited with a crackling roar. Howard leaped into the black liquid and swam frantically for the edge of the water pit as flames engulfed the gel-coated creature. Several yards away, the mouth section rolled and snapped furiously.

Howard pulled himself from the noisome fluid and scrambled toward Alaiya. A horrible vibrating shriek filled the air, and the pool churned with a maddened thrashing. Gray tendrils whipped blindly about them. Howard helped Alaiya to her feet, the larger coils dropping from her body to race across the floor toward the waves of heat beating outward from the struggling creature. A terrible stench was spreading through the room from the flaming mass of gel and tissue at the center of the water pit.

Howard and Alaiya made their way across the wriggling floor, up the ramp, and through the doorway. Clouds of foul smoke followed them as they stumbled through the darkness of the second chamber.

Howard halted in his tracks at the entrance to the first chamber. Flames were flickering in the archway behind them, casting an orange light into the great room. Alaiya tugged at his arm.

"We must reach the surface. The smoke will kill us."

"Wait. That little doorway." He pointed to where a second, smaller portal stood not far from the one that opened onto the first chamber and freedom. "I didn't notice it when we came through before." He sniffed the air. "Do you smell what I smell?"

"Only the corruption from the other room. We must go!"

"I smell the sweetness again. It's really strong right here. Wait." He hurried to the doorway, which stood narrowly open. Smoke began to pour into the chamber behind him, gathering in the high dome. "Give me a hand here. I don't think it's been moved in ages."

Together they forced the door wide. Light from the spreading fire fell into the room beyond, which appeared to extend for some distance beneath the floor of the first chamber.

The low-ceilinged room was piled waist-high with dried blossoms. In their midst were the bodies of small creatures, mostly animals and birds from the forest, along with a few others Howard had never seen before. Each one was wrapped in a sticky, translucent coating, only its head remaining free. Many had been partially devoured. Some of these were still alive, the coating apparently acting as a sealant that somehow permitted them to survive though major portions of their bodies had been removed. The effect was horrible.

The sweet smell was almost overpowering as Howard and Alaiya stepped into the room. In the far corner, Yam-ya-mosh moved weakly against his bonds, blinking at them in the firelight.

CHAPTER XVIII

Another Language Lesson

DAWN SAW THEM SPRAWLED ON THE CREST OF THE hill overlooking the city, lying where they had collapsed in exhaustion hours earlier after their flight from the burning chambers. Howard awoke to find Yam-ya-mosh's woolly head cradled in his lap. Alaiya lay close by, facing him. Her face was grimy with smoke and dirt; her vest and shorts were caked with greenish fungus and remnants of other corruption.

"Good morning, Ahwerd," she said softly. "I thank you."

Howard levered Yam's head carefully onto the soft grass between them and stretched to a sitting position, grimacing at the varieties of pain that accompanied the movement.

"I just woke up," he said, rubbing at his eyes. "I can't have done anything to be thanked for yet."

"I truly did not wish to die in that dark pit last night," Alaiya said. "I must thank you for destroying the beast and saving my life."

"Ah. You're entirely welcome. I owed you one anyway." He cracked his knuckles, then paused to examine his filthy hands. "As I remember, the last time I got powderbridge under my fingernails, it was while you were fishing me out of the rapids."

"I am sorry I mistrusted you when you asked for my belt," she said soberly. "On the Fading Worlds, belts

179

are removed when lives are taken. I was not thinking clearly."

"Forget it." Howard looked down, using his thumb-nail to scrape at a smear of something unpleasant on his vest.

"No," Alaiya said quietly. "That will not be possible. It seems I can forget nothing that you have done since I have known you." She reached out a hand and gently smoothed the dark hair back from his face. "Ahwerd, I have a thing to tell you."

Howard raised his eyebrows.

Just then Yam moaned and shifted position on the grass at Howard's side, his small hands opening and closing weakly. As they watched, the little warrior rolled onto his side and opened his eyes, blinking slowly in the growing sunlight.

"Hey, welcome back to the land of the living, Yam-bo." Howard ruffled the matted fur of the little head. "You had us worried there for a while."

"Ow-er-bel?" The Trilbit shivered in the warm morn-ing breeze, pressing closer to Howard's side. "Back you did come for me, after all. And Lai-ya!" Yam lifted his head, moisture shining in his eyes. "Certain you return for me someday!"

"Someday? O Yam of little faith—we were gone half an hour at the most. How come you took off like that? Were you kidnapped? Did that thing in the city send somebody after you for a little Trilbit take-out?"

The black eyes mirrored confusion as Alaiya helped Yam struggle into a sitting position.

The diminutive warrior had undergone a shocking transformation in the few days since they had seen him. Once plump and robust, he was gaunt and shrunken-looking, his fur dull beneath the vestiges of the sticky translucent substance Howard had peeled from his body before collapsing into sleep several hours earlier.

"Many days you are gone, Ow-er-bel," Yam said slowly. "Wait and wait for you and Lai-ya to reappear. Know-not time inside me, now I am gone from those Fading Worlds, but I count the days and see this sun tread the sky thirty-two times. Weather grows colder, and my firejelly is nearly gone. Finally I enter gray woods, mark my path for your return. Think to find that Averoy city Lai-ya says is there.'' He shivered again. ''Finding city, almost dying. Bad place.''

''Wait a minute here.'' Howard got to his feet and began to pace slowly through the purple grass. ''You think we were gone for over a month? Yam, that doesn't make sense. We spent less than an hour in that cave. But look at you.'' Howard shook his head above the emaciated body.

''Ahwerd, those marks on the trees were clearly made some time ago. And remember the date he scratched on the door.''

''I know, I know. Listen, Yam, how long do you figure you were down in that storeroom?''

''Know-not. Part of this memory is missing, other part confused. But know how I am caught by city-thing.'' Yam pointed a scrawny arm at one of the fat-boled trees in the orchard below them. ''Arrive in meadow, eat fruit from branches, six or seven, very tasty. Next day discover city. Go through gate, walk around, nobody home. Night comes, smell strong sweet—like fruit. Pull me, must start walk, stop-not.''

''Huh, like my sleepwalking last night,'' Howard said. ''I ate one piece of that fruit yesterday, and last night I took a little stroll. Alaiya had to snap me out of it.''

''No one here to waken me,'' Yam said. ''Walk, walk, deeper into under-city. Lie down in flower room with small things. Move-not. Sometimes hear noises in dark. Feel thing moving through flowers. Next thing is fire and you two standing in doorway.'' He shook his head wearily. ''Never eat fruit again.''

''You and me both. I only wish we could have saved more of the animals. I think most of the ones we freed made it to the surface, but the rest . . .'' Howard clicked his tongue, moving to the top of the hillside and gazed down on the silent towers. ''So the thing has been using the fruit to lure in prey from outside the city.'' He turned to Alaiya. ''I wonder if there are any more of them down there.''

''I do not know.'' She met his eyes gravely. ''This world is not as I expected it to be.''

''Would you rather we went somewhere else?''

"No. I wish to go back for the others on the Black and Blue World and see if they are willing to return with us, to cleanse this land of whatever evil has overtaken it. I wish to find my people."

"All right." He nodded. "The only thing that bothers me is this time business. Are we going to go back to the black mountains in a few days only to find that twenty years have passed?"

Alaiya looked thoughtful. "Ahwerd, when you operate the Key it is as if your fingers know what to do, correct? In your conscious mind you have no understanding of its workings?"

"Not so far, anyway. You've seen me adjust the bands on the shaft, but I'm always in sort of a daze when that happens. Although . . ." Howard left the thought unfinished, staring at her open-mouthed. After a moment he lowered himself to the ground. "You know something, this last trip I was really upset when it came time to use the Key. You were under the rock inside the suit, and all I could think was that I had to get you out of there. I couldn't seem to clear my mind like I've done in the past before using the Key. I was trying to help things along, and I know I gave one of the bands a little twist. I wonder if I changed something about the way it operated."

"Do you think your Key has the power to bring us to the future?" Alaiya looked uncomfortable.

"Maybe we didn't come to the future, exactly . . ." He shrugged. "Maybe we were stuck somewhere—in between the worlds—while time went on for everybody else."

Alaiya considered that idea. "It seemed that I passed an eternity inside the amoeba suit, but I had no sensation of being caught between one world and another."

"Neither did I, but then I've never noticed anything in between. Just cold and dark, and how can you measure that? It's a scary thought, though—that we were stuck somewhere in limbo while Yam waited out a Turn here." Howard ran his hand down his face. "I can't deal with this right now. Oh . . ." He stretched again, looking down at his stained clothing. "I need a hot bath, an expensive massage, and a Laundromat."

"There is in fact a cold bath available not far from

here, in one of the irrigation streams.'' Alaiya got slowly to her feet. ''Do you wish to come with me?''

Howard glanced at the ground by his feet. Yam was snoring quietly, his head slumped to one side on his shoulders.

''Uh, I guess one of us should stay here with Rip Van Trilbit. Maybe I'll just stretch the kinks out till you get back.''

Alaiya nodded. ''When I return I will provide the body rub you are craving.''

''Sounds great.''

Howard watched her retreat down the hillside, then turned with a sigh and broke off a stem of purple grass.

''What I wouldn't give for some OJ and a bowl of Frosted Flakes,'' he murmured, inserting the grass stem between his teeth. He spied Alaiya's pack and drew it close. ''There should be some sugary stuff left in here . . .''

''Food?'' Yam had opened his eyes again. He gave a great yawn that ended in a series of explosive sneezes.

''Yeah, you look like you could use a pick-me-up. Why don't I whip us up a complimentary continental breakfast? I don't think Alaiya will mind.'' Howard began to pull wrapped parcels from the pack. ''Anyway, we'll save her some. There should be a little bowl in here somewhere . . .''

''Food would be welcome indeed.'' The Trilbit sat up straight with an effort.

''Good. You know, there's a lot of leftovers in here . . . You don't mind if I mush it all together, do you? We can pretend it's meatloaf.''

''Taste-not anyway, Ow-er-bel. Nose full of flower pollen from storeroom.''

''Okay, give me a second here . . .'' Howard opened parcels, crumbling bits of food into the small bowl. ''Hmm. Here's some stuff I haven't seen before that looks like orange celery. Might as well throw it in. And let me chop up a few of these nutlike things.'' He used his machete to dice the bulkier items, finally stirring the mixture with his index finger before handing the bowl to Yam.

''Gratitude.'' The Trilbit scooped out handfuls and

swallowed them eagerly, passing the bowl back to Howard when half the contents remained. "Now your share."

"Don't mind if I do." Howard stretched out carefully on the grass next to Yam and began to devour the food left in the bowl.

"Ah, you are eating!" Alaiya waved at them from the bottom of the hill, where she was wringing out her clothing and hanging it on a tree limb. "That was to be my suggestion." Clad only in her short cloak, she climbed the hillside.

"Yeah, the Yamster and I raided the cookie jar." Howard pointed to the open pack. "Hope you don't mind. We left you some."

"Of course not. You are welcome to the food." She seated herself on the grass and began to comb her fingers through the damp mass of her long hair. "I will stay with Ya-mosh and eat my morning meal now, if you wish to bathe."

"Sounds like a good idea." Howard got to his feet. "Hey, Yam—I forgot to ask in the confusion last night. Do you have any idea what happened to my pack and stuff?"

"Your flying machine and supply pack are up a tree near the edge of the forest back by our first camp." The Trilbit nodded toward the orchard land to the east of them. "I could not carry them. I hope they have remained safe."

"Ah, terrific! Okay, I'll be back in a few minutes and we can have a strategy conference. I have a feeling none of us wants to spend another night in the vicinity of the city."

"Ahwerd," Alaiya said as he was starting down the hill. "Did you remove any of the small pods from this sack?" She emptied a half-filled bag of brown, nutlike objects into her palm.

"Yeah, I mixed them into my goulash. I'm sorry, were you saving them for something?"

"Well, yes." She looked back and forth between him and Yam. "You two have just devoured a large quantity of purge pods."

"Huh?"

"Purge pods!" Yam squeaked, his small eyes wide.

"I taste-not due to the pollen. Ow-er-bel, I wish I watch you prepare this food for us."

"Wait a minute, guys." Howard waved his hands as he reseated himself in the purple grass. "What are purge—"

"Ahwerd, do you recall what the Wossil grandmother told us about the parleybugs in our blood? That we should rid ourselves of them so the Keyholders would not be able to trail us?" She poured the remaining nuts back into the bag. "Do you remember that I said there was a way to do that, if I could purchase some purge—"

"Pods at Stillpoint," he finished for her, staring at the limp sack. "And we just . . . You mean in a little while we're not going to be able to understand each other? I don't believe I did this! How long do we have? Jeez, I'm sorry, you guys. What an idiot!"

Alaiya stared at him in silence for a few seconds, then leaned back and burst out laughing. She raised her hands to her face helplessly, tears beginning to course down her ivory cheeks. Howard reached out his hand in concern, but she waved it away, gasping for breath.

"I'm glad you're taking this so well," he ventured cautiously.

"Ah, Ahwerd, you are—you are so—" She wiped her eyes. "What is the proper word? Unique? Unequaled? Like no one I have ever known." She shook her head, chuckling as she dried her eyes with the hem of her cloak.

"My old high-school English teacher used to tell me I was a 'nonesuch,' " Howard said forlornly, propping his chin on his elbow. "I took it as a compliment, but I was never really sure how she meant it. Sometimes she'd call me that after I said something without really thinking about it and it turned out to be incredibly stupid—other times it was because she'd liked my latest paper. Either way, she'd shake her head and say, 'Howard C. Bell, you are one of a kind, thank the Lord—a definite nonesuch . . .' " He removed his own short black cloak and handed it over to Alaiya. "Here, in case you have to blow your nose or anything . . ."

"Thank you." Alaiya scooped the remaining nuts from the small bag and popped them into her mouth. "I might as well join you two," she said, chewing as she spoke.

"If we are to hide from the Travelers, we should do it completely. To answer your previous question, the onset of the parleybugs' demise is usually quite rapid. We should make our plans now, before it is too late."

"We must decide whose language to use," Yam trilled.

They drew lots. Howard was secretly relieved when the long twig fell to Alaiya. Though he looked forward to someday understanding the Trilbit tongue, he had serious doubts about his ability to produce the high-pitched squeaks and chittering that seemed to form the bulk of it.

"Where do we go from here?" he asked. "Yam, we found a message from a bunch of AWOL warriors on the Black and Blue World. They took off into the hills after they saw us vanish with the Key. They're waiting for us to come back and . . ." He glanced at Alaiya. "And I don't know exactly what—but they're definitely waiting for us. Alaiya says we probably have another Turn before they'll be leaving their current hiding place. In the meantime, I'd kind of like to get my stuff from that tree, so maybe we could hike back to where we left the overskin before using the Key again."

"This will give you two a good chance to take up Averant," Alaiya said with a smile. "I shall be a harsh teacher, I promise you."

"Okay, I guess that pretty much takes care of things. We can leave whenever you're all ready." He smiled nervously. "This is such a weird feeling. I guess I should go get cleaned up, huh?" He walked a few steps down the hill and paused. Squaring his shoulders, he turned back to where Yam was helping Alaiya reload her pack.

"Alaiya—if we're about to stop communicating, I want to—I mean I don't know how to say it, but—"

"I have things to say to you, as well, Ahwerd," she replied, all merriment vanished from her expression. "I could not tell earlier if you wished me to express these feelings."

"Of course I do, but—I mean, it's just . . . Oh, jeez, I can't believe we have minutes left to talk and I'm wasting them like this." He took a deep breath, his face burning. "It's just that I didn't know what to say, without messing things up for you. I know you're with this Omber guy and that's fine. I mean, it's not fine, but that's okay. I hope it all works out for you two—''

"*Eeyena.*" Alaiya raised her hand, her brow knit in perplexity. "Why do you *seplet* Oss in this context?"

"Well, because he's your mate and—" He broke off. "What did you say?" He frowned at Yam-ya-mosh. "What did she say?"

"*S'rrree-chee-ya.*" The Trilbit pointed to the top of his head, then made a small circle with his thumb and fingers. "*Ke-neen-che'rrree. S'rrree-neet?*"

Alaiya nodded and turned to Howard. "*Evedno*, Ahwerd?" she asked uncertainly.

Howard sank back into the high grass with a groan and stared mournfully into the lavender sky.

"Swell," he said. "Just swell."

Alaiya moved to his side, setting her palm against his cheek with a rueful smile.

"*Andweyo*, Ahwerd," she said with an elaborate shrug of her shoulders, a touch of merriment creeping back into her eyes. "*Meyen, meyen andweyo.*"

The language of the Averoy was complex but logical, and Howard and Yam were eager students. They made rapid progress as the three returned through the woods, and soon Howard knew words for many of the things around them, as well as how to express basic needs and wants. At first it was fun—as if they were playing a game that required them to use mime and exaggerate their facial expressions in order to communicate. After a few days, however, Howard had to come to grips with the basic unreality of the situation. It was easy to become frustrated when understanding was not achieved instantaneously. Here were two people with whom he had been exchanging thoughts and feelings effortlessly for several weeks. Suddenly they were strangers, their motivations hidden behind the unfamiliar sounds and puzzling gestures he had all but ignored before. Had Yam always had that habit of rubbing his ears while asking a question? What did it mean when Alaiya narrowed her eyes while repeating a phrase to him for the third or fourth time?

They took their time in the forest, resting often in deference to Yam's weakened condition and frequently extending their stopovers by an hour or two to conduct impromptu language lessons. To relieve the tedium, they began to exchange words in English and Ya'trrril, as well, although they continued to concentrate on Averant. It was seven local days before they began to see slices of lavender plain through the tall evergrays.

"Seee!" Yam squeaked proudly in Averant. "Rrrock!"

"Yes." Alaiya squinted through the purple trunks. "You have good, sharp eyes, Ya-mosh."

"Yes." Howard struggled to put his thoughts in grammatical order. "Is see tree?" he asked the Trilbit. "Is see tree close by where is my supply, where is my wing device?" He looked at Alaiya hopefully. "Is right?"

"Almost right." She corrected him carefully while Yam peered at the nearby treetops.

"That trrreee," he announced, pointing at a tall trunk whose crown was lost in shadows. "I go, I brrring, I give." Leading them to the base of the tree, he scampered quickly up its rough trunk. It took two trips for the Trilbit to retrieve both the pack and the flying suit. Howard and Alaiya exchanged nods with eyebrows raised, impressed by the swiftness of Yam's recovery after his ordeal in the city.

A tree-hanger had apparently started to pile twigs on the flying machine several days earlier, preparatory to utilizing the structure in an ambitious nest-building project. The little animal hooted indignantly at them as they made their way to the forest's edge.

They passed the last of Yam's arrow markers and stepped out of the woods.

Something had happened to the overskin.

The three walked across the lavender plain and gathered wordlessly around the rubble of shattered rock. Howard knelt and sifted black dust through his fingers.

"Surprise," he said, rising. "Is broken."

"It must have been time," Alaiya said. "I had not expected it so soon. Perhaps the process was accelerated when we were stuck between the worlds. Still . . ." She bent to run her fingers over a sharp fragment.

"Is not right?" Howard watched her closely. "Is not right with dead Awp?"

"I am not sure." Alaiya bit her lower lip. "I have only witnessed the procedure once before. But I thought there would be something left behind when the overskin crumbled."

"Yes." Yam pointed at the empty space at the center of the rubble. "Seee before, seee white." He outlined a small body with his hands. "Now seee nothing."

"Maybe the wind blew him away," Howard said in English. "He didn't weigh all that much to begin with." He puffed out his cheeks and moved his arms to demonstrate.

Alaiya and Yam looked doubtful.

"What you think?" Howard inquired in Averant. "Think animal take, eat?"

Alaiya made the eloquent hand-shrug of her people. "I had thought we would have something left to give to the fire and air," she said. "It seems we will have only our memories."

With Howard and Yam's assent, Alaiya conducted a short ceremony traditionally performed by the Averoy to honor a dead comrade whose body had been lost. They collected branches and long gray needles from the forest and started a small fire with a flint from Alaiya's pack. Then Alaiya spoke for a few minutes about her association with the Hant, after which Howard delivered his own brief eulogy, first in English and then in stumbling Averant.

Later Alaiya used the same fire to roast some crustaceans from the forest pools for herself and Howard, while Yam wandered off to nibble on a wad of Trilbit foodstuff.

"Soon go find warriors, other world," Howard said, picking his teeth with a slender claw.

"Yes, they should have just reached their second refuge." Alaiya had recalculated the best time to attempt to contact the defecting battle-gang members based on Yam's tally of his days spent waiting for them on Field of Flowers.

"Seee! *Ala-chee'rrra!*" Yam waved to them from far out on the lavender plain. He turned when he was sure they were coming and headed back toward the sea wall, gesturing vigorously.

"Seee! Seee!" he squeaked as they caught up with

him. He danced at the edge of the flower sea and pointed outward, his Averant vocabulary apparently unequal to the task of further explanation. Howard and Alaiya shaded their eyes in the direction of his trembling finger.

"Well, I'll be . . ." Howard gaped in amazement.

About half a mile from the shore a curious craft drifted lightly over the sea of blossoms, great multicolored sails belling out in the wind as its crew moved languidly upon the golden deck.

"Bingo," Alaiya said softly at his side.

CHAPTER XIX

The Butterfly Folk

"WHAT DO? WHAT DO?" YAM VIBRATED WITH EX-
citement, pacing back and forth on his short legs on the
ledge of rock. "Go seee, go talk?"

Howard turned to Alaiya, who stood staring raptly at
the apparition, her face as open and wondering as a
child's. He grinned.

"Yes, go!" He patted Alaiya on the shoulder. "Go
now, catch!" He trotted down to the edge of the plain,
the others at his heels. Launching himself into the flower
sea, he laughed with joy at the exhilaration of low gravity, springing away from the shore in a series of prodigious leaps.

The strange craft had drifted slightly closer to the land.
As Howard approached he saw a whirl of color rising
and dipping beyond the ship. It was a flock of butterflies,
keeping pace with the newcomers as they had escorted
Howard and his companions shortly after their arrival on
this world.

The three moved quickly through the flowers, mindful
of the whip-armed creature they had seen attack one of
the butterflies weeks earlier. At last they came to rest on
a ridge of red-orange blossoms that put them nearly in
the path of the ship.

"Look," Howard panted, pointing to the wide sail
yearning toward them above the low, flat deck. At a distance of about fifty yards, he was able to identify the

191

material from which the iridescent patchwork had been constructed. "Wings!"

"Butterfly wings." Alaiya nodded at his side, her expression wary. "Yet the butterflies do not seem to fear them. Perhaps they are gathered after the creatures die."

The body of the vessel seemed to consist of flower stems, slightly thicker than those they had yet seen and bound together in some fashion. It curved gently upward fore and aft, the prow gleaming golden with a layer of pollen as it slid noiselessly over the multicolored blossoms.

Yam sneezed at Alaiya's side, fumbling through his pockets till he had located Howard's sock.

"Many peeeople," the Trilbit observed as he tied the makeshift filter at the back of his woolly head.

The ship was perhaps twenty feet from side to side and about twice that in length. As it neared them, its crew began to gather at the low sides of the port bow. Howard felt Alaiya stiffen as they received their first clear look at the approaching sailors.

From a distance they had seemed human. Perhaps they had been, long ago. The sailors stood between eight and nine feet tall, towering above the deck on impossibly slender torsos, their arms and legs attenuated into spindles. Narrow heads all cocked in the same listening attitude as the ship skimmed closer, dark eyes watching without expression.

"How many?" Howard murmured. "Fifty, sixty?"

Half a dozen delicate flower-stem poles appeared in holes along the low sides and were thrust through the blossoms to the yielding earth below, as the ship drew alongside them and ghosted to a stop.

They wore loose robes of butterfly wings, each individual's falling within a particular range of hues, in contrast to the brilliant motley of the great sail. Skin color varied from pale violet to purple-black, with a golden sheen that came and went in the sunlight. Faces were thin, with high cheekbones and small mouths that turned slightly downward at the outer edges. Dark eyes were dominated by huge irises that showed only slivers of white to either side. The skin lay close to the bone, with few muscles in evidence to lend expression to the solemnly beautiful countenances.

Alaiya gave a small shake of her head and stepped forward, extending her hand to the figures nearest to her in the prow. At once a dozen narrow hands reached out to cover hers, spidery fingers moving lightly up and down her wrist and arm.

"We are friends," Alaiya said to the sailor in front of her, a plum-colored individual in robes of indigo, violet, and iridescent green. The angular head turned almost imperceptibly in her direction, no change registering in the great dark eyes. There was no clue to the gender of the sailors; all of them were slender and fragile-looking beneath the thin garments.

Howard watched the scene in fascination. The ship rocked gently in the mild wind as the anchor-sticks held it in place, dipping slightly to one side under the combined weight of its crew. Thin fingers slid like feathers over Alaiya's hand and forearm; dark eyes stared impassively out of the narrow faces.

Abruptly there was a commotion on the far side of the ship. Yam craned his small neck around the golden prow as the sailors' heads turned as if all blown by the same breeze.

"Think bad slake-thing rrreturrn," Yam trilled. "Want eeeat!" Howard and Alaiya hurried downslope on the ridge. As before, the butterflies milled above the blossoms in a flurry of churning wings. The whipslake was not yet visible, only a slight stirring of the flowers betraying its presence. Alaiya drew her dagger and stood poised.

A dozen of the sailors stepped lightly from the ship and moved off in the direction of the flock. They carried shorter versions of the anchor-sticks, six-foot-long flower stems that appeared to have been sharpened on both ends. After a moment, Howard realized that the sailors were walking on the surface of the flower sea itself, picking their way with unconscious grace from blossom to blossom. Leaning out from the ridge, he gently prodded the hull of the fantastic vessel. Heads turned as the ship swayed.

"Sorry." Howard held up his hands and moved back

to the center of the ridge. "Ship is easy break," he said
to Alaiya. "Like leaf."

The sailors had reached the whirling flock. They spread
out into a loose circle and waited, flower stems held casually.

Howard clutched Alaiya's shoulder as a thin whiplike
tentacle shot suddenly above the petals, narrowly missing one of the larger butterflies that floated near the center of the flock. Instantly the sailors came to attention,
the two nearest the eruption dropping gracefully to one
knee, while the others pulled back and hefted their sticks.
Fifteen seconds passed, and the tentacle ventured forth
again. Bracing themselves, the two kneeling sailors thrust
downward with their flower stems. They held on grimly
as something began to thrash wildly beneath the surface,
flinging them through the air as if they were made of
twigs.

Alaiya waded into the neck-high blossoms. Howard
unsheathed his machete before following her into the
thick forest of stems.

The remaining four sailors darted back and forth above
the unseen whipslake, their sticks rising and stabbing with
a mechanical regularity. By the time Alaiya and Howard
reached the scene of activity, it was over.

The sailors ignored the two intruders. One of them
drew a coil of fine, silky line from within a robe of ver-
milion and deep scarlet. At one end of the line hung a
small weight, which was lowered slowly through the
stems above the creature. The procedure had to be repeated several times, three of the sailors lying prone on
the surface of the flower sea, heads almost touching as
they let out the line inch by inch, their dark eyes intent
on what lay beneath the blossoms. Finally satisfied, they
sprang to their feet. Two of them unwound the line in the
direction of the ship while the others stood guard over
their victim.

The line was fastened to a small projection at the rear
of the vessel. As Howard and Alaiya slowly returned to
the ridge, the anchor-sticks were lifted and the trembling
ship slipped forward over the flowers. The hunters waited
by their prey as the silken line grew taut. Probing with
their weapons, they pushed and pulled in the direction of

the ship's movement. Something like an end of frayed black rope appeared above the blossoms. The hunters strained at their flower stems, urging the creature onto the surface. It was about five feet long, with a flat narrow body ending in a tangle of whips that added another six feet to its length. A few of the tentacles still twitched, coiling fitfully around the thin line that disappeared into the center of the whip-mass.

The ship crawled forward, butterfly sail stretched in the wind. As the whipslake was dragged slowly past, the three on the ridge could see dark fluid gleaming from a dozen wounds along its side.

Anchor-sticks appeared again as the ship began to pass over a section of the ridge. Sailors swarmed silently from the vessel, surrounding the carcass. With great effort they dragged the creature the few feet necessary to place it above the high point of land. There, in an area marked by a stripe of pale yellow blossoms, they began the task of butchering their kill.

The flatter ends of the sharpened killing sticks were used to slice the creature's hide open, several of the hunters working together to saw slowly through the warty skin. Alaiya, Yam, and Howard moved closer to observe the grisly process. Numerous organs were removed and carefully set aside. One, found just behind the juncture between body and tentacles, was treated with extreme care.

"Perhaps that is a poison sac," Alaiya said. "It is located next to the mouth, which contains a deadly sting in most whipslakes."

"This different," Yam observed, outlining with his hands the creature's long, flat body.

"Adapted to the low gravity, I imagine," Alaiya said.

"Yes, yes. Think right." Howard had arrived at the same conclusion but was at a loss as to how to express it in his limited Averant.

Every portion of the whipslake's corpse seemed to have a purpose. The various organs were deposited in shallow bowls that looked to Howard as if they had been constructed out of papier-mâché. The long tentacles were severed at the base and taken back to the ship, where half a dozen sailors worked to slit them lengthwise, removing the rubbery outer coverings from the lengths of pink-white sinew beneath. Then both flesh and hide were hung from a horizontal bar set on the mast below the great sails.

"I think for keeping together," Howard said, pointing from the black rubbery strips to the dark ribbons that bound together the bundles of flower stems that made up the hull of the ship.

When the butchering was done, two of the sailors lifted a bowl containing a narrow, translucent mass. They carried it into the flower sea, the rest of the group escorting them to a spot several yards from the golden vessel. There the pair deposited their burden and stepped back to join the crowd. At once the butterflies, which had been circling high above the ship since the kill, descended to form a loose sphere above the bowl. As the sailors stood by, an elaborate dance was enacted above the offering as each butterfly in turn dipped into the bowl for a few seconds, took to the air, and was replaced by a relative.

"Is eeat sugarrr sac," Yam commented as the three watched the graceful aerial ballet. "Help kill, now get eeat."

"There seems to be some sort of mutual dependency here. I wonder if this is what the butterflies expected from us when the slake attacked that other time," Alaiya mused.

"Think so." Howard nodded. "Big surprise on them."

The feeding of the butterflies took over an hour, Howard and his companions returning to the nearby ridge to seat themselves while the sailors remained stolidly standing throughout the event.

When the butterflies had consumed their feast, a different pair of sailors retrieved the bowl and the entire group marched back to the ship. Anchor-sticks were removed once more, and the fragile vessel slid forward over the blossoms. Heads turned as they passed the three on the ridge, scores of dark eyes staring at them from the beautiful, expressionless faces.

Alaiya looked after them with a wistful yearning in her own eyes, her hands moving restlessly at her sides as if she was fighting the urge to wave.

"Want go?" Howard touched her on the shoulder and pointed toward the retreating vessel. "You want go these people, get know more?"

The butterfly folk showed no surprise when the three came bounding up behind them minutes later. Though they were obviously aware of the new companions that traveled in great leaping bounds at the side of their delicate ship, they interacted with them seldom in the time that followed, those few occasions made all the more remarkable by their rarity.

Once, when Yam-ya-mosh was engaged in a protracted sneezing attack while attempting to clean his argyle face mask, a group of solemn sailors approached the little warrior bearing a bowl of yellowish paste. Curious, Yam allowed them to apply the substance to his nostrils. Shortly thereafter his allergy to the pollen disappeared, and the next day he triumphantly returned Howard's sock to its rightful owner.

They witnessed two more kills during the four weeks they traveled with the butterfly folk, each a reenactment of the first. Every part of the dead creature was used in some way aboard the golden vessel. Alaiya had guessed correctly about the nature of one of the whipslake's internal organs; several times between kills the sailors gathered to dip their sharpened flower stems in the shallow bowl containing the poison sacs.

No form of communication was evident among the crew of the golden ship. Many of their actions had the feel of ritual to Howard, and he wondered about the type and level of intelligence that suggested.

A dying butterfly was discovered one morning. The crew gathered around the creature fluttering weakly against the blossoms, all other activity suspended as long hours passed.

Finally it was over. At once a dozen slender hands joined to pluck the gorgeous wings from the body. Then a basket of woven stems was opened, and a score of robes in various stages of completion were brought forth. Another substance gleaned from the whipslake was used as an adhesive as the shimmering black-and-gold wings were carefully added to a nearly finished garment of royal blue, gold, and black.

It was an idyllic time for Howard. His and Yam's proficiency with Alaiya's language grew rapidly as they traversed the flower sea, the ship leading them in a strange looping course that repeatedly sent them far out to sea only to return them to within sight of land a day or two later. The sailors bent to the will of the wind, gathering supplies and resting when it was calm, raising the anchorsticks as soon as the breeze returned. A small canopy curving up in the rear of the ship provided protection on those few occasions when the strength of the wind threatened to blow the sailors from their own deck. They sailed by day during normal weather, and if the moons were up they sailed by night, as well. Howard and his companions went ashore from time to time to keep their bodies used to normal gravity, returning gladly to the blossoms and the silent folk who waited patiently for them beyond the rocky shoals. It was a temptation at times to climb aboard the golden ship and glide above the petals with the sailors, but it was obvious that not even Yam could set foot upon the fragile craft without destroying it. One night near the end of their stay with the butterfly folk, a sudden gust of wind blew the ship off course and it drifted against a jut of purple rock. Two days were needed to repair the damage. An expedition into the blue-green deeps returned with a quantity of sturdy flower stems that were trimmed, bound into bundles with whipslake hide, and then cemented in place in the hull using whipslake adhesive.

"Do you wish still to come back and kill all whipslakes?" Howard asked Alaiya as they sat upon the offending rock and watched the leisurely repairs.

"It would seem to be impossible." She shrugged. "These folk could not survive without the monsters."

"It will be strange to walk another world again," Howard said, watching the sunset blaze violet and crimson amid the silver clouds behind Alaiya's bowed head. They had decided to return to land soon and walk to their base camp at the edge of the forest for a day or two of rest before using the Key to go back to the Black and Blue World. Fortunately, the golden ship had reversed direction two weeks earlier and started back up the lavender coast. By the time they left the butterfly folk they would not be far from their destination.

"I wonder, will they understand when we leave?" he said in a tone of gentle melancholy. "I hope they are not waiting, waiting for a long time after we go."

"Who are these people, Ahwerd?" Alaiya laid her cheek upon her folded arms and watched as the sailors went about their methodical work, gracefully sidestepping Yam, who bounded here and there among them, making offers of assistance that he knew would go unacknowledged. "I thought that by taking this time with them I would have answers to my questions, but instead I have found more doubts. Are they my people, after all, transformed by millennia and their long-ago desertion of the land, or are they something else, something new that has sprung up on its own?"

"I do not know," he said, watching her with concern. "I will feel sorry to leave them. But we must meet the others, I think. Tomorrow at dawn we go ashore, all right?"

"Yes, we must leave tomorrow if we are to catch them at their next refuge," she said softly, and lifted her head, the breeze catching her unbound hair. Finding his eyes on her, she added in lightly accented English, "Not sad for me, Ahwerd, please?"

"All right."

She reached out and shook him lightly, her hand on his shoulder. "Okay?" she asked.

Howard looked away, smiling. "Okay."

CHAPTER XX

Reunion

IT TOOK THEM THREE DAYS TO REACH THEIR camp. Despite their preparations, their muscles were sore as they hiked the last few miles along the edge of the forest.

"I wish I brought the flying suit," Howard said with a groan.

"Nice plan," Yam-ya-mosh chittered at his side. "You fly above, poorrr frrriends walk below, make fist at you."

"We should be running," Alaiya commented. "By walking like this, we are not using the muscles we strengthened while we leaped from ridge to ridge."

"Fine," Howard said in English. "You jog on ahead and put on a pot of coffee. Yam and I'll pick up a cheese-cake at the deli."

Alaiya exchanged glances with Yam.

"Speak Averant," she said sternly. "I only understood a little of what you said, but I do not think I liked it."

"I only understood one word," Yam said glumly. "My name."

"Oh, leave me alone. You guys just want me to talk Averant because it makes me more polite. Damn! There it goes." Howard halted and lifted his right leg, staring in dejection at the tattered remnants of his sneaker, which had just separated completely from its sole. From his cloak he drew the pair of thin sandals he had taken from the bath tent near Stillpoint. With a sigh he sat down on the smooth rock and exchanged footwear, lacing the sandals securely around his calves. He tucked the sneakers under his arm and got to his feet.

"I should have these bronzed, they've done such a good job for me. I wonder if they'd put me in a commercial if I wrote them a letter . . ."

"Averrrant!" Yam squeaked, as Alaiya swatted Howard with her pack.

"All right!" he grumbled. "Stop attacking. I speak this language now, make you ever joyful."

They walked in comfortable silence for a while. Howard unsheathed his machete and began to polish the flat blade with the corner of his cloak, whistling as he worked. Yam covered his ears with a grimace and dropped back a few paces.

"Ahwerd," Alaiya said. "There is the possibility of fighting when we go to meet the other warriors. We cannot assume they have outwitted the Keyholders, and there may be Travelers or worse awaiting us when we appear."

"What could be worse than a Traveler? I know." He raised his hand. "Something with tentacles. I wonder why bad things always come with tentacles here?"

"Perhaps because they are most often slakes, and all slakes are so endowed. My point is that I have done little to prepare you for actual battle. You are skilled at destroying monsters and dealing with the unexpected, this you have proven. But if we are met by warriors loyal to Stillpoint you will face a different challenge."

"This is true." Howard frowned at the gleaming blade before sliding it back into its sheath. "What is your suggestion on this matter?"

"That you stay behind Ya-mosh and myself if trouble arises," Alaiya said frankly. "We have both been trained in hand-to-hand warfare for many years. Your best occupation would be as one who stands at the rear and encourages us to victory."

"I see." Howard nodded thoughtfully. "I have come all this way and had these many experiences in order to become—you must forgive my English, but I do not have the word in Averant—a cheerleader?"

"It is helpful that you are familiar with the role."

Alaiya patted him on the back and moved briskly into the lead. "Come, we are almost there. Let us run for a while."

The campsite was unchanged, their belongings where they had left them by the rubble of the overskin. Howard spent the afternoon practicing the rudiments of swordplay with Alaiya, while Yam built a fire and went into the forest to refill their water bags.

When he returned he reported a strange sensation. "As if a thing is watching behind the trrrees."

"A bad thing?" Howard glanced at Alaiya, wiping the sweat from his face. "Like from the city?"

"I do not know." Yam attempted the Averoy handshrug. "Maybe my mind is trrricky on me."

"It might be wise to keep watch tonight," Alaiya said.

They ate a light meal and went to their nests of soft needles shortly after twilight, eager to be underway and at the same time sorry to leave Field of Flowers. Alaiya took the first watch. Howard yawned and sat up at her tap on his shoulder.

"My turn already? Did anything occur?"

She sniffed in negation. "All has been quiet."

The two moons bathed the campsite in silver light. Howard got to his feet with a grunt and stood next to Alaiya as she gazed out in the direction of the flower sea. The night air was cool and redolent of a dozen subtle spices.

"The others will be amazed when I tell them that we have walked on Field of Flowers," she said softly. "And more than that when they learn what we have found here." She leaned against his shoulder, yawning.

"You need to get some sleep." Howard walked her to her bed-nest. "I am going into the woods for a moment."

He passed the double-trunked tree and wandered into the forest, finding his way more by memory than by the occasional silver moonbeam that penetrated the close-set trees. He stood next to a tall trunk and waited for his eyes to grow used to the dimness, smiling at the tightly curled shapes of a family of tree-hangers that festooned a nearby branch like a collection of Christmas ornaments. Moonlight gleamed from the edge of a silent pool.

"There is something to be said for outdoor plumbing," he murmured to himself, fastening his shorts and moving away from the tree.

Something huge and pale rose in front of him.

"Urk!" Howard said, stumbling backward into the trunk. He groped for his machete as the tall shape moved toward him.

"I am doubly honored, Hawa," a resonant voice said in flawless English, "but if you will not take offense, I prefer to retain the noble appellation you bestowed upon me at our first meeting."

"Huh?" Howard blinked in astonishment.

"Another pleasant choice," came the hearty reply. "Though of the two, I think 'Urk' has the—"

"*Awp?*" Howard said.

"You do remember. I was beginning to experience doubts. But perhaps the light is not sufficient for your optic organs." The pale form extended a massive arm and guided Howard gently to the other side of the round pool.

"I don't believe it—you killed yourself!" Howard squinted upward as the two stepped into a shaft of moonlight.

"On the contrary, I decided to grow up. Hawa, it is a profound joy to see you once again!"

"Same here." Howard reached out his arms and felt himself being lifted off the ground in a smothering bear hug. "Hey, Awp—you got bigger." He stumbled back and stared at the figure standing before him in the silvery light. "A lot bigger . . ."

"Indeed," the Hant said. "The overskin had become quite confining by the time I emerged from it."

"But how—Alaiya said you were doing a final molt. She said you must have gotten bored with things. She's seen it happen to other Hants."

"Ah, I thought I had told the Redborn of my intentions. But my memory of those final childhood days is still hazy. Hawa, I have remembered and forgotten much while undergoing my transformation." The great head turned from side to side in the dimness. "I did not even recall traveling to this world before constructing the overskin and was quite disconcerted when I emerged on the plain of stone beneath this unfamiliar sky.''

''No, we brought you here—Alaiya and I. That is, we went back for your body. We have a whole lot of catching up to do, Awp. And how come you're speaking English? Alaiya and Yam and I took some purge pods to get rid of our parleybugs, but I can understand you better than ever.''

''Now that I have matured, I have discovered quite a few heretofore hidden capabilities, Hawa. My own parleybugs did not survive my transformation, my body's blood attaining a temperature at one point that must have proven fatal to the tiny creatures. However, I no longer require them for most communication. Through their use, I have gained a knowledge of many languages by hearing them simultaneously in the original and in translation. We all have. Now, after my metamorphosis, I am able to consciously utilize this knowledge.''

''This is so great!'' Howard reached up to squeeze the massive shoulders. ''Come on, little buddy, we've got to go tell the gang.''

Alaiya and Yam were waiting by the fire with weapons drawn as the two emerged from the forest.

''We heard voices, Ahwerd,'' Alaiya said as he stepped from the woods. ''Were you—'' Her eyes widened and she took a step forward as Awp came into the firelight.

The once diminutive Hant had indeed been transformed. Standing more than twice its previous height, the huge body bore powerful muscles beneath a sleek white hide. Moplike hands sported fingers the size of cables. No longer perched upon a thin, flexible neck, the head had altered as well, its complicated eyes gazing down at them above a broad lipless mouth whose upturned grin gave the pallid face the look of a polished clamshell.

Awp was introduced to Yam-ya-mosh, who stared up at the giant in wonderment.

''This is tiny Hant frrriend you mourn?'' he squeaked, looking sideways at Howard and Alaiya.

''Yeah, death seems to have agreed with him,'' Howard said.

''Noble Hant, we rejoice at your return,'' Alaiya said.

"But how is this thing possible? When I found you in the overskin, I assumed—"

"My apologies, Redborn," Awp replied in Averant. "As I lay in the cave in my aftermolt, my mind was afire with novel concepts. My new friend Hawa'bel represented a fascinating puzzle, one that I was determined to unravel. In order to best accomplish that I knew this body would have to undergo some modifications." It smiled sheepishly. "Unfortunately, I had forgotten the extent of my options. It is a consequence of such a long life, I am afraid. Many Hants grow tired of the world and enter their final molt without ever reaching maturity. You see, adulthood is a voluntary undertaking for us, something that occurs only when the individual is truly ready to initiate the process. As I lay in the cave with my mind fixed on the future, the doors of the past reopened for me and I began to recall many things." It paused. "Still, many of my memories, both recent and ancient, remain fragmentary and incomplete. But mystery is what makes life worth living, *henh*?"

"So, we were associating with a child all that time," Howard said with a shake of his head. He turned to Alaiya. "Remember what Grandmother Wossil called him—'that old baby'? She knew what she was saying."

"It seems that I am not the only being to undergo a transformation," Awp said, looking at Howard closely. "And now, my friends, you must be kind enough to share with me some of what has befallen you during the time I was in the overskin."

They were still talking when the sun rose above the flower sea. Awp was fascinated by their tale, stopping them often to ask questions or to request amplification of a particular incident. Descriptions of their interactions with the Wossil Grandmother were of great interest to the Hant, as was the unusual condition of the gravity on Field of Flowers—or Tai Inimbra, as it was called in Averant. The Hant's many-lidded eyes grew thoughtful at Howard's recounting of his experiences with the Key.

"I suspected you bore a connection to the Keys back in the red desert which you named Kansas, when you were able to sense our Fade to the Black and Blue World before it had properly commenced. Your lack of insight concerning the functioning of the instrument suggests that mine is not the only memory to suffer impairment.''

"What," Howard blurted out in English, "you think I once knew how to operate the Key and then forgot?" He looked skeptical. "Sorry, I seem to have missed that course in high school—I think I took Shop that term instead."

The Hant translated rapidly into Averant for the others, then spread its hands. "I merely attempt to assemble a readable pattern from available information, Hawa. Perhaps we will both experience revelations in the time to come."

"I know you try to help," Howard said. "But this Key matter causes me concern. Each time I use it I feel that we take a chance. I do not wish to be trapped in between again, while time goes on."

"Yes, that is a perplexing occurrence." Awp narrowed a few of its eyelids. "But perhaps together we may banish some of your uncertainties. Are you willing to try an experiment, noble Hawa?"

First Awp asked Yam to brew a pot of bigtassle tea. Before handing Howard his portion, the Hant stirred the steaming liquid with one of its ropelike fingers.

"I am working a small change in the chemical makeup of the beverage with my skin secretions, Hawa," the Hant explained. "This is to render your mind more amenable to suggestion."

Then, with Yam and Alaiya as uncomfortable spectators, the Hant positioned Howard several yards from the campsite, standing for a few seconds with its many-fingered hand on his brow as it spoke gently into his ear. It released its hold and stood back.

"What do I do now?" Howard asked, feeling his apprehension give way to a growing sense of calm and relaxation.

"Simply wait until you are ready, adjust the band as you did before, and then turn the Key," Awp said, moving to rejoin the others.

"But where am I trying to go?" Howard closed his eyes and tried to clear his thoughts. "Don't I have to have a destination in mind?"

"I suspect so," the Hant said. "Therefore what you should do is concentrate on traveling to the precise spot upon which you are standing."

"Huh?" Howard's eyes flew open.

"I believe we agreed to continue to use 'Awp,' " the Hant said. "Please trust me, Hawa. I do not believe you will be harmed if you do what I suggest."

Howard made a quick scan of the area. Then, his eyes still open, he attempted to focus his mind on the lavender plain beneath his feet. He turned the Key.

To those who watched he simply flickered out of existence. A second later he was back, his eyes wide as he stumbled toward his friends.

"Ahwerd, what happened? Are you all right?" Alaiya ran to his side and supported him on her shoulder.

"Yes, I—Awp, will you translate? I think I cannot tell this in Averant."

"More tea?" Yam asked with concern as they helped him sit down at the edge of the woods.

"Thanks. Whew, that was so . . ." He shook his head and drained the cup in a few noisy swallows. "It wasn't all blackness this time. It was like—like worlds flashing past me, hundreds of them, thousands! Awp—" He turned to the massive Hant. "What was it? How did you know?"

"While I lay in the overskin I had a dream, Hawa. A dream at once familiar and utterly strange. I saw worlds passing before my eyes, much as you have described, though not so swiftly. When you spoke to me of your experience with lost time, a portion of that dream returned to me. I believe it was my true remembrance of the time we spent between the Black and Blue World and Field of Flowers. I think the setting you made by adjusting the second band of the Key activates a sort of map that allows you to view other worlds before you choose to go to them."

"Like a directory," Howard said slowly. "But why didn't I see it before?" He frowned. "And what was that you whispered in my ear before I took off? I couldn't quite make it out."

"It is my theory that the first time you employed the Directory function your eyes were closed," the Hant said

matter-of-factly. "Before you left this time I told you to
watch where you were going."

"But where were we before?" Alaiya asked. "Where
does Ahwerd go when the Key tries to show him all of
these worlds?"

"I have no idea," the Hant said. "This trip, Hawa
returned as soon as his eyes fell on Field of Flowers,
which was both his starting point and his destination.
Before, he was caught in the Directory until it had run
its course."

"Four weeks . . ." Howard said quietly.

"But your dream," Alaiya persisted. "Why were you
able to perceive the other worlds when we were not?"

"For that I have no true answer. You were in the
amoeba suit, which may account for your own blindness.
Hawa's eyes were shut. I have no explanation at all for
my dream. As I said, my knowledge is fragmentary."

They decided to make the trip to the Black and Blue
World after their noon meal. While Awp and Yam made
luncheon preparations, Howard took Alaiya for a walk
by the shore of the flower sea.

"Part of me would like to stay here now, Ahwerd,"
she said as they watched the breeze move through the
many-colored blossoms. "I find myself with little desire
to resume a life of fighting and destruction."

"It is beautiful," Howard agreed. "Perhaps someday
we—you, I mean—can return here and stay for as long
as you like."

"Yes, perhaps." Alaiya turned abruptly and walked a
few paces down the shore. "If you do not mind, Ahwerd,
I would prefer to be alone for a while."

"Oh." He nodded. "All right." Puzzled, he returned
to the campsite, where Yam-ya-mosh was in the process
of teaching the Hant a Trilbit folksong.

They stood in a close circle, Awp and Yam on either
side of Howard, hands on his arms. Their other hands
were linked with Alaiya's, who stood opposite Howard,
her eyes on the lavender plain between them. Their various supply packs were strapped to their backs, the Hant
carrying the flying suit atop its pack. Howard had replaced his cloak with his worn blue jacket, which had

become somewhat tight about the chest and arms. He raised his eyebrows to Awp and smiled at Yam. Then, careful to make no preliminary adjustments to the second band, Howard cleared his thoughts and turned the Key.

A sharp noise, a blast of freezing cold, a moment of darkness in which, for the first time, Howard thought to see a hint of movement and color.

They stood upon the pathway from which he had first glimpsed Stillpoint. Wind tugged at Howard's hair and clothing, and low clouds filled the sky with gray. Tucking the Key into his jacket pocket, he looked out over the empty plain of rose-red moss.

"The hiding place is on the inner rim of the great crater," Alaiya said briskly at his side. "We should move quickly in case the Keyholders have detected our arrival."

She turned away, the others moving to follow her up the narrow passage.

"Sure," Howard said under his breath as he brought up the rear. "Lead the way."

It was cooler on this world. If Field of Flowers was entering autumn, the Black and Blue World was near winter. A flock of whiskerwings passed slowly overhead as they climbed toward the rim of black rock. Awp paused to watch them.

"They go east to the great steam pools," it observed. "There to blacken the air with their wings as they battle for the privilege of mating during the long cold months."

"I suppose that's one way to settle it," Howard said darkly. "More civilized than pistols at dawn."

When they reached the top, Alaiya stood for a moment scanning the far horizon, her breath coming in white plumes. Pink flower buds covered the black rock along the rim, their stems protruding from tiny cracks.

"Called rocktongue. Strong winter growth," Yam said, noting Howard's surprise. "Seeds come in spring from droppings when whiskerwings return, sleep all summer, start to grow in late fall. Good to eat."

"If you can forget about the spring part," Howard replied.

"I have located the hiding cave," Alaiya said, her eyes

on Yam and Awp. "We must go around this way in order to descend safely."

They made their way slowly down the black cliff face. Alaiya halted them after about fifteen minutes. They stood on a ledge that had taken shape ages earlier when a large section had shifted outward from the body of the cliff, as though driven by a wedge, forming a narrow passage behind a thick wall of rock that would render them invisible to anyone below them. Howard moved cautiously onto the ledge, wondering how much weight would be required to send the entire structure crashing to the valley below.

"Once we leave this place we will be in full view of the ground," Alaiya told them. "If our timing is accurate, then our allies wait for us below, though I have as yet seen no activity inside the cave or out." She turned to Awp. "Noble Hant, your eyes are superior to ours."

"I will search for signs of life," the Hant said, moving to the far edge of the rock wall. Yam followed, peering out cautiously past the Hant's knees.

"Well," Howard said when the two of them stood alone. "You will see your friends soon."

"That is true." Alaiya allowed herself a short nod, keeping her gray eyes focused on the backs of their companions.

Howard thrust his hands into his jacket pockets, his throat tightening. "Alaiya, suddenly you seem to find my presence an annoyance," he said quietly. "Forgive me if I do not understand my error. I merely want to wish you and Oss the best. It has been—"

"Again you mention Omber Oss to me!" Alaiya whirled on him in the narrow space, speaking in a fierce whisper. Yam's ears twitched at the other end of the passage. "What is your obsession with a warrior you have never even met, Ahwerd? Can you tell me that?" She raised a slender hand between them, her fury evaporating as quickly as it had risen. "Forgive me. Your reasons are your own, as your life is your own. You need explain nothing. We are merely comrades-in-battle, as you are quick to emphasize."

"I am sorry if my comment causes disturbance to you." Howard chewed his lower lip, his face hot. "I am not yet familiar with all Averoy customs. I have assumed that you would be eager to see your mate once again.''

"My . . ." Alaiya stared at him wide-eyed. "Why would you—Oh, no!''

Howard blinked in astonishment as Alaiya's face turned red. She slumped against the rough wall of the passage and stared at him.

"At last your behavior is made clear to me. Damn the parleybugs!'' she said vehemently, striking the wall at her side with her fist. "We are well rid of such meddlers.''

Howard shook his head in bafflement, unable to read her expression. "Alaiya, please,'' he said in English. "Will you tell me what the hell is going on here?''

"Ahwerd, listen closely to me now, for I must explain a thing to you.'' She reached out and gripped his wrists. Her hands were trembling. "When the Keyholders come into possession of a talented warrior, particularly one who is Redborn and seems to come by her skill naturally, they strive to preserve this bloodline. Thus they match the successful warrior with another favored one and order the two of them to breed children, hoping thereby to gain more slaves of high quality. Two years ago my hated masters informed me that I was to produce offspring for them with Omber Oss, should both of us survive our fighting time.'' She took a deep breath. "Do you understand, Ahwerd? That is what it means to have a 'mate' upon the Fading Worlds. It is ugly, like another slavemark.'' She released his arm and raised her own, showing him the three small emblems tattooed on her ivory wrist. "And this bond is never of our own choosing. Oss finds his heart's desire in a warrior named Shing, who fights for the Dreadful Noise, while I . . .'' She made a sound that was half hiccup and half something else and turned away.

"Hey.'' Howard had stood motionless through her passionate speech. Now he moved toward her in the narrow passage. "Does this mean we can start going out?''

He took Alaiya's face in his hands as she turned to him.

"Ahwerdbel, you are one of the kind,'' she said softly in English. "Thank Lord!''

As she drew him close Howard was swept by a sudden wave of nausea and vertigo.

"Hawa! Redborn!" Awp boomed from its station at the edge of the rock. "An enemy appears. We must prepare to fight or flee!"

"What incredible timing," Howard snarled through clenched teeth. In Averant he cried, "Show me where they are, noble Awp. I am filled with anger—we will fight!"

"Ow-er-bel!" Yam squeaked, skittering between the Hant's legs and diving for the safety of the rock wall. "They are many in number—and they bear a mountain gun!"

"Oh." Howard exchanged glances with Alaiya, then shrugged. "In that case, perhaps we should flee."

"Do not fear this weapon, Hawa." Awp carefully removed the flying machine and its pack, setting both at the base of the rock wall. Then it squared its massive shoulders and moved back to the edge of their shelter. "I am not so swift as when I was a child, but I am far more durable. I will handle the mountain gun while you defend the cave."

Rounding the wall of rock, the Hant began to climb downward over the rough cliff face.

"Ya-mosh!" Alaiya raised her voice to the diminutive warrior, Silversting glinting in her hand. "Shall we fight them?"

"Indeed!" The Trilbit drew an object resembling a complicated slingshot from its belt and brandished it in the air. "For freedom we shall fight and an end to the Keyholders! *Cheee'rrra!*" He disappeared around the black wall and started down.

Alaiya turned at the edge of the protected area.

"We will return soon, Ahwerd," she called to him, her gray eyes shining. "Remember your promise to remain out of danger."

Howard nodded obediently, making a thumbs-up sign as she clambered over the edge, her red-gold braid swinging in the wind.

"Yeah, right," he muttered when Alaiya was out of

sight. "Rah-rah-rah, go team, go." Drawing the machete from his belt, he gave it a final swipe with the edge of his sleeve and moved swiftly to follow.

CHAPTER XXI

Gray and Black

HOWARD CLUNG TO THE SIDE OF THE CLIFF JUST under the rock wall and looked out over a deep valley. About a hundred feet below and to the right there was a large hole in the cliff wall. He could see tiny figures clad in black peering from the cave mouth. From his vantage point he could also see the group dressed all in gray that peered back at them from behind a great tumble of rock on a slightly lower level some fifty yards away. Those must be the Stillpoint warriors, he decided, his hunch confirmed seconds later when the unmistakable hulking form of the Dratzul came momentarily into view. Above them all, midway between the ground and Howard on a narrow plateau on the other side of a small but torrential river, more gray-clad soldiers swarmed over a partially assembled object that glinted with bright metal in the sunlight. The Traveler he had sensed earlier must have delivered both groups, he realized, as the mountain gun was clearly too large to have been hauled up the side of the plateau. He squinted at the faceted black rock around him but could see no sign of the strange creature.

He searched the cliff face below him anxiously. Awp, Yam-ya-mosh, and Alaiya were nowhere to be seen. Howard hoped they had found places of concealment before either of the enemy emplacements had spotted them.

His attention was caught by a flicker of movement from below. The gray soldiers were slipping out of concealment by twos and threes. As they scurried across the wrinkled folds of rock and began to creep from both sides toward the cave mouth, Howard realized that those inside the cave were unaware of their approach.

Some of the Stillpoint warriors carried bulky weapons whose tips flared continuously with a searing light. Howard remembered the glowing sparks that had pursued him and Awp into their cave above the rapids miles from this place. As the grays found hidden pockets from which they could draw a bead on the cave mouth, he groped with his free hand on the ledge above him for something loose. His fingers curled around a fragment of black rock the size of a bowling ball. As the first of the attackers lowered its weapon toward the cave mouth, Howard heaved the stone downward with all his might. It landed with a resounding crack several feet in front of the gray soldier. As the attacker reared up in surprise, searching the sky, a black-clad figure appeared suddenly above a nearby rock and leaped on the warrior, a strident war cry on her lips.

Howard grimaced and started rapidly down the cliff face, his hands and feet slipping dangerously as he kept his eyes trained on Alaiya and her opponent. The enemy was an Attercack with a tall crest of blue quills. Four sinewy arms clutched and tore at Alaiya's lithe form with deadly claws as the two rolled on the uneven ground, Silversting flashing in the sunlight.

Abruptly something like an incandescent bee arced past Howard's nose and turned to circle his head as he batted at it with his free arm. They were shooting at him from behind the rock spire. As he struggled to protect his face, the blazing object caught in his jacket sleeve. There was a sudden flare of heat. He swayed precariously on the side of the cliff, working furiously to shed his jacket as the skin of his arms and back began to burn. Finally the garment sailed flaming toward the rock far below. Howard turned and clambered shakily back up the rock face, his palms and knees cut by the razor-sharp projections. Gasping at the pain, he pulled himself up onto the ledge and dived back behind the rock wall. Breathing rapidly, he stuck his face around the edge to see black figures pouring from the cave mouth as gray soldiers rose to

meet them. Alaiya and her opponent were hidden from
him by a bulge in the cliff face. He cursed and tried to
edge out farther from behind the protecting wall.

Another bright projectile arced toward him. It followed him behind the wall as he ducked and flailed,
swatting at the relentless spark with one of the tattered
Reeboks from his pack. He felt the tiny impact against
the worn sole and crawled to the edge, drawing his arm
back and aiming for one of the gray-clad snipers still
crouched behind the spire. He released the sneaker just
as it became white-hot. Peering over the edge, he grinned
with satisfaction as the burning missile fell at the Stillpoint soldier's feet, sending him racing from concealment and into the several arms of one of the black-clad
defenders.

He was ready when the next flash of light from behind
the spire alerted him to the launch of a third projectile.
He raised his remaining Reebok and stood motionless,
the pattern followed by the tiny objects when in flight
clear in his memory. Once again he sent a fiery missile
down toward the grays.

The fighting seemed to be dying down on the ground
below. Bodies littered the valley, most of them gray. Howard searched the fallen blacks for a red-gold braid, but
he saw no sign of Alaiya or his other comrades.

There was still a small knot of grays behind the rock
spire. Howard had run out of objects with which to catch
their incendiary pellets. He waited on the ledge, fuming
in frustration and daring occasional glimpses at the scene
of battle. Gradually the rebels were withdrawing into the
cave mouth, carrying their wounded with them. The grays
began to follow, then halted at a bellow from their head-
quarters at the foot of the rock spire and turned to run
for nearby cover, their fallen comrades left behind them
on the rough plain.

Lifting his eyes from the scene of carnage, Howard
understood the reason for the sudden retreat.

The mountain gun stood poised at the edge of the plateau, its heavy snout pointed down at the cave entrance.
Two soldiers were making final adjustments at the base
of the device as their fellows backed nervously to the
other side of the strip of rock.

A gigantic white shape rose suddenly behind them. A gray-clad Trull turned and squealed in terror as Awp climbed ponderously onto the top of the black mesa. Scattering the grays like toys, the Hant made its way toward the mountain gun.

The soldiers left at the gun jabbed frantically at the targeting mechanism. The blunt muzzle began to swing slowly around as Awp neared the edge of the plateau.

It was too late. Lowering its head, the Hant moved forward, its massive shoulders plowing into the great weapon. As Howard watched in awe, the huge gun was pushed irresistibly to the lip of the mesa, its operators scrambling for safety. The gun teetered for a long moment at the edge of the plateau, then plunged over like some mammoth beast, landing seconds later with an earthshaking crash on a smaller jut of rock halfway down the side of the cliff, its muzzle pointing impotently at the cave mouth below.

"Whoa!" Howard waved at Awp, his voice lost in the sound of the river. "Nice going!" The Hant returned the wave, then lumbered to the other side of the mesa and began to climb slowly back over the edge.

Howard turned his gaze below. No one was moving on the black rock. The few remaining grays who had crouched behind the spire were gone.

He frowned. It was all over in a surprisingly short time. If the Traveler that had caused his earlier discomfort was still present, it remained in hiding. Perhaps it had merely acted as a doorway to deliver the Stillpoint warriors, then folded in upon itself and returned to whichever world the city currently inhabited.

The Hant had reached the bottom of the plateau. It waded into the river and moved slowly through the chest-high torrent, seemingly unaffected by the tons of water crashing against its body. Then it climbed to shore and made its way across the battlefield. Black-clothed warriors emerged cautiously from the cave mouth and ran to greet the Hant.

Howard laughed with relief as Yam and Alaiya came forth from the cave and the three turned and shaded their eyes in the direction of the rock ledge, waving at him to come down. He waved back and turned to gather his pack, wedging the flying machine into a crevice at the base of the wall until he could return for it later.

As he was edging his way over the ledge, a small movement caught his eye. He searched the nearby walls of fractured black rock, finding nothing.

Finally he noticed the single gray-clad figure crawling stealthily up the side of the plateau across the river. As he watched it reached the secondary ledge and crouched at the side of the mountain gun.

"There's no way that thing is still operating," Howard murmured to himself. Dangling his feet over the rock ledge, he called to those by the cave below. The river noise was too great.

At last Alaiya looked up, and he waved wildly for her attention, pointing toward the mesa.

Rocks sprayed upward as a hollow explosion echoed through the valley. Howard cried out in horror as the Hant pitched forward, rubble raining down as smoke rose to obscure the scene. The gray-suited warrior had been thrown from the ledge by the force of the firing. Now it was crawling back to the damaged weapon as Yam and Alaiya ran to kneel at the side of their fallen friend.

Feeling as though he was moving in slow motion, Howard threw off his pack and fumbled the flying machine onto his back. He yanked the straps tightly around his chest and jabbed at the button set between his shoulders. Not waiting for the answering hum of the motor, he launched himself from the ledge, the huge wings unfolding stiffly behind him as he plummeted downward. After an endless moment he was jerked backward as the wings began to beat. The river glittered below him. He gave the control rods a savage twist and hurled himself at the side of the mesa where the gray soldier was preparing to fire again. He had a confused image of a face that was part bull and part bat screaming up at him in rage. Then he crashed into the figure and both of them fell from the jut of rock. Part of the blackness beneath them seemed to ripple as the Dratzul fell into it ahead of him. Howard felt a strange detachment, his fingers tugging nervelessly at the control rods as he hurtled unchecked toward the rocks. A different sort of blackness rose in his face.

CHAPTER XXII

The Tale-tell

HE AWOKE TO A DARKENED ROOM, FIRELIGHT flickering in orange webs across the ceiling of faceted black rock. He turned his head slightly, wincing as pain rolled like boulders behind his skull. He was lying on a low pallet in a cave. Carefully he shifted his gaze to the other side.

Yam-ya-mosh sat cross-legged on the floor by the pallet, snoring softly.

"Hey, you." Howard reached out and rubbed the woolly head affectionately. "Who's the patient here?"

Black eyes opened instantly.

"Ow-er-bel!" Yam dove for his neck, hugging him with soft-furred arms, then sprang back in concern. "Do you hurrt? Sorrry! Sorrry!" The small warrior clambered to his feet. "Wait! Stay!" he admonished, then turned and fled into the darkness.

Howard was dozing again when he felt a smooth hand on his brow.

"Ahwerd."

His eyelids fluttered open, and he watched relief flood Alaiya's face.

"Hi," he said weakly, struggling to lift his arms. One of them seemed to be restrained in some manner. "How's it going?"

"It goes well, now that you are returned at last," she

219

replied in accented English. "I thought you are lost to me."

"Not this mouseketeer." He shook his head, clenching his teeth at the resulting pain.

Alaiya winced with him.

"You might try the Averoy way for a time," she said, touching his nose with a gentle fingertip while she wrinkled her own by way of illustration. "There may be less discomfort."

"You could be right." He closed his eyes as she draped a cool cloth across his forehead. "What's been happening? How long have I been out?"

"It is nine local days you are asleep, Ahwerd." She knelt by the side of the low pallet. "Sometimes you are speaking, but your mind is . . . away." She waved her hand. "I do not have the words."

"Hey." He struggled to clear his thoughts. "You've got a lot of words. How come you're doing so well with English without me around to tutor you? You didn't take a transfusion from somebody, did you?"

"No, I will have no more welcome for parleybugs in my body." She shook her head carefully from side to side. "Awp starts to teach us your language. We drink the tea, and the Hant speaks to us while we almost sleep. It says we have the words already inside if we have heard them with the parleyblood."

"Awp is all right, then?" Howard tried to sit up but fell back weakly. "The mountain gun—I saw him go down."

"It was not a center hit," Alaiya said, removing the cloth for a moment to smooth back his hair. "Though I believe even that is not enough to kill the Hant in its new form."

"Thank God. When that gun went off I thought you guys . . ."

"We are well." Alaiya smiled. "But it is clear we owe our survival to you. If the Dratzul is able to fire a second time there would be many deaths."

Howard looked at the rough ceiling. "I was so worried about you guys. This warrior stuff makes a lousy hobby when you've got loved ones in the business."

Alaiya's face grew sober in the firelight. "In truth, we

lost two brave comrades to the Dratzul's followers. Ser-mantry and Kattalpin are dead.''

"I'm sorry, Alaiya." Howard reached for her hand with his good one.

"We honor their memory tomorrow night at the tale-tell. If you are well enough . . ."

"Yes, I'd like to be there." He closed his eyes again as she stroked his brow. "What happened to me, any-way? How come I'm alive—did I land in the river again?"

Alaiya was silent for a long moment before answering.

"You are fortunate to come down in the broken rocks and dust produced by the mountain gun," she said at last. "It softens your landing and prevents your hurts from being much worse."

Howard was watching her face. "And?"

"There was a strange occurrence, Ahwerd," she said hesitantly. "To some who watched through the smoke and confusion, it seemed that a Traveler appeared in the air beneath you and the Dratzul as you fell. You both disappeared into its darkness. We found you lying in the mound of rubble near the Hant. The Dratzul's body was never located." She gave a shrug, a gesture she had learned from Howard. "The meaning of this incident is not clear to us."

There was a noise from another part of the cave, and Alaiya turned her head and smiled into the darkness. "Ahwerd, a friend is here now that I strongly wish for you to meet."

"Sure."

A tall Averoy with dark skin and curly black hair came into the light and knelt next to Alaiya. He had light gray eyes and wore a mustache above his handsome smile.

"You must be Omber Oss," Howard said in Averant, holding out his hand.

"I am in your debt, Ahwerdbel, as are we all." They clasped hands. "It was magnificent how you dropped upon the Dratzul like a meteor from the heavens. But your companions have told us of your other fantastic deeds, as well. Truly it will be an honor to serve in your battle-gang."

"Nice to meet you, too," Howard said, blinking as

the dark warrior rose. Alaiya had a hurried conversation with Oss at the mouth of the cave.

"My what?" he asked as she returned to his side. "I don't have a battle-gang."

Alaiya ran her finger lightly over his brow. "We will have a discussion of many matters when you are well enough, Ahwerd. Perhaps tomorrow. For now, you must get some more sleep."

"No, I'm wide awake." He gave a prodigious yawn. "Anyway, I don't want to go back to sleep. Suppose I wake up in Boston?"

Alaiya leaned forward and put her arms around his shoulders, bringing her face close to his own.

"I will not allow this to happen," she said playfully. "Not even if I am required to hold you in this manner for many days in order to prevent it."

Her breath was warm.

He laughed weakly and touched her cheek.

"Hey, if you want the job, it's yours. I don't see a line forming. So what was this about . . . battle-gangs?" He was growing weary, his voice slurring into another yawn.

But Alaiya's reply seemed to come to him from a great distance, and her words, reverberating in the cave, meant nothing to him as he drifted into dreams.

When he awoke again the cave was flooded with morning sunlight. His thoughts were clearer, but the headache pounded relentlessly as if in compensation. Awp was there to give him a cup of the fragrant bigtassle tea, gently holding his head in one of its great, many-fingered hands as he drank. The pain receded and he slept again.

It was dark when he next opened his eyes. He lay quietly, luxuriating in the absence of pain from his skull. After a while he heard voices from the cave mouth. He turned his head as Alaiya entered, Yam-ya-mosh walking behind her with a torch.

"How is the pain?" Alaiya knelt at his side, her fingers cool on his brow.

"It isn't." He grinned and stretched. "Am I in time for the tale-tell, or did I sleep through another week?"

Yam and Alaiya looked at each other.

"You are in time," she said. "It will commence in a few hours."

"Do you wish us to brrring you anything, Ow-er-bel?" Yam squeaked in Averant.

"Yeah." Howard crossed his arms behind his head. "A mug of hot chocolate with a little peppermint schnapps in it, and about six months' worth of Sunday funnies." He smiled at the Trilbit's expression. "No, thank you," he added in Averant. "I wish only to leave this soft bed soon and stand upon some strong feet—my own, if possible."

The sheeplike muzzle wrinkled comically.

"This is good, that you learn to perform humor in Averrrant," the little warrior said. "I did never hear your Ingliss through my parleybugs and so my own lessons will be long."

"No problem." Howard lifted the blanket and glanced underneath. "As I thought," he said, raising one eyebrow. "Has anyone knowledge of the current whereabouts of my shorts?"

With Alaiya's assistance, Howard dressed in a fresh outfit of vest, shorts, and cloak, all of black piped with silver as before.

He suffered a moment of panic when he suddenly recalled the fate of his jacket.

"My God, the Key!"

"Yam-ya-mosh scoured the valley and recovered the remnants of your garment once we realized that it is missing," Alaiya reassured him gently. From her cloak she drew forth a sturdy thong of leather from which the golden object twinkled brightly in the torchlight. She placed the Key solemnly around his neck.

Later he limped from the cave on her shoulder, one of his legs still stiff and aching from disuse. In addition, his left arm had been wrapped in bandages and hung in a sling of black cloth from his neck.

"Where are we?"

The landscape was unfamiliar to him. They crossed a sward of rose moss toward a wooded area, a range of black mountains rising through the twilight at their backs.

"It was felt wise to leave the place of battle," Alaiya said as they made their slow way toward the patch of forest. "So far we have detected no pursuit from Still-point. The Hant has concocted a liquid that functions much as purge pods, and after the tale-tell all will rid themselves of the parleybugs."

"I wonder if Grandma Wossil's got any eyes or ears nearby," Howard mused, looking at the darkening woods.

The land fell away past the first few trees, then rose again at a lower level, forming a natural amphitheater that was hidden from all but aerial inspection. Firelight shone ahead. Alaiya held a branch aside for Howard, and the two entered the tiny valley.

About thirty warriors representing a variety of races sat at different levels around a flat area where a bonfire snapped, sending up orange sparks and filling the valley with the tang of woodsmoke.

Awp and Yam-ya-mosh awaited the new arrivals at the bottom of the moss-floored bowl. Howard took a seat gratefully on the soft ground, his back against a fallen trunk of gray wood.

Alaiya walked to the center of the clearing.

"We gather here in this place to give honor to those who have died," she said solemnly, "as well as to celebrate the deeds of those who yet live." Howard heard a soft chorus of other voices as she spoke. Turning, he saw that Omber Oss, Arpenwole, and the other Averoy were repeating Alaiya's words so that they might be understood by those who still relied on parleybugs. He smiled at Arpenwole as she glanced his way, but the short-haired warrior made no response.

Alaiya paid tribute to Kattalpin and Sermantry, then relinquished the floor to others who did the same. Without the parleybugs in his blood, Howard marveled at the variety of alien speech. This time it was Awp who quietly translated the several tongues into Averant for Howard, Alaiya, and Yam.

When the eulogies were at an end, the tale-tell turned to descriptions of the battle of the black cliffs. Growing drowsy as he listened to the many versions of what had transpired there, Howard was amused by the exaggeration that seemed to invest the tales. Especially disconcerting was the amplified role his own actions had been given in the event. He shook his head in bemusement as speaker after speaker extolled his valor and ingenuity.

"This is getting embarrassing," he whispered to Alaiya. "I'm tempted to get up there myself and set these folks straight."

"They are almost finished," she replied. "Do not worry, your chance to speak will come."

When the last of the tale-tellers had assumed its seat, Alaiya once more strode to the center of the small clearing. She thanked those who had spoken, then stood for a long moment as if contemplating the words she was about to say.

"Now, my comrades and friends, we reach the moment we have all awaited for several days. The time of decision. We are united in our wish to end the tyranny of the Keyholders and throw down the walls of Stillpoint. United but leaderless." Her gray eyes flashed as they roamed the crowd, coming to rest at last on Howard, who smiled sleepily and winked at her.

"For the past nine days we have discussed this issue, and it is the will of the majority that I am to announce." Glancing around the firelit amphitheater, Howard noticed Arpenwole's scowl as she softly repeated Alaiya's words.

"It is our decision this night of mourning and celebration," Alaiya continued, her voice rising in the darkness, "to form a battle-gang such as Stillpoint has never known—a final battle-gang. And it is our further decision to name as our battlechief one whose strange and noble gifts are equaled only by his bravery and honor."

She paused as Howard scanned the crowd behind him. Who would it be? Omber Oss, the born rebel? Arpenwole, the schemer? Or was it the Hant, whose strange gifts had won the admiration of this warrior band? He shrugged and returned his eyes to center stage, only to find Alaiya staring directly at him with her dark gray gaze.

"My comrades," she was saying. "I present to you your leader—Ahwerdbel of Massachusetts!"

Howard sat thunderstruck for a few seconds; then he laughed in delight, looking around at the solemn faces.

"What is this?" he said to Alaiya. "An elaborate practical joke?"

"Not at all." She came to his side and took his hand.

He remained where he sat. "Alaiya, I'm too tired for this. I think I need to get back to bed."

"Awp?" At Alaiya's word, the Hant appeared next to them, holding out to Howard a cup of the ubiquitous tea.

"I saw your fingers in there, Awp," Howard said suspiciously. "What's going on here?"

"Merely a small chemical change to bring you wakefulness and vigor," the Hant assured him.

Howard took the cup and drained it, feeling warmth and energy spread through his body.

Alaiya led him to the center of the clearing, where he stood blinking stupidly at the black-clad figures as his head slowly cleared.

He turned slowly, taking in the rows of expectant faces.

"You guys are serious, aren't you?" When he spoke there was a hum of other voices, as Awp translated his words for the Averoy, who echoed them in turn for the rest of the crowd.

Howard rolled his eyes at Yam-ya-mosh, who sat at the edge of the mossy space.

"Tell them they're crazy, will you, Yam?" he pleaded.

"You have saved my life more than once," the Trilbit declared, rising to his full height. "More importantly, you have acted with compassion and intelligence, humor and bravery—all qualities that I require in one who is to be my leader."

"Oh, swell. You're no help at all. Alaiya?"

"Ya-mosh knows that he ably expresses my own opinion in the matter, Ahwerd."

He groaned and looked over at the massive Hant. "*Et tu*, Awp?"

The Hant translated his words into Averant, then nodded slowly. "Hawa, you must stop protesting and bow to the inevitable. Many mysteries and much excitement await us, this I feel to be truth."

"I can't. I won't. Battlechief?" Howard shook his head and faced the crowd with his arms folded. "For God's sake, guys—I was an English major!"

Alaiya conferred softly with Oss and the Hant, then moved to join Howard in the center. "If it is the title that auses you concern, Ahwerd, I think we can provide another, perhaps more suitable one.''

"Oh, yeah? And what about this battlechief stuff? I don't know anything about fighting.''

Yam-ya-mosh took a step forward from the sidelines.

''I propose Redborn Lai-ya to act as war councillor to Ow-er-bel,'' he squeaked grandly.

Alaiya looked startled, then nodded slowly as the Trilbit's words received vigorous approval from the assembled warriors. "If you wish.''

''Fine,'' Howard said. ''With that condition, I agree to serve—for a short time only—in whatever temporary, ad hoc, advisory capacity will be useful to you folks.''

Alaiya raised his hand in hers as the crowd cried out in joy.

''I hereby name you leader of this glorious battlegang.'' She paused dramatically. ''Ahwerdbel—the Nonesuch!''

''I'll get you for this,'' Howard whispered in her ear. Aloud he said, ''And do I at least get the privilege of choosing a halfway decent name for this glorious battlegang?''

Alaiya looked apologetic. ''Ah, Ahwerd, I am afraid the name was voted upon and passed while you slept. There is no changing it now.''

''Swell,'' he muttered. ''And just what am I leader of—the Ponderous Pugilists? The Inconsiderate Nailbiters?''

''Nothing so trivial.'' She gestured grandly to the crowd with a bow in Howard's direction, her eyes twinkling in the light from the bonfire. The strange assortment of creatures climbed to stand on whatever served them as lower limbs. ''Noble Ahwerd, great Nonesuch, I present for your inspection your magnificent battlegang—the Breakneck Boys!''

Howard turned to Alaiya in disbelief as a cheer rose from the assembly.

''Where on Earth did you develop this bizarre sense of humor?'' he asked her.

Later Howard and Alaiya walked back to the cave together. The sky above them was clear and dusted with

stars. They held hands and spoke softly as they crossed
the field of moss.

"Are you content with this decision, Ahwerd?" Alaiya
peered at his face in the darkness. "I felt that you needed
a measure of prodding to accept the wisdom of our
choice, but if you wish to change your mind . . ."

"No problem." He tilted his head back and watched
the night sky. "As long as everyone understands that it
isn't a permanent position. I mean, there are things that
I have to do."

"The work of fiction," Alaiya said with a nod. "Your
profession as a repairman."

He laughed. "I'm not too concerned about the second
one. There'll always be things that need fixing, no matter
where I am. As for the book . . ." He shrugged. "Maybe
someday."

"You have the Key now," Alaiya said. "I have wondered if you have thought through the implications of
that."

"What, that I could go home? Yeah, it's occurred to
me. I do have a few loose ends to tie up." He looked at
the woman at his side. "Not very many, though. How
about you?"

"I also wish to accomplish certain things." She started
to walk again. "My people must be freed from their
Holding. Stillpoint will not be easy to conquer. I wish
to look one day into the eyes of a vanquished Keyholder.
After that, there will be other challenges, other mysteries."

"Yeah, I have a couple of my own to unravel, both
here and back on Earth." He gave an Averoy hand-shrug.
"It should be interesting."

"Indeed."

They stood before the small cave, light from a nearby
torch falling on their faces. Howard put his fingers on
Alaiya's cheek and kissed her on the mouth.

"So, is that something you guys do, or what?" he
asked a few seconds later.

"It is not a practice common to the Averoy," she said,
staring calmly into his anxious face. "But I believe it is
one that may be worth investigation. I was taught to be
respectful of different cultures, you see."

''Whew,'' Howard said, ''that's a relief.''
They went inside.

It was decided that the battle-gang would travel to Tai
Inimbra once the elimination of the remaining parleybugs
had been effected, thus removing them temporarily from
the Fading Worlds while they devised a plan for their first
true assault on the Keyholders.

Accordingly, Howard stood two days later in a meadow
of rose-red moss, on one side of a wide circle of black-
clad warriors, a slender shaft of golden metal in his hand.

Alaiya stood at his right, and Awp held Yam-ya-mosh
in its massive arms on his left.

''Everybody touching?'' Howard scanned the line of
eager faces. All eyes were on him. ''Okay, then, we're
out of here.''

Holding his arms out in front of him, he suddenly
frowned and stared at the gleaming object in his hands.

''Wait a minute,'' he said softly. ''This isn't *my* Key.''
Nearby faces turned to him in shock.

Howard grinned. ''Hey—I'm kidding,'' he said.
Then he turned the Key.

About the Author

Paleontologist, cryptographer, stunt pilot, longshore-man: Geary Gravel has learned the correct usage of these and many other words during his career as a writer and sign language interpreter.

He lives in western Massachusetts with several gold-fish and a thesaurus.

DONALD MOFFITT'S
SCIENCE FICTION

IS OUT OF THIS
WORLD